Heaven Sent

A Legacy of Love from Human, to Angel, to Canine

To: Kimmy
You are such a
Love, and so thoughtful!
Best friends forever
BFF!

Written By:

M. ENDSLEY

XO
MiSchelle

Edited By: Mikayla Taylor
Cover Illustration By: Mikayla Taylor

Photography and Picture Editing
By: Susan Centilla Photography

AuthorHouse™
1663 Liberty Drive
Bloomington, IN 47403
www.authorhouse.com
Phone: 1-800-839-8640

Published by AuthorHouse 04/30/2013

ISBN: 978-1-4817-1402-0 (sc)
ISBN: 978-1-4817-1401-3 (hc)
ISBN: 978-1-4817-1315-3 (e)

Library of Congress Control Number: 2013902529

Heaven Sent Reviews

"Mischelle's writing is warm and thoughtful, I laughed and cried and was totally drawn into the story. It was very thought provoking. I was unable to put it down. Heaven Sent gives you a warm feeling of what might be after death and how one's life is watched over and guided by a higher power. Well done."
-John Avink, Avink Funeral Home
Iron Man Tri-Athlete and Marathon Runner

"Heaven Sent is a TRUE LEGACY of Love. Love of God, Family, and the human connection to our pets. I loved all the verses that precede each chapter and the message we receive from God's word. This is the perfect book to share with families of all ages who so appreciate their pets and the power of angels in our lives."
-**June Grannis, Member of the Pelee Island Book Club,**
Ontario, Canada

"Sophie the lovable Chihuahua entertains readers and tugs at their emotions when sent by heaven to look after and protect her former family. *Heaven Sent* , the story of Sophie the spunky Chihuahua is the perfect book for any pet lover."
-Dennis Kehoe, Financial Planner
Portage, Michigan

"Heaven Sent is a delightful family read. If you enjoy animals you will be thoroughly entertained."
-Randy P. Kohler, CFP, Author of *"Living the Good Life" Essential Financial Information Everyone Needs to Know*

"This book is a warm, delightful story about a loving relationship between a husband and his wife, and how their love for each other overflows to their daughters, grandchildren, friends, pets, and God. Anyone that has ever developed a special bond with a pet will enjoy reading Heaven Sent."
-Mary Law
Competitive Dog Obedience Trainer and Exhibitor

"Heaven Sent is an amazingly sweet and charming tale (or perhaps I should say "tail") of the power of a love that lasts forever. It is impossible not to smile as you read about the adventures of one of Heaven's littlest guardian angels. I found myself laughing out loud, and, at times, blinking back a tear or two. Anyone who has ever loved a little dog will know right away that if dogs *could* talk, they would tell you how perfectly Ms. Endsley has captured their spirit. Read it. You'll Love it!"
-Jamie Marsman
Author of "*The Knitting Fairy*"

"A heartwarming and imaginative tale for pet lovers and a tribute to the eternal bonds of family love!"
-Douglas S. Nelson
#1 Best Selling Author of "*Catch Fire; How To Ignite your own Economy*"

"When you read *Heaven Sent* each event that takes place is very easy to picture and relate to. You will be drawn into the characters and chapters so much you will envision the scenes as if it were a movie. The relationships developed by Sophie are endearing and magnetic. Share this story with all ages and pet enthusiasts."
-Rand Pauler
Author of "*Ambushed*"

"Trusting God, no matter what, can be difficult, and so can teaching a child this principle. *Heaven Sent* makes the job easier by teaching this principle in a fun, down to earth way. It takes a concept that is hard for many adults to grasp and brings it to a level that kids will understand and enjoy."
-Jeff Selph
Youth Pastor , Kalamazoo Community Church

"*Heaven Sent* is a delightful romp between heaven and earth – fantasy and realism – families and beloved pets. It's a funny yet poignant tale told by a grand storyteller. You will want to share your laughter by reading aloud Mischelle's lighthearted way with words and endearing thoughts through these whimsical adventures."
-Harriet Swartz
School Teacher

"How far you go in life depends on your being tender with the young, compassionate with the aged,sympathetic with the striving, and tolerant of the weak and strong. Because someday in your life you will have been all of these."

-George Washington Carver

"Look at everything as though you were seeing it either for the first time or last time. Then your time on earth will be filled with Glory."

-Betty Smith

Contents

Note from the Author,

I wrote this book in loving memory of my father "Robert George Endsley" who has been deceased since 1983.

Dad, you have never been forgotten!

My mother's inspiration for this story made it fun to write, and since so many of the events are from our real life, it is a tribute to the joy she brings us all.

Therefore, I am dedicating this book to my parents, who loved me unconditionally and allowed me to be me, and never put limits on my imagination. Also a special thanks to my wonderful children who unconditionally love and believe in me, and most of all, Ron who has totally supported and loved me throughout this endeavor.

Also I want to thank everyone who encouraged me and contributed their input and help in any way, especially Mikayla and Melanie Sue who made this easier.

Thank You All,

Without your love and consistent support, I could have never accomplished this! XOXO Mischelle

PS—Thank You Sophie, Jlo, Tinkerbell and Blue, without you, our furry family, this story could never be. All of you are a delight and the best pets ever!

I would like to introduce myself. I am JLO, the actual star of this book. Even though you will think this is written about my silly sister Sophie, it is truly about me. As you can see I am helping my mom . . . "Mischelle or AKA Monica in the story" write all the good parts. I sit with her while she is writing to make sure she does not leave out the parts where it explains how beautiful I am.

After all it was me who got this ball rolling. If it were not for my mom "Mischelle", bringing her girls Mikayla and Victoria to the puppy farm then you would not be reading this book. That's where they fell in love with me, so I will take credit where credit is due. It is only out of the love and adoration for "me" that they even considered getting another beautiful Chihuahua.

So back to the same puppy farm they went, where I came from to choose another Chihuahua. Luckily for my half-brother (He is truly a brother from another mother as they say) Blue or "Scruffy" as Sophie calls him in the book, my Aunt Kathy, went with her sister Mischelle to see the puppies. Of course Aunt Kathy adored Blue and adopted him, and that was just plain good fortune.

Then the unthinkable happened, my mom picked the littlest, sickest puppy and low and behold it was Sophie. Let me tell you it's true, she has not been quite right from day one. First I thought we were a halfway house for un-adopted pets, nobody would adopt her in their right mind, but instead she became a part of the family. I can now see she will never be normal, she is still a sissy and a little on the goofy side. The expression "she's a few French Fries short of a happy meal" fits. Speaking of French Fries (one of my favorite traveling treats), I'm hungry right now! So just read about my wonderful life, you can skip the other parts they are boring anyways.

P. S. I was born with a white star in my fur, right on my chest. God probably knew I was destined to be famous!

Happy Reading, JLO

Heaven Sent

A Legacy of Love from Human, to Angel, to Canine

Psalm 34:6 This poor man called, and The Lord heard him; he saved him out of all his troubles.

1

TIME TO REMINISCE

"Calling all angels, Calling all angels! It's an emergency, Please help us!" The words were ringing in my head, I was panicking and out of breath. I opened my eyes and recognized I was in the bed I had slept in before. I looked up realizing I was reliving a nightmare, and Hernandez was at my bedside, "Is she here?" I asked him. Hernandez placed his hand on my forearm to comfort me, shaking his head,

"You have a few more hours of rest before you can catch up with your thoughts and understand. Go to sleep, you need your strength. This will all come together and make sense when you wake up." His voice was calm as he then placed his hand upon my head and I closed my eyes. I was so exhausted I couldn't bring myself to respond, quickly drifting back into a dream state. The memories of my past beginning to flood in . . .

As I began to start dreaming again, I thought about my life. When I looked back it sometimes seemed like the nice guys finished last. There were moments during my life I thought that was true. As a kid it often seemed hard to get ahead, or to make progress the way I knew

I wanted to. That might be because I grew up knowing the meaning of poverty. Growing up, times were more often than not, difficult for my family. But despite those troubles, since I was young, I've felt sort of strangely lucky. When I look back at my entire life and sift through all of my endeavors, I've come to the understanding that "luck" is not always easy to comprehend. But no matter what has happened I still feel fortunate for my journey, even if my luck was sometimes the dumbest luck you could ever imagine.

As I drifted through my thoughts I saw myself growing up during the Great Depression. At that time I was a teenager. Coffee was ten cents a pound, but back then no one had ten cents to spare. It was truly a time in history that our economy was stuck at an all-time low.

I was one of the fortunate few. I took the chance to become acquainted with a man uptown because I liked his dog, Huey. Over time, I found out Huey's owner, Gus, was a millionaire. I actually happened to find this out only after he hired me as his personal driver and "errand boy." This was not just luck, because each day that I passed his house, I would wave at him and if his dog was out I would always take the opportunity to stop and pet him. "Huey" had this sweet spot right behind his ears and wagged his tail as I rubbed his head. Huey liked being scratched so much, and over time I would find him waiting at the front gate for me to pass by, or watching for me in the foyer of his owner's house. It came down to the point where it was obvious that this dog knew I liked him and he liked me.

One day while I stopped to pet Huey, as was now my daily routine, and Gus his owner strolled over to me, catching me off guard, "Rob, can you drive a car?" he asked, I lifted my head after a moment and replied,

"Yes sir," I watched him tap his finger against his chin before he donned a comforting grin.

"I'll tell you what, wear your nice clothes tomorrow and you can drive me to town, how does that sound?" Taken aback, I blinked a few times nodding so eagerly I swear my head could have rolled off my shoulders,

"That would be amazing, thank you sir!" I remember shaking his hand and being so grateful that day before rushing home to pick out some clothes that would be right for the job.

Since that day I worked diligently six to seven days a week on average for Gus and couldn't have been more thankful for the opportunity. This gave me the chance to provide for my family which in the end allowed us to keep our home. Since I was the third of four boys growing up in a small house, this meant four teenage sized appetites for my parents to provide for. Finding food to feed everyone was hard enough for my parents, so being able to assist with that burden in such difficult times gave me great satisfaction.

As much as all us boys would love to have a pet at home there was no room and no extra money for such a luxury. A pet was another mouth to feed and it was out of the question. Our family could not afford to keep one, so I learned to come to terms with that fact. Thankfully, there was Huey, the millionaires' dog. He was a black lab and our friendship was enough to fill the evident gap in my home life for my fondness of pets. Huey went everywhere with Gus and when I dropped him off for an appointment, Huey rode right beside me in the front seat. Huey and I had many conversations while we were driving around, and he would just stare at me, as if he could understand every word I was saying. During the times I was in need of comforting he would lick my face or hand. Even when people wouldn't listen to me, Huey always would. His big brown eyes took in every word I said, he seemed to blink and gesture at the exact perfect time as I rambled on to him about everything. He was the greatest companion I had ever been exposed to up to that point in my life, Huey and I had mutual admiration for each other.

After ten years of service to Gus, his time on earth came to an end. I hadn't even noticed the way time was wearing him down until his last few months when he told me he was ill. It was then that his state of being seemed to suddenly change from young-hearted to old and frail. I had lost a great friend with his passing, but was also given a new one. Huey! His will stated, "I Gus leave my most prized possession to Robert Harper, my dog, Huey, along with my 1930 Ford, and one thousand dollars." Even though he had passed on, my old friend found a way to still be the most generous man I ever knew.

I treated his car as if it were a Rolls Royce; it was my first car, and I would have never expected my first one to be as nice as it was. I was so grateful for everything he had done for me, the job, the money, and the car, but by far the greatest treasure he could have ever passed on to me after ten years serving him was Huey. I felt like he was partially mine to begin with, but calling him my own meant the world to me. Sadly, Huey only lasted about eighteen months after his master's death; he was almost fourteen at the time and absolutely heartbroken when Gus passed away. It was shattering to see that dog long for him. I was his friend, but no one could replace Gus. I learned at that time exactly the undying love that a dog can have for a human companion. He was looking for Gus every day after his passing. He would lay waiting on the front porch curled up on the rug nearly all day for his master to return. After watching him this way for so long, I was certain they would be together again someday; their bond was just too strong. Gus always used to tell me "Don't forget, a good dog will replace a woman any day." I personally believe that's because even though Gus was married three times the consistent partner in his life was always Huey.

My life was, well, to say the least, the best it could be. The fact that my parents were strong Christians made our family solid. In good times as well as bad, we always had each other and our faith to keep us together. Often in these sorts of times, a man without faith could easily fall to gambling and booze. We were lucky to have such a strong bond and devotion; it was what kept us on track through the rough times. I had a decent job, and married at the age of twenty-five to a woman five years older. Together we had a son, and it was a good thing but because of the unfortunate times, I found myself single again due to divorce fifteen years later. I never considered it bad luck; it was just the way my life happened to turn out. I never really thought I would be staring over at forty, and I never really planned to, but like the old saying goes, "when life gives you lemons you make lemonade." From that point on, I aimed my focus towards being the best father I could possibly be to my young son, "Rob Jr." I worked hard, but was sure to set aside time to go to his ball games and help him be successful in school. Being quite the athlete, he played all sorts of sports. I was and will always be so proud of him and what he accomplished in life.

During my spare time I collected antique and unusual guns. I refurbished them in my basement that I turned into a gun shop. I adored the history of where they originated from. Almost every rifle and pistol had a story, some more fascinating than others but each one in itself never boring. It was a hobby that kept me busy. Rob Jr. and I loved working on them together and I carried this tradition on in my life with all the children I was to be blessed with. My son went to gun shows when he was young and even as he became an adult he enjoyed going. He and my future kids were troopers helping daddy enjoy his day at the guns shows and just spending memorable bonding time together. After the shows we would pack up our things and go for ice cream as a family or even a burger; they had the choice of what treat they wanted for being such good little scouts at the end of the day. I'm pretty sure growing up that gunning on a Sunday afternoon would not always be their first choice, but they wanted to spend time with me doing my hobby. These bonding days were some of the best days of my life, for sure. The memories are fond.

Proverbs 2:11 Discretion will protect you and understanding will guard your soul.

2

A NEW BEGINNING

When I thought my luck had run out, my fate turned. I met the most amazing woman. She and I worked at the same factory where I was a welder, and she worked on a line at the factory packing and was going to school for hair styling on the weekends and evenings. Her name is Ellie. She was young and beautiful, so much so that I couldn't resist glancing her way with at any given opportunity. I tried to cross her path every chance I had when we worked the same schedule. When I came into work or took my lunch break I would take the long route through the building, just to pass by her and nonchalantly smile at her every chance I could get. When I wasn't working, I would fantasize about her voice. I wondered what it would sound like if we ever had the chance to talk. What would I even say if we could talk? After weeks of the same routine, it finally broke, and to my surprise she noticed me, more than likely because she caught me staring. Swallowing hard I spat out a few words, "Hi how are you today?" my smile faltering a bit, I was nervous as ever, but when she smiled it's as if my nerves were overtaken by pure exhilaration,

"I'm fine, and yourself?" My heart was beating so hard I was sure she could hear it.

"I'm great," I replied, *I'm great now that you responded to me,* I thought to myself.

From then on we chatted regularly. Just for a few minutes here and there, but it was frequent enough that after a month or so, I finally felt comfortable with asking her on a date. I was so nervous, at the time she was about twenty-seven and I was forty-one, and she was absolutely stunning. My nerves were in my throat when I asked. The palms of my hands damp with sweat as I finally shoved the question out, "Ellie, would you do me the honor of spending an afternoon with me?" my voice cracked and I swallowed hard. It felt like eternity before she replied, seconds feeling like hours,

"Yes, I'd love to," I almost jumped out of my boots with a triumphant "Yes!" but instead I somehow managed to play it cool,

"Great, I'll pick you up Saturday at 1:00 p.m. then!" I was giddy for the next two days. I decided I would just stick to smiling brightly as I walked past her at work, afraid that if I said too much that she would find an excuse to cancel our date.

Finally after much anticipation, it was Saturday. Our first date was a picnic at my uncle's lake house where I took Ellie for a pleasant boat ride. I packed sandwiches, fruit, potato salad, and brownies for dessert; I was hoping that with such a variety to choose from she would be able to pick something to eat that was to her liking. She seemed to really enjoy it, thank goodness, and for sure like the outdoors, so I would say that it went rather well. In fact, to my luck, the first date led to a second and then a third to follow that. It was the fourth date that seemed to solidify our relationship and to make a long story short, by the time I was forty-five,

Ellie and I were married and that same year had my first daughter Kathy. Later, at fifty, we had another daughter, Monica. Gosh, my life sure did an about face in a hurry and lucky for me, it was all for the best. I will always cherish and remember our wedding vows, as if we said them yesterday, “I will honor and love thee until death do us part.” Little did I know our love was going to transcend even death itself?

This life was merely the beginning of a wondrous adventure. During our time together we had two beautiful daughters, six felines, four dogs, a hamster, a guinea pig, some turtles and a few other *all-female* pets. Even the goldfish were girls I don’t know why but I was destined to be surrounded by many women. Of course I managed to not have them all at the same time. As one pet passed on it would only be a short time until Ellie or the girls would bring a new one. My youngest daughter Monica always seemed to find the hurt or ailing animals and bring them home to nurture them. She always convinced us that they would not live without the special love and tender care of our family, and I could tell she truly believed it. I would always say “No, no more pets,” but their smiles and adoration for their animals was a blessing to give. Kind of like Gus and how he was lucky to have his dog Huey, and Huey was lucky to have him. I suppose it didn’t affect me, I was treated wonderfully and they all, even the pets loved me immensely. Whether I wanted to be or not I was a King of a mixture of a human and animal kingdom of women since I was the only male in the household. Rather humorous one of those dumb luck things in my life that I ended up adoring.

My beautiful wife Ellie was fourteen years younger than me, so being agile, fit and staying involved with the girls was very important to me. I was of a slight build, strong, but considered thin by most. Our family and home life was the best, I couldn't complain about our lifestyle even now. I always said if you don't create the fun it may pass you by, or in other words "The party does not come to you; you have to go to the party." It was for this reason that Ellie and I had a date night almost every Saturday evening once the girls were enrolled in school. With the girls we did many things such as playing games, attending school functions, roller skating, and sledding in the woods as well at a hill in the park. The girls and I would often hike a quarter mile back through a woods to a pond so we could ice skate. We also camped with our trailer, traveling down south and out west as a family. Of course, each time bringing along which ever precious pooch was a part of our lives at the time. The cats and other pets would stay home, lucky to be fed by Grandma, Ellie's mother Mable, so we had the chance to go away and not have to worry about taking them.

Psalm 49:18 Though while they live they count themselves blessed—

3

SPOILED ROTTEN

I swear there were no other pets on earth treated better than our own. They were cared for day in and day out, fed too much, and pampered to death. Oh, did I mention loved? Our pets were for sure a real part of the family, and I was as guilty as the rest of the family when it came to spoiling them. But I have to admit, I loved the dogs the most. They had a way of communicating that surpassed the rest of the pets. You could just talk to them and they seemed almost human the way they would respond with their gestures. There was no mistaking their unconditional love for the family, you could see that when they looked at you. When talking to them, I would look into their eyes I could just imagine what they would say if they could form words. I know my experience with Huey gave me the pet or dog instincts that helped me relate better to my furry friends that came along later in my family life.

We started out with two cocker spaniels named Peachy and Patsy,and then years later came two terrier Chihuahua mixes named Cindy and Tasha. All of them were "*cute as bugs' ears.*" That's my saying when you can't describe the look to others or maybe they would not agree. In any case they were the center of attention in every sense. My daughters Kathy and Monica would dress them up and take them on the bicycle, in the wagon, in the baby buggy and everywhere they went. I'm sure the pets didn't appreciate the clothes but they loved the girls' attention so much that they tolerated a lot. You could almost see their eyes roll when the girls were wrestling them around to put the latest fashion concoction on them. In the summer I would ask them "Don't you think it's too hot today to put clothes on the pets?" But the girls would giggle and squeal,

"Oh daddy it's never too hot for a dress up day!" *Well okay,* I thought, *if you say so. I'm just glad I'm not that pet right now.* Shaking my head I snickered, knowing that even though it was obvious the girls enjoyed it, the pets enjoyed the attention in some odd shape or form as well. Even if it did mean sitting still in some fancy dress that belonged on a doll, or even riding in a stroller, sometimes even both.

Ellie would even take the dogs for rides in the bicycle basket, and we would put a child seat on the back of her bike for the grandchildren, which turned into a dog seat when the grandchildren weren't there. The Chihuahua terriers would sit behind her balancing and thoroughly enjoying the scenery. People used to ask me, "Do they just stay there?" Well of course they do, there is no other place they would want to be. Those dogs would go for a ride anywhere, anytime, especially with Ellie.

Our dogs even slept with us every night, doing the usual pacing around just before bed, letting us know it's time to go upstairs. They sometimes begged for one additional potty break or just a little sniff outside before retiring. At any rate, they kept us on track to go to sleep and wake up at the same time night and day. We did not need a time clock they were very adamant about their schedules. They kept us on schedule no matter what the events of the day beheld. Every day at about seven in the morning they would start walking around the bed to wake us up. They did this sometimes even with a nudge of a wet nose or a paw on the arm. Either one would do the trick; they definitely achieved their goal of getting us up and going every morning without fail. No alarm clock needed.

I've always said if I ever come back to earth and was not human, I would want to be a Harper Dog, for sure! No doubt about it! Life day in and out does not get any better than that of a Harper dog. I personally can guarantee this is absolutely true! Even though I've told others this, my mother in-law Mable would always laughed at this and say "Rob, I would absolutely have to agree with you, there are no dogs more spoiled!"

We would both laugh as the pooches were being pampered again on a daily basis for some reason. Just existing in our house made you a pampered pet.

Psalm 26:6   Those who go out weeping, carrying seed to sow, will return with songs of joy, carrying sheaves with them.

4

NOT WHAT I PLANNED

Tasha was the last dog I had. She was a favorite, a Chihuahua-Terrier with an adorable face. We always picked the Chihuahua mixes because the full breeds were too high strung. Unfortunately in my early seventies my soul parted from this wonderful earth, leaving my beautiful wife whom I adored, my loving girls and pets behind.

I wish I could tell everyone, to “Live everyday as if it were your last” because you never know what the higher powers has in store for you. Oh and I’d like to tell everyone to “Do unto others as you would have them do to you.” Because I now know the difference it can make in the outcome of your life.

One day I went in for an operation and expected to come out and see my family in a couple of hours. It was a simple procedure and I wasn’t too concerned. After all, I was fit about 5’10” and 170 lbs. active, ate well and expected to live at least another ten years minimum. But mistakes happen and I guess there was an opening in Heaven just for me. Wow, who would expect this? Neither me nor my family, that’s for sure!

That day the weather was cool, I remember because it was early Spring. Ellie was beyond nervous. I said that I would drive to the hospital being that nothing was wrong with me to not drive and she was already a wreck. I told her we needed to do the garden planting when I get home and that cards next Friday with friends should be good as long as it was held at our house. It would help pass my recovery time faster to look forward to things. I kissed her hand as she folded her fingers sideways into mine as I drove. I told her she was beautiful and how much I loved her and the girls. The last thing I remember is kissing them all before the surgery and saying "See you later alligators." Well, to my dismay, that would be much later than we all expected.

Upon waking up, or should I say, leaving my earthly body. I was in a panic, I was shouting, "Wait, wait, I have to help my daughter with her remodeling project and Ellie will never forgive me if I leave that huge mess in the basement!" I had been finishing some wood work and left the project in the middle of its completion. I was watching the surgeons work on my still and lifeless body, the monitor showing a flat line where there should have been a pulse. I began to panic and thought, this can't be happening, I was healthy. This operation was just a simple procedure, I should be out and recovering. What's going on? No, stop everything, I'm not ready! My mind was racing and yet trying to process what has happened.

"I have to tell her goodbye, I'm sorry this was not the plan, and mostly how much I love her," I was sort of yelling and speaking to anyone that would listen to me at the time as I was trying to reach out to her in the hospital waiting room. I could see her there quietly talking to Kathy and Monica, still nervous. I was pacing back and forth and not a soul would listen to me, not the doctors or the beautiful people in white and gold clothes that stood there patiently as I finished my ranting. I felt helpless and to the best of my ability tried to scream, “Ellie I love you, I’m sorry, this wasn’t supposed to happen, please tell the girls I love them and my son and his family!”

As I knelt with my head in my hands I began to feel somewhat helpless as tears formed in my eyes. When I looked up, I felt a warm feeling around me, and then, poof! I was in a glowing cloud; with the kind people in the robes surrounded me with love and comfort. I was floating and feeling very warm and secure, like a warm blanket on a cold winter day. I was wondering where I was going as I started to see people in the distance and hear beautiful music that I had never heard before. I approached them in this warm cloud and as it slowly dissipated, I could see all my loved ones who passed before me and they stood there with outstretched arms. It was like looking into a beautiful rainbow that was glowing with the most radiant colors. Angels have glowing auras of color around them; this shows the goodness in their hearts and angel hood. The ones with the most colors and have gold around them, shows their works are very high so they have special ranking, and have done well serving on earth as well as in heaven. I knew this at the moment I saw them, it was a sight to behold and Jesus was above them holding his hand out as if to welcome me. I was suddenly overwhelmed with happiness to see him and I found myself running to them with joy and love outpouring like the heavenly music filling my soul. I was so engulfed in so much love that I momentarily forgot about leaving my family behind.

3 John 1:14 I hope to see you soon, and we will talk face to face. Peace to you. The friends here send their greetings. Greet the friends there by name.

5

REUNION

After meeting them all and saying our long overdue hellos, I told them that this was probably a mistake and that I'm probably going back, but they unfortunately assured me that it wasn't. This was a bummer; I was totally caught off guard. This was not supposed to happen, not now. Oh, I miss my family already, but also such a joy that has come over me that it's hard to relate. But the truth is stranger than fiction, I'm in Heaven, and I'm sure this destination is due to the wonderful life I had led since meeting Ellie. I'm filled with happiness and regret all at once, yet calmly comforted as these feeling rise and fade.

I was taken to a greeting area, where you are briefed about what lies ahead. This is where you gain all the knowledge you may have not had on earth. This process is amazing and very awakening to realize your faults as well as the feats you have overcome during your time on earth. This process is necessary to become an angel. It allows your mind to adapt to what just took place and what is going to happen from here on out. Realizing your shortcomings, lack of kindness, love and just wrong doing is sad, it becomes something you greatly regret once you are here. No one needs to tell you when you were wrong about something it is blatantly obvious how bad of an effect this was on yourself or others in your life. It is extremely humbling and I begged for forgiveness. On the other hand, it is instrumental to making good decisions from then on, and believe me, as an angel there are a lot of decisions you have to make.

So now that I am here I guess I better learn the ropes. Heaven is nothing like what I imagined. It is a real place like a resort, but better. It is perfect weather not too hot or too cold, sunny all the time and just right. There is no crime, hate, bad thoughts, violence, or stress, just relaxing and social communion. Everyone is polite, cordial and helpful. Since I've come here we have information learning sessions all the time. There is a lot to learn to be a helpful and good angel in heaven.

After arriving and being greeted by loved ones angels took me to a room to rest and get my angel programing. I sort of just relaxed in a huge fluffy easy chair that fit me perfectly and I just seemed to absorb so much pertinent information. Sort of like I was watching it on a screen but there was no screen there. After that I reviewed my family life and I was so thankful for my parents, siblings upbringing and how miraculously I was blessed with Ellie and my family for the last years of my life.

I've now seen all my old friends and relatives that have passed away before me, that part is wonderful. I have spent months telling them all about my son, Ellie, our girls, the grandchildren, and how much they have grown and their lives. It has been great catching up. I've even seen my old pets that have passed away. When I saw my old pets, they ran right to me in a full out sprint, jumping into my arms. By just looking into their eyes, they told me how much they loved me and our family and how happy they were to have belonged to us. They showed their appreciation and it was obvious they would be eternally grateful. I still get to see them regularly, those things are a blessing here.

Oh, Gus and Huey they are here and still inseparable, Huey never attends animal events and Gus pretty much won't do anything without Huey by his side. Because they can communicate by looking at each other they reminisce about their days on earth and seem to snicker a lot. It's definitely a good thing. Gus has friends and relatives here but never had a solid lasting relationship, Huey filled that void in his life.

Philemon 1:4   I always thank my God as I remember you in my prayers,

6

LEARNING THE ROPES

All the angels have been constantly telling me that soon I will get "assigned." They never explained to me what that meant, but I just believed them. Then one day a supervisor, one of the hierarchies, came to me and wanted to meet one on one. This was new. Until now I have stayed with groups and a few people at a time, learning new tasks and daily routines that take place in Heaven. "Today is special," they told me.

I was in a beautiful sort of board room type area with silver and gold decorations, along with white and tan furnishings. In walked a man who looked like he was of Mexican descent, he was quite large and had an accent. The man smiled at me, "Welcome, Rob. I am your mentor and superior angel," I stood up to shake his hand and he just put his hand up as to say take a seat, "My name is Hernandez. You'll find that we will be seeing a lot of each other from now on," he said.

"Very well," I replied with a nod.

"So" said Hernandez, I thought this was an unusual name for a superior, "What are your concerns since you have arrived?" I told him about my concerns about Ellie since I have been gone and how I worried about her,

"She needs someone; she's not cven 60 years old and now she is alone," I expressed, as I mention this Hernandez nods, assuring me she had special angel attention as we speak and that her earthly needs were being met. That message alone made me feel better, right away, but I was still wary, "How do I know if this is the truth?" I asked, trying not to be skeptical, but this is my family we're talking about. Giving a half smile he faced me,

"Look here . . ." Hernandez waved his hand and like a movie playing for me, I saw Ellie, our girls, Ellie's family and friends were all assisting her and she was okay. I could see all of the family more clearly than ever before, I could see their beauty radiating from them and how gentle and pure their souls were. This was new and comforting. I then realized that anytime you think thoughts of an earthly person in Heaven their image is perfectly clear in your mind. I told him how great it was to actually see her again with the girls. A knot formed in my throat and I just wanted to reach out and touch her. I stood up to get a closer look, I wanted to jump into the scene and hug her so badly.

That is when I received the good news. Hernandez told me I am allowed to pick one particular person on earth to be their guardian angel. That meant I was assigned to them for hours each day to help them feel safe, guide their decisions and look over them. When Hernandez asked me who this would this be, I was still looking at Ellie and the family. I turned around suddenly, "Of course it would be my wife." Hernandez smiled, they seem to know everything here, and nodding his head I could tell he was pleased by my decision.

Ruth 3:12 Although it is true that I am a guardian-redeemer of our family, there is another who is more closely related than I.

7

GUARDIAN

Besides, since I could not change the way things are, this gave me an alternative. From this day forward I would be Ellie's guardian angel, so every day I was able to watch over her and help her with small decisions. I could even contact my superiors if I thought she needed more assistance. I learned that in heaven God hears everything even if you don't pray; they already know what you are thinking. But it is respect to pray, properly ask and be specific when you want direction or you are asking for a blessing. Boy, if I only knew this when I was on earth that there are no coincidences. My life would have been a lot easier. I learned that humans cannot control their fate; but they can rearrange it greatly by being good or being bad. Your fate is laid out in a direction your life follows you can change it greatly, it's up to you. Some people receive rewards and some face the consequences of their ways. Boy, I sure wish I would have put this all together when I was young because I'm sure if I would have known this, my life would not only have been easier, and I could have had a more positive affect on those around me.

This is because Heaven strategically arranges all things that are positive and good for people. It is pretty amazing. I just watch over Ellie so some of these things are arranged appropriately for her to meet her needs. As her guardian I am given the opportunity to set up life situations so things go smoothly for my Ellie. It is a wonderful assignment, and I would not want to be guardian of anyone else. I've found that sometimes people on earth are given new assigned guardians, I'm not positive why, but I know there's always a good reason for everything done here.

It has now been over twenty years since I've passed on. It is amazing to me because up here it seems like only a few years. When you have forever and ever, weeks are like minutes.

I have been notified that I will be having another meeting with Hernandez. He was assigned to me when I entered Heaven and we meet on a regular basis. He is very pleased with my guardianship with Ellie. They act as if I consider this a job, which I find humorous. If this is a job, I could take on a few, but I don't bother to mention that, since I want all my attention on Ellie. This is a mission of everlasting love that I never want to give up. This guardian position is perfect for Ellie and I, and it has turned into the biggest blessing.

Ellie is older now, in her early eighties, and still as active as ever. She is so beautiful. She has taken care of herself and has been very involved with our grandchildren. I knew the older grandchildren, my first grandson J.R. is a successful accountant, and our first granddaughter Courtney is a famous hair designer, they were born before I died. They always were blessings to us. My youngest daughter had two beautiful girls' years after I passed and they are still young, so we have four altogether. Oh, and Ellie has a little female Chihuahua and a large tortoise cat. They actually both belong to my youngest granddaughters Kayla and Tori, but these pets adore Ellie. Ellie began to watch the youngest granddaughters that Monica had when they were born and continues to do so even now when they are enrolled in school, so watching over the family pets is just another part of her daily routine. The Chihuahua looks somewhat like our last dog Tasha, and the cat is an active part of the family. These pets get spoiled with turkey treats, special food, a daily walk, and a soft place on her lap full of scratches with her nice fingernails. What pet wouldn't absolutely love Ellie?

In Heaven you have the chance to see what is going on. They, Ellie and our daughters, often say "I wish Dad could see this," and I do! That is the best part of being appointed someone's guardian; you get to watch their life. My family has been so blessed and I am grateful every day. My prayers and heavenly guidance for their success and safety has been more than answered.

Deuteronomy 15:16 But if your servant says to you, "I do not want to leave you," because he loves you and your family and is well off with you,

8

THE ASSIGNMENT

Today is the day I have my appointment with Hernandez. I enjoy meeting with him, he always has the best insight since he is an angel who is full of knowledge and understanding. When we met today he gave me some pretty bad news and when I say *bad*, nothing is "bad" here, so this was devastating. Hernandez told me I had graduated to a new guardianship level and I would be put on an assignment that would have me earthbound. I shook my head, "No, no, I don't want to change, Ellie needs me more than ever now, she is older and I watch over her diligently. I absolutely cannot leave her now," I told him, but Hernandez told me not to be concerned and that in Heaven all things are attended to, but I still did not understand, why now?

He told me my assignment would be particularly important and in order to progress, I must take it. Then another guardian in Heaven would be assigned to Ellie. I was in total disbelief. This cannot be happening. For the first time I felt a longing in my heart at the thought of being away from Ellie. My passing was hard enough to accept but now I really feel like I am deserting her all over again, but I had no choice except to follow my superior's instructions. Up to this point he has never leaded me astray, but I for the first time in years have begun to worry.

After thinking a few minutes I was asking all sorts of questions, "What will I do? Will it be similar to what I do now? Will I get to see my home or my family or most importantly, Ellie? How will I know what to do?" Hernandez just smiled. My mind was racing, will I be old? Will I be young, or just born? That is a scary thought. I wanted to know exactly what I would be doing.

"This will all be explained, please trust in our decisions they are the best for everyone involved." With that confident grin he nodded towards the door and I knew our discussion was over. As I slowly got up to leave I tried to give him a smile but not much came through. Hernandez could see my disappointment and just gave me a pat on the back, "Rob you must believe this is for the best," he tried to assure me,

"I know I will do my best," responding low, still not convinced of my thoughts.

The next day I went into an extension of my prior angel training. I was still Ellie's guardian but unfortunately not for much longer. They told me that I would be gone for a period of time which was still to be determined. I'm not sure how long that would be but I want to get back quick, so I can take over once again as Ellie's guardian. They told me I would not have any recollection of familiar things that were once in my life, people, faces, places, names, etc. Everything would be new to me. I would understand how the world works after all I was there for seventy two years; I hope I have a clear enough understanding. After all, a lot has changed since I've been gone. I will understand that I am myself and I am on a mission, but my identity and new persona will not be revealed until I arrive.

My new identity will be given upon arriving to earth and my mission will be revealed as I progress on earth in my new identity. I was told that when I see other earthly assigned angels that I will have communication with them by just looking into their eyes, when our gazes meet we will be able to communicate without speaking. There will be *a twinkling* and automatically we will have a form of mental telepathy. We just think of what to say and we can understand everything between the two of us. I found out that the longer I am on earth the less I will remember about Heaven. But I will know my identity as I was previously, Rob, for seven decades on earth. I will be able to draw on my past life experience, but I know a lot has changed over the years. This new identity which remains to be seen will be interesting.

I will return back to heaven when my assignment is completed on earth. Of course, I wanted to know more than anything how long I would be away, and how I will be able to know Ellie is being looked after properly. Hernandez just looked at me with half open eyes almost reprimanding me with a nod, "You will know in time, trust in our heavenly decisions Rob and you will be fine." With that he turned and left the room while I sat at the end of the table, my head in my hands so full of worry and longing for Ellie. In a moment with one last plea I jumped to my feet and asked Hernandez,

"Can you please talk to whoever assigned me to leave heaven as Ellie's guardian, I don't want to be disrespectful but no one can look after Ellie with the love and care like I do, please!" Hernandez stopped for a second and just proceeded nodding his head. I can only think, fretfully, *that this is not good.* I instantly overlooked Ellie as her guardian to help her, as much as I can before I have to leave for my assignment.

They also told me that I will go to sleep for two whole days and when I awaken I will be on earth. Then my journey will begin as an carthly angel. I do not yet know why I have been chosen to do this as I did not understand until now there were such assignments. I have been reassured that each mission is perfectly assigned to each earthbound angel, and apparently, this is perfectly fitted for me, whatever that means.

In Heaven they tell you what you need to know, when you need to know it, you never have to think or worry about details. So I just want to get this mission over and get back to heaven so I can watch over Ellie once again.

Psalm 4:8   In peace I will lie down and sleep, for you alone, Lord, make me well in safety.

9

TIME TO GO

A few days later, Hernandez came to tell me it was time. Again I told him of my concern for Ellie and he reassured me things were going to work out perfectly. I asked for one last look at Ellie, and I felt what used to be tears and that huge knot in my throat, "Hernandez, promise me nothing bad will happen to her, especially while I'm gone," I spoke softly, Hernandez nodded and took my arm and led me to a corridor I had never seen before. I felt like a child being punished and there was nothing I could do, I had to obey my heavenly instructions. I walked slowly as if I were going to a torture chamber instead of on a heavenly mission to earth. My doubts were high and confidence low. What I should be looking forward to I was dreading, only because I'm leaving Ellie behind.

Before opening an unusually big golden door, Hernandez gave me a full view and rundown on my entire family. I felt better at first better because they were all well, but then worse since I won't see them until I get back to Heaven. I felt a little like I was dying a heavenly death, if there was such a thing. At any rate I was again leaving my family.

He opened the large golden doors and we went into a beautiful bedroom. It was a dreamy baby blue, with silvers, whites and cream colors and it had the softest most comfortable bed I had ever seen. I climbed in and it felt like a cloud engulfing me. I fell into a deep slumber and dreamt wonderful dreams about being able to see Ellie back on Earth. Of course if I did see her I would not know it because of not being able to recognize people, but either way it was a good dream. As I'm drifting in my dream I was smiling and gazing into Ellie's beautiful brown eyes, I began to compose a love letter that I would recite to her when I hold her in my arm's again.

To the End of Time, I will Love You,

To my Beautiful Wife Ellie Marie Harper,

It has been decades since we have looked into each other's eyes.
I remember the very last touch and glance you gave me at the hospital.
Your love and concern has never been forgotten.

I have been with you in spirit every day since my passing and have watched over you daily with love and pride. You have been so strong with our family and children, I realize more every day why God allowed me to have you as my mate.

When we see each other again in heaven I can hardly wait to embrace you and hold you in my arms once more.

You are the love of my life and until the end of time,
I will always love and adore you . . . . Rob

Then Hernandez appeared, and that scared me, and interrupted my peacefulness.

"This is the final debriefing," he said, making sure to remind me I would not recall anything familiar at all from before. I will only recall my experiences as Rob on earth and can draw upon them to guide me for wisdom. Soon I will not even remember Hernandez. I will only have the contact with the earthly angels which would be closer than I initially thought. I am to stay diligent and strong throughout the entire mission no matter what challenges I may face. "Rob, what is my name?" he asked, and I replied,

"Harry, of course!"

"No guess again," he said with a laugh,

"Herman!" I exclaimed, he just shook his head,

"Good Rob, the transition is taking place," Okay? I'm not sure exactly what that meant, but I fell back asleep and slept like a baby. In Heaven you don't need sleep, but boy I sure do now, and it feels so good. Somehow this seems strange and good at the same time. While sleeping a voice came to me and said,

"My words will be guiding your path, they will ring through your memory and stay in your soul, you will never be alone, now sleep and have trust in your faith . . ."

Job 19:13 "He has alienated my family from me; my acquaintances are completely estranged from me.

10

THE AWAKENING

I finally woke up, expecting to feel invigorated, yet I felt terrible! I was damp and clammy and my eyes were closed. Maybe I'm coming through the atmosphere or something? I think I've been in an accident, I'm not sure what kind of accident but this is bad. I feel yucky and quite out of place. I'm either in a bad dream or I'm not yet on earth.

It feels like people are moving me around, rubbing me then they try to force feed me. I have not eaten earthly food in over twenty five years. "Oh man, yuck, whatever is in my mouth is dreadful!" I tried to spit it out and I can't seem to talk, I'm trying, but I only whimper. "Boy, I sure wish I knew what was going on." Then I remembered what's his name had told me, *"When you're afraid just pray and a guardian will listen."* So, I began to pray, asking things like, "Where in the world am I, and I can't see, what is going on?" Then in the middle of my prayer, it dawned on me. Maybe I'm a blind man. Oh, my goodness. Come to think about it I have no idea. Right now all I know is I'm in a place that smells bad, I'm damp, it feels cold, and I don't hear many people voices. I may be in an asylum? People are howling and whining enough, that's for sure I remember visiting the nut house to see a great uncle when I was a kid; people were making these kinds of sounds there.

"Hello, Can someone in Heaven hear me? I'm very alone here!" For the first time in over twenty years I'm very afraid! Then I heard a voice I had not heard before.

It said "Rob this is Patience, your Heavenly contact, I am here,"

"Oh, thank you, thank you, Patience," I praised, whew, that's a relief. I asked her to help me to get out of here so I could see what's going on, but Patience told me that in good time my assignment would unfold. She asked if I was hurt and when I thought about it I told her I was okay. She kindly told me to be patient before leaving me,

"Be patient, Rob. Your destiny lies ahead. You are a wise man and you can do this, or you would not have been sent."

So I waited for a sign to come to me and when nothing happened I fell asleep. Maybe I'm being taught a lesson so I can talk about it like they do at the information sessions we have in heaven. Yep, that's probably it. I can do this, I'm going to do it and do it well. I'm going to get it done and over with and go back soon. These were the thoughts I kept repeating as I fell in and out of sleep. "I'm going to do good, I'm going to complete this mission . . ."

The next day I woke up and still had no sight, I'm sure this means I'm blind. Someone keeps washing me, Whoa, this is weird, I'm trying to tell them to leave me alone but they keep feeding me this awful stuff. They force a tube in my mouth and squirt liquid in. I'm trying to swallow, but I can't seem to find my hands to help the process. Being blind does not help either, I feel quite a mess. I'm going to stay asleep till this makes sense, but boy, things sure smell strong, kind of like urine and gross food.

Suddenly I was being rubbed really hard and woke up to the words: "She's going to die, she's going to die! Help her!" All I could think is there must be a damsel in distress. Then I realized I have some sort of vision now. I could just barely see a face and it was massive. I must be hallucinating, I felt like this face was as huge as a bed. But my vision was so blurry and I was so disoriented that I'm not sure what's happening. Next thing I knew, someone was looking at me and poking at my eyes and putting drops in them. Maybe I have a weird eye disease? Anyway, I decided there was no other explanation and that this must be my doctor. I just was so tired again; I didn't put much thought into it and fell immediately back to sleep.

Today I woke up and could actually see a little bit more, although it was still quite blurry. It seems that I am in a prison type ward. I only have blankets on the floor to sleep on and a bowl of water set on the floor, it looks more like a troth than a bowl. I can't believe this is my assignment; to be in prison. What in the world? Did I do something wrong? Am I being punished? I need to figure out why am I here? There must be some mistake. I hate to doubt heavenly decisions, but I'm worried this is not where I am supposed to be. No one wants to be a Doubting Thomas. There is already one of them in Heaven and we are reminded never to doubt the Lord's word. This just seems unusual; I guess maybe at this point I'm hoping this is where I'm supposed to be, and not a mistake.

I'm alone and trying to talk to get someone's attention. My voice is raspy and it sounds like some sort of whine. The people show up again and there is a woman; I think she is the nurse. I'm surely still hallucinating, they look huge. They look so unbelievably huge and it feels like they are dangling me in the air. Boy the drugs I'm on are powerful, and I don't like this at all. None of it makes sense. I feel dizzy and extremely weak. Then they set me down again on the cold damp floor.

Now for sure I'm hallucinating, they just put a dog in my ward. I am seriously on big time drugs or something. This dog is huge, like everything else here, and it is licking me. I feel damp and clammy again. This is a dream, I'm sure this really cannot be happening. Suddenly overwhelmed, I pass out.

In my dream I'm convincing myself that *this for sure, is not reality.* In my subconscious sleep I called out to Patience in prayer and she assured me that if I was not in pain, everything is alright. I told her about the drugs and the dog experience and she told me I will be fine. I just needed to adjust. I tried to explain I have never been a drug user and this is why they are affecting me so badly. Patience just told me to rest and it will all work out. I was doing my best not to have doubt, but maybe I'm out of sync with humans and earth. I need to stop panicking and give my body time to adjust. So again I slept, deciding that was what will give me strength to get this mission started. After all coming through the universe back to earth has to take a toll on anyone. Maybe I'm older now and will die soon so I can go back, yeah, maybe that's why I'm not adjusting very well.

Upon waking I was lying next to a dog, or what appeared to be a dog like figure at least. Maybe I've been dreaming about my past pets? What is going on? Before I could call upon Patience again, to figure this out she came to me. Thank God, "Patience," I said, "please explain this I have no voice and I'm still hallucinating!" Her voice was calm as she spoke,

"Just wait, your identity will be revealed today," *Great*, I thought, *Maybe I will come out of this crazy faze and get out of this loony bin.*

Genesis 27:23 He did not recognize him, for his hands were hairy like those of his brother Esau: so he proceeded to bless him.

11

IDENTITY UNFOLDS

A few minutes later the nurse came, it's time for my daily force feeding of the awful food. They make me choke it down; even if I am a convict I deserve better slop than that. I'm glad when that's finally over. Then she took me and washed me up. Which is good because it feels like it's been days since I've bathed. I don't even care this nurse is going to bathe me in this hallucinating state I definitely can't do it myself. The drugs are so powerful I can barely stand sometimes. As she bathes me I feel soothed and relaxed, I wonder if I am going to get a shave, I feel quite furry and scruffy. Maybe it's the warm water or just knowing the information that I will understand more today is a relief in itself. But I have to admit now bathed and a little food in my belly I feel surprisingly better.

She then took me over to an area and used a blowing machine to dry me. This must be a new thing on earth for people. Ah, this actually feels quite good. Then she sat me up in front of a mirror. I was shocked let alone horrified at what I saw! I looked like a DOG! A weird little DOG! I feel faint I think I'm hallucinating again, and before I could straighten out the thoughts in my head I passed out.

I kept dreaming and thinking that this cannot be true! Where is Patience, is Heaven testing me? I need to have faith in this mission. I need to find a Heavenly being on earth so I can communicate. Patience came to me while dreaming and assured me that everything was going according to plan. I asked her, "Am I a dog or am I going crazy?" Sternly she replied,

"Rob, you are what you are and you are not crazy. If you are not in pain try to be patient," I let her know I was being as patient as a human angel can be.

Upon waking I was whimpering again. I wish I could talk clearly, but I can't. I wonder if there is something wrong with my throat or my voice box. The words are garbled and sound unfamiliar. Maybe I'm going to speak a foreign language. I need to find out my mission and get away from this craziness. I am going to take on this mission with gusto. I am Rob, I know who I am, and I can do this. This is what I have decided. I am going to use the determination I used to have in my former life and do the best job I can. Just as I was thinking this I got a proper look at my arms, since my vision was finally clear enough for me to see.

Oh my God, I am a dog! I just got a look at paws, *my* paws! And I have these enormous things on my head, I think they are my ears, they are the size of basset hound ears or at least they feel like it except they stand straight up! I am a weird tiny white dog. Why didn't they tell me this? No wonder I was feeling unshaven. I am in a pen with other dogs and they are sneering at me. I hope I'm dreaming. Maybe this is a phase on my way to earth? Possibly this is just temporary or maybe even a mistake? "Whoa! Get away from my behind! Quit sniffing me!" Oh, I felt that and it sure felt real. Maybe this is permanent? I may have to think like a dog. Stand up for myself, or sit down so I won't be sniffed. There has to be a reason for this. My mentor, whatever his name is, would not have let me come here without good reason. I squirmed back into a corner to observe and think this over. I wanted to stay clear of the other bigger dogs, which they all were *big* since I was so very small.

“I never did grow into my ears, maybe if I keep them down I will look normal.” . . . Sophie

Proverb 6:30   People do not despise a thief if he steals to satisfy his hunger when he is starving.

12

HUNGER

Soon, I realized I had hunger back. In heaven I never got hungry, but this is familiar. Then I smelled the food. In the pen it came in three big bowls. So I ran up and tried to get a bite. I fought tooth and nail just to reach the bowl because I was the smallest and more often than not I was pushed aside. So when us puppies were fed I had to try and muscle my way in just to get a bite of food. That's all I got, one bite, one measly bite and it's not even that tasty, but when you get this hungry you'll eat anything. The others growled and snarled bad dog words at me. They did not like me at all. They warned me to back off and I was just a runt, and a sicky. Okay, yes, I was always a thin man, but this is ridiculous! I stayed as aggressive as possible trying to stand my own, but I never received much food.

The nurse and doctor people sometimes came and put me in a small area and gave me my own serving, but that only made the others dogs sneer more and call me runt, spoiled or baby. There was only one dog that was remotely nice to me, he was a shaggy haired sort of breed, and he seemed to try and let me get into the food bowl and never growled at me or called me names.

I call this guy "Shaggy" for obvious reasons, and he told me I have a reputation for getting all the attention, and the other dogs think I am faking being sick. He said that sometimes I just lie there and shake a lot and if the people see it they come and scoop you up, this annoys the other pups. Wow, that explains why I feel so dizzy and sick sometimes. I just wake up disoriented and feel like I need sleep. I asked him what this is from, but he did not seem to know. He told me he has protected me when I was spacing out and shaking on the floor. Once a dog was trying to push me and paw at me when I couldn't do anything, Shaggy said he stood between me and the other dog to protect me. I thanked him and told him he was a good friend, in which he just looked at me and gave me a nudge.

I have to think about this and set up a strategy. I keep reminding myself, I am on a mission; I have to figure this out. So I hide sometimes in small places to dart out first to get a good bite or two of food before the gang woke up and the feeding frenzy began. From my calculations I'm at a puppy farm! Yep, I'm just one of the mill. What could that have to do with my mission? I doubt that I'm here to help these dogs? I have not even thus far seen any angels in any form? What does this all mean, where am I supposed to be? I'm pretty sure it is certainly not with here.

This is Blue or "Scruffy" at an Oktoberfest
with a short haircut.

Proverbs 15:30 Light in a messenger's eyes brings joy to the heart, and good news gives health to the bones.

13

FIRST CONTACT

The one thing I did get was attention from all humans that visited this puppy farm. They all seemed to pick me up and want to hold me until they learn something about me. Not sure what but they never take me, I'm just put back in that smelly pen. Then one day a lady came to look at all of us dogs and when I looked into her eyes it happened. My *eyes twinkled* and so did hers. I was so excited; I knew immediately that this was it, part of my mission! I asked her just by looking only, *"Are you going to take me home with you? Are you my mission?"*

*"*No, I'm just a locater,*" she* said. I then asked her what that meant, and she explained that she is here to make sure I'm where I should be. She also told me that she would help to get me out of here and that it won't be long. Her name was Cathy and she told me she was sent here to check on me and see how to arrange things. Arrange things, well that's good. I knew this had to be temporary! She was pretty and had smells of other puppies on her, she must be a puppy angel, if there is such a thing. Anyway, I'm so glad she came to find me, I feel much better, I just wish she could have stayed and held me longer. She pretended to be interested in me

when talking to the breeder and I was just hoping she would take me with her, “Oh, well.”

After she left, I was filled with hope, and for some reason I really liked her name “Cathy”. *That’s a good name for an angel,* I thought. Whew, this is a big, big relief. I’m getting out of here. Although the woman and man are nice to me, I figured out they are not a doctor or nurse they are the breeders. Can you believe it! I came back to earth as a dog. Remember what I told you about luck, it is hard to define. Well this is definitely *goofy luck.*

Job 7:14   even then you frighten me with dreams and terrify me with visions,

14

THE VET

Today, the breeders took me to the Vet. I hate the smell of this place; it smells like antiseptic, which nauseates me. Now I understand why my pets panicked when I brought them to their appointments. Also I feel quite intimidated by other dogs that are trying to sniff me. Your nose as a dog is a hundred times more powerful than that of a human, so now that I smell all these crazy new smells, they scare me. Some of these animals are really sick, not only physically but mentally too. You should have seen the Great Dane in the lobby, he was winking at me, and I think he must be gay. If there is such a thing as gay dogs or maybe he's just confused? Jeez, what was he thinking? I'm afraid to think about it, so I just told him "Please, let's be real here and not so weird and goofy, you big disgusting drooling thing!"

Oh boy, it's my turn. The breeder lady carries me into a little room; meanwhile I look back at the other dogs in the waiting room. One had her paws over her face, another was sniffing anything that moved, I think they all acted or look a bit crazed here? Maybe the puppy farm is not so bad; the pups there are just mean. Ewe, I just caught sight of that Great Dane, he was still winking and licking his lips at me. Maybe he wanted to eat me? Oh, that's an unpleasant thought. I was frightened enough, so my mind was trying to erase all these wild thoughts and think pleasant things but it's not working this time.

Now I'm in the little room, sitting on a cold metal table. The Vet prepared a shot and I couldn't even look anymore, because "OWE, Those shots hurt!" Then they clipped my nails and I hate all of this. I have never had long nails and definitely don't like these. I can't stand it; it's like a slow torture chamber getting my nails clipped. It's like nails on a chalkboard but somehow even worse. I always kept my nails very short as a human, these are absolutely crazy. I just kept screaming like a little schoolgirl getting her hair pulled when they were clipping them. I wanted to bite the Veterinarian, I hated it so bad. I was trying to listen to what the humans were saying, but my whimpering was getting in the way. I heard them say something about "Caesars"; I used to love those salads. Maybe I'm going to get one? That was the only pleasant thought that came to mind.

Then I hear "Chihuahua, Female three month's old 1lb. 9oz." Wait—WHAT!!!? Female!!!? What do you mean?! I cannot be a female dog! Can I? My human soul is a man; can my canine soul or body be a girl? I guess I better check out my parts . . . Yep! I'm a girl alright! For heaven's sake, really? Am I a girl? How or why is this possible? How could I have met this unfortunate fate? I guess just trying to survive and get my earthly bearings again occupied my time so much that I never bothered to pay attention to what I was. At the farm we are all just puppies. Boy, oh Boy, this is truly dumb luck. I'm not only a dog but a *girl* dog! Wow, wow, wow, this is totally crazy. I bet someone is getting a good laugh at this, I'm not sure who but this is ridiculous!

I hope if this is my mission I can play the part. Well, I guess either way I will have to. I hope the female hormones kick in, up until now my heart and soul is that of a seventy-two year old male. I feel like a man in a girl's body. Holy Mackerel, This must be some kind of lesson or pay back for something I did wrong on earth. I am a purebred Chihuahua, with something definitely wrong with me? I can't believe this; I didn't even like the pure breed Chihuahua's when I was a human, they are usually so high strung. Come to think about it, I was strung about as high as I could be in that appointment a few minutes ago. Why couldn't I be a big strong male dog? I just don't understand how this could possibly be my mission?

The vet is using all sorts of terms I don't know. After even more poking and prodding they finally take me back to the puppy farm. It doesn't smell good at the breeder's either but the breeder's place is way better than the Vet. Now that I think about it, no wonder that male Great Dane liked me. How ridiculous! We couldn't even, oh no, oh no. Besides what would people call them? Great—HuaHuas? Great Chi-Chi's? Chi-Chi Danes? That is a horrible thought; I'm just totally worn out and need sleep. My butt hurts from the shots and my head is pounding from a mix of stress and the awful scent in the air. On the way home I tried to watch out the window of the car. I can only see countryside and lots of grass; I'm getting kind of dizzy, besides I don't recognize anything anyway. I was told I wouldn't remember or recognize any people or places, but I guess it doesn't hurt to try. It exercises my brain back to earthly thinking even if it is useless. Last thing I remember after falling asleep, is contemplating, where in the world have I been placed? Then I fell asleep and didn't remember a darn thing till morning.

James 1:6 But when you ask, you must believe and not doubt, because the one who doubts is like a wave of the sea, blown and tossed by the wind.

15

VISITORS

When awaking I was still sore from the shots. I began thinking that this whole mission was becoming a huge mystery, but I have not called upon Patience yet since I am trying to sort things out on my own. Instead, with my thoughts of wonder, I lie still waiting until it's time for food again, hunger is truly a real issue as a puppy here on earth. I'm beginning to appreciate eating anything as long as it's edible and I'm able to digest it.

Today a lot of people visited the puppy farm, but again, no one took me. They all held me though, I like that the best; they hold me and pet me. If there's one part of the mission I enjoy most, it's the human touch.

I don't know why no one will take me, and I don't think being here is part of my mission. Today two ladies came by and the one held me for a long time and the other one held my shaggy friend. They were inspecting us and the one who held me was very gentle, "Aw, she's so little to have such issues," she said as she kept petting me and even held me close to her neck. Oh, she smelled delightful; I liked her touch very much. She gave me a little kiss on top of the head and said softly, "I like you, little one . . ." Well, I liked her too; I just wish she would pick me. The other lady kept petting and holding Shaggy, and then she gave the breeder lady something. I was hoping they liked us both, but who knows. People often hold me but they always pick the other dogs to adopt. I think the lady holding shaggy will be back, she was talking baby talk and scratching him all over. Shaggy was wagging his tail and being especially loving.

Immediately after they left Shaggy and I had a talk, he thought the lady who held him would come back to see him if not take him home. I told him I'm very hopeful the nice lady liked me. Up until now I have not mentioned any angel stuff to Shaggy, but today I asked him "Do you think those ladies were angels?" He cocked his head,

"I don't know, why do you ask? Besides, what's an angel?" Then I remembered I'm talking to a puppy that's only month's old,

"Forget it, just thinking," I said. He scampered off to boast to the other puppies about the attention he had from the visitors. I just watched how the other dogs listened and a few peeked over his shoulder and glanced at me. I did not look them in the eyes as they all outweigh me by at least double and I did not want to provoke them for any reason.

It was a few days later and one of two ladies came back. I was happy to find that it was the one who held me! She had two small girls with her and I was picked up and handed to them one at a time. They giggled and passed me back and forth, the one squeezed a little too tight, and the other put me in one of her shirt pockets. I could get used to them but the squeezing makes me kind of nauseous. I thought this might be my chance to leave, but again, no. They just seemed to enjoy petting and holding me then they left without choosing me. Why does no one take me? Visitors seem to inspect me and put me back as if I'm a reject or something. Darn, I really liked these people. I'm really sad they didn't like me. I walked over to the sliding door where I could see my reflection. Maybe I'm too weird looking? Never thought about looks as a dog, who would? But when you're hoping to go to a good home, I guess it's important.

As time goes on, I still fight for my food, and now they all call me runt and don't play with me at all. I miss seeing and looking after . . . what was her name? I can't even remember what she looks like but I know I used to be her guardian I wish I still was. I do remember . . . *I loved her.* Shaggy is even nicer to me now, he helps me with the bullies and even blocks them from pushing me. He is a real friend, my first friend I've made in this new life. I hope I meet other's as nice as Shaggy as I progress in my mission.

I did not realize that dogs have such real feelings. I'm actually depressed and the breeders are worried about me. They are constantly checking me over and I still wonder why. Then one day the other woman came back, the one who visited with the lady that I liked and it was on that day that she took Shaggy away with her. As she was giving the breeder lady something and the breeder was explaining things to her, Shaggy already in her arms managed to look back, "I'll miss you runt cakes," he said, I wagged my tail and said,

"Me too, take care, Shaggy and don't forget me,

"I won't," he replied.

I was happy for him, but now I have no friends here. He was three months old and glad to go to a new home away from here. I am four months old, much older than most the puppies that are here, but smaller than all of them still. I'm still getting shots because apparently I'm not growing well and I weigh one pound fifteen ounces. I've learned that I actually am kind of a reject . . . and they don't suspect I'll live very long. Yeah, that means back to Heaven. That would be okay with me; I've been lonely here and miss my family in heaven and my old assigned position as a guardian. Shaggy leaving makes me extremely sad, and I know now that these earthly feelings are very real. I just tuck my head into the corner and curl up, wishing for morning, praying that something would happen soon. I told Patience I was trying to be patient and strong for the wimpy little girl dog that I was and that I'm trying not to doubt why I'm here but it is hard. I also prayed for all of the bigger dogs to leave me alone. The less noise or motion I make the more they ignore me, so I just lay still till I fall asleep this gives them no reason to bother with me.

1 Chronicles 16:27   Splendor and majesty are before him; strength and joy are in his dwelling place.

16

NEW BEGININGS

Within the next few days there were lots more visitors looking to adopt puppies. I think every one of them held me but after they learned some dreaded news my adoption was a no go. I heard one man say "who's going to pay that for a sick dog?" Well there you go. No one wants a *new sick puppy.* I feel doomed to be stuck here until I get well. Besides, not one of the visitors smelled as good as the lady with the little girls. And she even kissed my sick head. I'm trying to stay positive but it's a daily challenge to be here alone and so small.

Weeks passed before that lady with the two small girls happened to come back to the puppy farm. For the first time, it felt warm and hopeful. They all held me and I was praying, "Please don't set me down, I don't want to stay here anymore." Then low and behold they put me in a towel wrapped me up and then I was riding in a car. The little girls were ecstatic, and were arguing who was going to hold me first in the car. The lady said,

"Now girls, you can both take turns holding her, just be careful, she's tiny and frail," I knew it; no one wanted a new *frail puppy.* Thank the heavens or Patience, that this wonderful lady wanted me for some unknown reason. I know someone heard my prayers, as usual. But truly heaven and their angels always hear everything; they could be wearing ear plugs and still get the message. Ha, I'm feeling a little more confident, now, let's just hope this streak of luck doesn't run out too fast.

Hey, it just hit me; this must be the start of my mission! I was apprehensive and excited at the same time and just so darn glad to get out of the puppy farm. This is the first day of my assignment. These people must be the reason I am here. There is a mom and two daughters and they kept saying "Thank you, Mommy," I just kept looking around and smelling everything. The girls took turns holding me and they smelled good, kind of like lunch meat and cookies. I liked the towel they brought along to wrap me in as well, it smelled clean and was soft. I just really want some of that familiar smelling food of lunch meat and cookies. It's funny what you recall from previous earthly thoughts and pleasures. I licked them and tried to snuggle into them tight. I wanted them to like me so I wouldn't have to go back to the farm.

When the car stopped we arrived at a home. It was kind of cool outside; it must be Spring since I see some flowers. I have not been free outside since coming back to earth, this feels great. They put me down in the grass, it rubs on my belly. I have to pee, ahhh that feels good, kind of natural. It's funny to use the outdoors as your toilet. At the puppy farm we went on old papers. I looked around and there were big houses all around. We were in front of one. If this is my new home then wow, it looks like a castle.

They picked me up and brought me inside this big house and everyone was ooh-ing and ahh-ing over me.

The man seemed less than happy about my presence, actually kind of mad. I'm just tired and needed sleep; I think the excitement of today has left me exhausted. A chubby tough brown dog came over to me and sniffed me and wagged its tail apprehensively, she sneered "You are only visiting, I run this house and you are only a guest," murmuring in dog words.

"Okay are you from Heaven?" I blatantly asked, but she would not answer or look into my eyes. Then a cat, a massive cat, came up and stared right at me. I stared back hoping that she would be from heaven, but unfortunately no. She just washed herself and looked unconcerned about me. Boy I must be really small, either that or she is just really huge. They call her Tinker. I only know this because they stuck her in my face and said "Tinker this is your new friend." Then the little girls took me into a room with a little bed and some bowls. The other dog, cat and I, all have separate food dishes. Wow, my own plate! This is already way better than the puppy farm, breeders, or where I came from. I'm so happy to be at this new place.

Next the little girls put a collar on me, which was two sizes too big. I don't like it but its okay if it comes with this territory and these people that helped me out of that puppy farm place. After all, each of my pets in my past life had a special collar, and I guess that's basically what this is. It's kind of heavy, and quite clumsy, but I will have to get used to it. If it's part of my mission I will wear it with pride! Ha, it's not as if I could take it off anyways.

They put me in a room that had a night light with a little bed, the towel I came here in, and some water in a bowl. I don't like being alone in this room but it is an improvement over fighting to eat or even sleeping on a damp floor. They put a funny looking type of pad on the floor and told me go potty, go potty and patted the pad. I tilted my head as I looked at them . . . I guess I'm supposed to pee on that diaper thing. Ha, I remember, diapers are for babies. They petted me more and the little girls were arguing about what my name is. I tried to tell them "Rob," but it sounded like a whine. They were saying names so fast; I just kept looking from one to the other, and not sure of what exactly they were saying. They would hold me up and say a name then squeeze me in the blanket. The big cat sat on the counter up high looking at them on the floor with me. She seemed totally unconcerned but never bothered to leave.

Finally, the mom came by and told the girls to put me to bed, since I must be exhausted, which wasn't far from the truth. They kissed my head about twenty times and were still arguing over names when they shut off the light. I sat in my new little bed with my blanket; there was a little dull light next to the floor giving the room a glow. It was better than the farm, but I whined because I was lonely for them and I wanted more pets, I like that part. I felt like a sniveling kid who was home sick when spending the night at a friend's house for the first time. I just wanted it to be morning soon. It wasn't like the little girls didn't want me to go with them to bed, they begged, but their mom said "No, you may roll over on top of her in your sleep and suffocate her. She needs her own bed." The man was just shaking his head and seemed very unhappy about me.

"That dog or me! You choose!" I heard him yell. Oh boy, that is not good for me, and I know it, I snuggle down and begin to worry about going back to that awful puppy farm. I'm lonely for Shaggy and his warm demeanor. I remember how important friends are in life, even for a dog.

The cat jumped over the barrier during the night, her litter box is in this room. I asked her again if she is from Heaven. She just scoffed, "You silly thing, what have you been told?" I tried to tell her that I was once human and here on a mission, but she just rolled her eyes and continued to ignore me, jumped over and out, bidding me a good night. I realize my voice is very high and I had never talked to anyone in conversation except Shaggy. I don't think I come across very serious in a conversation at all. I've decided that I'm going to try to develop a strong talking voice so the other pets will actually want to hear me and possibly converse with me.

I took the time to pray to Patience and thank her for getting me here, even though I'm not sure where *here* is. I was very afraid I was going to be left at the puppy farm to be a guardian over those mean dogs. She came to me during the night and reassured me that everything would work out just fine. I am so thankful that angels or messengers from heaven are assigned to little pet angels like me, or I would be so lost without her guidance and her constants wisdom. This made me feel less anxious and maybe even a little less afraid.

Psalm 49:13 This is the fate of those who trust in themselves, and of their followers, who approve their sayings.

17

THE MAID

The next morning a maid or someone came in to help the girls get off to school, "What's your name, little one?" she asked softly, I just looked at her quizzically and she scooped me up and talked to me in the goofiest voice. The little girls squealed,

"Her name is Sophie, we agreed on it this morning!" The girls ran right in and took me from her arms. I was exhausted from a worrisome sleep. The mom took me from her daughter's and kissed my head, taking me outside with the brown dog. Ah, that feels good. The grass is wet on my tummy but I needed relief. Once back inside the little girls came into my room to pet me once more, then they were out the door and off to school. Soon the mom and dad followed out the door, the man said nothing and barely looked at me but the mom kissed me a few times and told me she would be back soon. So, now I was left with the maid. I really like the mom, she has a natural loving nature and I like her smile and smell, she brought me home even though she knows I'm almost too frail.

Whenever the maid had time she came over to check on me and pick me up. She doesn't know what to think of me, "You're just another mouth to feed and thing to look after, aren't you," she said, but at least she said it with a smile. She seems older but nice and quite busy; I like her gentleness and she smells yummy too. As a dog you can sense and smell everything on a person, like food, fear, hate, love, even pain and even something as fatal as disease. The nose of a dog is a great tool. I smell a kindness and tenderness on this maid, along with some morning breakfast which smells just as wonderful and delicious.

I have only been here one day and it is a million times better than where I had been. It smelled rancid to me at the breeders and everything was absolutely filthy, though it's not much of a surprise why, since puppies are not very clean. Here everything is large and clean. This house is huge and I don't travel far from my bed since I fear I may get lost. My dog voice is not very good it is only a muffled whining sound but I am practicing whenever I am alone. In my head I try to form words but it does not come out very good, let alone clear. I kind of whimper, it is sad and I feel like I'm behind when I need to learn everything as fast as possible to get going with my mission. Maybe Patience will show me a "Puppy Angel Manual" or something that could give me some sort of direction here.

It has been days and I still do not know what my reason for being here is? The girls have a lot of visitors; the mom and dad work and the dog and cat have absolutely no information about anything except their daily agendas. I'm trying to watch the activity and try to learn whatever I can.

Let me tell you, this feels like I'm living in the land of the giants. The world needs to know to treat small species with concern for their size; it's truly frightening down here! There is so much activity I usually hide under something or beg to be picked up; otherwise I'm afraid I'll be stepped on. From this view it looks like the people are skyscrapers with feet that can crush you! At the puppy farm humans were never in the pen, I just had to watch out for the clumsy and mean puppies. I'm going to get good at scooting out of their way and passing by when the coast is clear. I will have to become my own traffic police to watch for moving giant people.

Job 12:7 “But ask the animals, and they will teach you, or the birds the sky, and they will tell you;

18

PET AGENDAS

The cat always appears very aloof, but it is obviously an act. She hears and sees everything. She always eases my worries, like when the people are gone, and it feels like they might not return, she'll say "Don't worry kid the people are coming back soon, after all they live here." She also has a great meow and cat gestures that everyone appreciates. She pretends to be washing herself or purring but is really listening to every word and movement in the house. She knows where everyone is, where they all are going and about how long till they come home. She never goes outside, which I kind of feel sorry for her, but she has the run of the entire house which is huge. I've only been in a couple rooms and it is a nice place to live. I think I like this "Tinker" cat. She seems to know all the ways of the people that live here, so I've decided I need to watch and learn from her.

I was listening a few days later and heard Tinkerbell say "Put me down, please put me down right now," Then I heard a few grunts of displeasure. I peeked out from my little bed to see blonde haired Kayla, one of the little girls, running through the hall with Tinker in her arms, but she was holding onto her underneath her front paws in the air and her back legs dangling down. It looked like she was choking or something with her paws over her head. Yet Tinker never wiggled or protested other than her low meowing pleas. Kayla was laughing and telling her how they were planning their hiding spot. Then I heard Tinker meow lowly, “If I had known this sooner, I would have hidden from you.”

After this escapade she was sauntering by and I decided it was a good time to ask her why she can’t go outside. She told me she was declawed, “Oh” I said, “That’s because, Why?” Tinker explained that she was to be an indoor cat and she would not need claws if she didn’t have to protect herself in the wild. *I wish my nails were gone*, I thought, *Getting them cut them is the worst torture ever.* Then Tinker piped up,

“If I could change one thing that would be it, I would want my claws back.” After I had been so willing to give mine up I said,

“Well Tinker, when life gives you lemons, you make lemonade.” Ha, I love it when those human thoughts just come. Tinker cocked her head at me, and gave me a peculiar look,

“Have you lost your mind, little dog?” asking me skeptically. I sat up straight,

“No, no, what I mean is its like, if life gives you weeds, make catnip.” Tinker looked at me, and after a few seconds said,

“Seriously, have you been dropped on you head or something?” I huffed at that,

“No tinker, really the lemon thing is a human saying; I was just trying to use the weed thing so you might understand!” She shrugged,

“The only thing I understand is that you’re a confused little dog,” Instead of trying to explain, I just laid back down, feeling like I didn’t very well convey the fact that I was actually sympathizing with her. Oh well,

I will do better. It's hard to get pet and human thoughts straight.

Then there's that brown dog, she is the maid's favorite. She is quite the performer too, even though she is not very receptive to me. But she knows the ropes around here. I must pay attention and learn her dog-like ways. She is so good with her ears, eyes, tail, raising her eyebrows, tipping her head at the perfect angle, she jumps up at the right time and can stand on her hind legs, like a human. I have a lot to learn and I have to learn it to the best of my ability. This dog will teach me the ropes; I just have to stay out of her way. I will begin to follow her. Now as I look at her more, she kind of looks like me, except bigger.

I've been here a few weeks now, and I've come to really like my new home. The maid lady took me for a walk a few times. I refuse to walk with that harness contraption on me though. It pulls my ribs and my neck I hate it, it seems way too big and clumsy and it's stressful. So I just plant my legs and then, she just picks me up and carries me while the big dog walks. I would only slow her down anyway, and besides, the view from up here is just spectacular!

The brown dog has made it clear that she is not happy I'm here and has tried to sabotage my stay on multiple occasions. She peed on the floor where I did accidentally the other day. I was waiting by the door to go out, but couldn't hold it any more. This is embarrassing but my bladder was going to explode, and no one was there to let me out so I just let it go. She knew they would never blame her for wetting in the house so she just snickered when I got into trouble for it. By the way this brown dog is definitely not an angel; she is actually sometimes a devil. I keep saying, “My name is Sophie!” and she just says gruffly,

“I know that,” I think her name is Jello or something silly like that.

At times I can hear her telling the Tinker cat how she’s sure I’m just temporary and I won’t be here long. I replied to her, “Hey, who says?!” and that was not a good decision on my part as she just stared me down,

“I do!” she growled. Tinker just licked herself, glancing in my direction,

“She’ll soften up, just give her time,” she said calmly.

I pretended not to have said those words. I found myself wishing that I could take them back somehow as I trotted away, admittedly frightened. I was scooting away as fast as I could, not wanting to look back.

Kayla is the ONLY person who Tinkerbell allows to carry her, or hold her this way.

Romans 14:19   Let us therefore make every effort to do what leads to peace and to mutual edification.

19

FRIENDS?

I decided to try and make friends with the brown dog, so I said "Hey Jello, you want to finish my food for me? I'm full," She snapped at me,

"Call me your Majesty,"

"I thought your name was Jello . . ." I mentioned,

"What?" she said "Jello—what is that?"

"Well it's a squishy wiggly food they must have named you after?" It kind of made sense, I mean, she was a little plump and squishy; she has extra fur around her neck from her plumpness. I was smiling at the thought of Jello the food and the resemblance. Hey, how did I remember Jello? I adore these déjà vu moments!

"For heaven's sake are you crazy or something? My name is Jlo, named only after a most famous actress; don't you see my diamond collar? I am probably more beautiful than her! Jello? Where did you get that word? Did you make that up to make me mad?" she began to growl, eyes narrowing in my direction,

"No I really thought that was what they were saying! It's hard to tell when you're listening to words flying over your head so high up,"

"Oh, well the name is Jlo, but it's Your Majesty to you," Just to please her, I gave in,

"Okay Jlo, Your Majesty,"

"That's much better," she muttered as she held her head high, nearly sashaying over to the rest of my food and quickly gobbling it down. I swear this dog could eat more than a third world country if given opportunity. I can barely eat a few bites and she even sneaks a bite of Tinkers fish food whenever no one is looking. Yuck just the smell of it turns my stomach.

While she was licking her lips in delight, I wanted to engage her in more conversation. I tried to tell her that I think I was named after someone famous named Sophia Loren. She just snorted with her mouth full of my food, "There neither is nor was such a person, silly, I would know if she was famous, the girls read all the latest magazines to me and there is no such person," It was then that I remembered, Sophia Loren was from my day, a beautiful actress with dark hair just like that special person I loved. Oh, I do wish I could remember her more. Somehow I miss that part of my past, unfortunately it almost seems erased from my memory. As I was trying hard to recall the thoughts from my past, I was distracted, which happens constantly. Then seconds later, the best surprise yet since I've come back to earth happened!

We heard a voice and the door opened, when I looked over I couldn't believe my eyes. It was that lady who took home my friend Shaggy, and she had him in her arms. I went running up to him and nearly slid right into him as she sat him down, "Shaggy, Shaggy, do you remember me?!" I hollered happily, he looked right at me,

"Runt cakes!" he barked, then proceeded to lick me all over my face. Jlo was so taken aback,

"How do you know her?" she asked, her tone revealing her confusion. Shaggy, now named "Blue Boy" but called "Blue" for short. Was adopted by the maid's daughter and I'm told she comes to visit on a regular basis. I was so excited and asked if an angel had talked to him, but he just said no, not that he knew of. He just licked me again,

"Glad you ended up in a good home; I was worried about you for a while there, Besides now we get to see each other again, I visit pretty often and Jlo and Tinker are like my cousins!" he chimed. Oh thank goodness, angels, God or just plain luck worked for me this time, I feel better to know I have someone on my side. Even if he is four legged and furry, this is great. Angel or no angel, Shaggy or Blue is good in my book. This is a good day! I hope he comes back soon! Wow, this is a great day, actually; my first real friend on earth is going to be a part of my life. I don't think dogs get to choose their owners so we are just lucky. I'm chalking that up on my life-or maybe "life after death" lucky chart.

I said a little prayer, and thanked Patience, she probably had something to do with this since absolutely nothing is a coincidence when it comes to heavenly matters. It was a happy puppy day, it hadn't even been a month and my first friend on earth showed up! As I finished my prayer I said out loud "Amen and Thank you, whoever is listening!"

"Don't you think I am way more beautiful
than the original Jlo?" . . . Jlo

The three little Chi-Chi Musketeers,
Jlo thinks two and one-half Musketeers
Jlo–Sophie–Blue

Proverbs 5:21 For your ways are in full view of The Lord, and he examines all your paths.

20

NEIGHBORS

Today on our walk a lady walked over to say hello to the maid. She told her that she was new in the neighborhood, a childcare nanny from up the street. She introduced herself as Darlene and she told our maid that she took care of the children a few doors away from our home. Our maid was very kind and asked her to stop by for tea or coffee sometime. I was drowsy and almost asleep from the soothing walk, in which I was actually being carried by the maid in the sun. Then when I squinted and looked at her, it happened! *The twinkle!* I was so thrilled to see another angel. She told me that she was sent to be sure I ended up in the right place. I was so excited; she told me I had been perfectly placed and not to worry. I asked her if I was going to die soon, "No, just be patient, I will be close by to keep check on your status," she assured me. I'm so glad that there are Heavenly angels are out here. She told me to just love and protect my new family, and I told her that for a tiny, weird female dog I will do my best. Then it hit me a bit, I am a pet guardian angel, maybe that is my mission. I will have to look after the she-devil dog and that Tinker cat. I asked the angel that and she merely told me to do my best. Of course she was saying this only by looking into my eyes while continuing a conversation with the maid. She was sly about it and by petting me she could communicate and look directly at me. I tried to smile, which proved to be nearly impossible, being I was a dog of course. But I know since she's an angel she knows my gratitude.

These days, I'm thinking less about heaven and more about the task I have at hand here, or should I say "at paw." I can't believe it but today I have digressed even more. I'm not only a weird little female dog who has something wrong with her health, but I now wear dresses. Yes, dresses. It's those little girls that dress me up. They chose a dress I think used to belong to Jlo but she grew too big. So now lucky me, I get to adorn these fashions—and I just hate it. Not only should creatures with paws not wear clothes but they don't fit at all like clothes do for humans. Even though it's embarrassing and uncomfortable I try to cooperate. Once dressed, I walk slowly or lie down so that the maid understands my displeasure then she takes them off me. I found a mirror that goes to the floor in the hallway. I can't believe my eyes, I look so ridiculous that it's hard to not think "Pinch me I have to be dreaming, I can't really look like this or be this size, can I?" I just lie there and hope for help from a person who takes pity on me. Tinker just snickers and walks by, once she licked me and said,

"Kid I've been there, I know how you feel," I want to tell her, maybe you understand the uncomfortable clothes, but inside this head is a wise old soul, who is trying to be serious. Communicating is hard enough, but wearing a dress and not even weighing 3 lbs., this really messes with your psyche when you're trying to learn the ropes.

But that is the least of my problems; my teeth are not coming in correctly. There is a problem with them since my adult teeth have started to arrive. Therefore they feed me soft good food and some meaty treats ground up, that's the good part of being not quite right. Jlo gets jealous and still tells me I'm not staying. It seems like the family likes me but she thinks differently and still tries to convince me they don't really care for me. It doesn't seem like I'm leaving but Jlo seems convinced this is truly a temporary situation. I hope not, I hate change and I am really trying to be a good girl, I mean a good dog, a good pet, good angel or whatever I'm supposed to be.

I'm not growing well; at my first vet visit with my family they said I have seizures. Well that cleared up the "Caesar Salad" thing, and it's probably why I get dizzy and disoriented sometimes. The mom seemed to know I was not normal before they took me home, I'm glad she still wanted me, but they are still concerned about my health. Couldn't I at least be a normal dog? I'm sure I must have done something wrong, or I'm going to die soon and go back to heaven, who knows? Maybe I should call Patience? No, not yet, I will try harder to stay diligent and work through this bizarre assignment. Thus far, I seem to be adjusting to my family and new home fairly well. I think?

“I’m just posing for them today, I let Jlo and
Sof wear the clothes.” . . . Tink

Jeremiah 10:19 Woe to me because of my injury! My wound is incurable! Yet I said to myself, "This is my sickness, and I must endure it."

21

ACCIDENTS HAPPEN ON EARTH

The other day it was a beautiful warm day, Jlo and I were outside in the yard with the maid. Kids in the neighborhood were playing and I was just taking in the whole ambiance of the day. Then as I was gazing around, I saw the neighbor lady Darlene, the angel. I was so excited to see her again that I ran straight out to greet her and unexpectedly ran right in front of a huge contraption. It must have been a truck. I thought I died—again! The maid panicked and asked Darlene if she could watch the house as I needed medical attention, and she grabbed me up and off we went in the car.

I ended up unconscious and at the vet's office. The maid explained to the vet I was bumped by a big wheel plastic tricycle. I thought "you've got to be kidding. It felt like a Mac Truck." A little four year old was riding by the house on the sidewalk, and I ran right in front of him on this trike trying to meet Darlene. I had a bruised rib and a concussion. It felt like a semi hit me, instead it was a small plastic tricycle. The vet gave me pain killers and sent me home with the maid. I had a taped up torso where my ribs were bruised and I felt a little delirious, almost like when I was at the puppy farm. For me medication or that slightly dazed feeling is not good. This tape is tight but it seems to protect my sore ribs. Boy I was sure a moving automobile hit me, not a small plastic trike. That makes me truly realize for once how small I really am.

The maid felt responsible since I was with her and she would not put me down all the rest of the day. I hated the accident but I loved being carried around by her all day. I definitely could get used to this. The maid smells familiar, maybe it is just a people smell, but I like it. I just nuzzle into her and it is a great smell which makes me feel much, much better. I think she's starting to like me. She smiles at me and pets my head a lot; my favorite thing about being a puppy is receiving so much petting.

That night I slept with the mom and dad in their bed. They wanted to check on me since I was hurt. They put my bed and blanket right on their bed right next to them. Even the dad gave me a few pets, yeah, this is good, I could get used to sleeping in this bed it is soft big and warm, it smelled good like special perfume and soft hair smells from the mom's head. This bed was up the large staircase, the staircase in the back of the house, this home is so big they have a staircase in the front also. I can't get up the stairs since they are twice as tall as I am so I had never been where they all sleep. Later that night, I woke up whimpering and I was in pain so the mom took me out of the bed and put me right next to them in my towel. She gave me another pain pill. She put it in peanut butter, even as a human I could never turn down a good peanut butter sandwich. I licked and licked and licked until I got all the peanut butter out of my mouth then I licked her fingers and snuggled back to sleep.

Even though I'm hurt it is nice to be cared for and loved so much. My family is great. They took me to bed for the next four nights. After that they put me back downstairs at night so I whined most of the night for them to come get me. Then about when I gave up the youngest daughter came down to my room and scooped me up and took me up the staircase and into her bed. Yeah, being a whiny girl isn't so bad. As we passed Jlo on her pillow bed I smirked. Did I really say that? "Whiny girl?" Oh well, I found out one venue to get my way, whiny girl or not it worked, or at least this time it did.

Luke 22:43   An angel from heaven appeared to him and strengthened him.

22

SHOPPING

Today the girls took me to a big shopping complex; they put me in a bag or purse type contraption. Believe it or not! I was a seventy-two year old man and now I'm in a purse. I slept most of the day in the purse, partly out of exhaustion and partly from nausea from being swung around. But we did meet a lot of people and I got a lot of petting from strangers; now that part I like. The girls found me a new little collar, much smaller and softer with a bell on it. I think it is a cat collar, but it is more comfortable. I licked them in thanks for replacing the old cumbersome one I had.

The girls were holding me up in the air admiring their new purchase around my neck, I was wagging my tail. As the girls were putting me back into the purse, an old man with a funny, real furry dog came along and said what is your dog's name, "Sophie!" they said. I actually realized that is what they call me, still hard to believe. I'm having a hard time remembering my old name and my assignment, so "Sophie" it is! Along with all the rest, this takes the cake. Oh well, it's all part of the earth based mission I'm supposedly on.

Then the hairy dog looked straight at me and *the twinkle!* I asked excitedly, "Why are you here?! What message do you have?" I raise myself higher out of the opening of the bag to look at him better. He told me that his task is almost over that he is old and was sent to be a guide for his master. He was to be the protector, alerter, and the one to never let his master be alone, "You, a protector—But how? You can't be much bigger than me," Alfonso was his name and he assured me he was all of six pounds and managed to say it like he was sixty pounds,

"You are as mighty as your will and you have someone or something here on earth to protect or engage with," he told me.

"I can still barely bark just a sort of low woof and I'm not even three pounds!" I said. Alfonso assured me that my mission will be clear soon enough. This was the first animal angel contact I had on earth. I was elated! That whole day I understood more of everything around me. When we left Alfonso and his owner bid Tori and Kayla goodbye. Ah ha! The girl's names are Tori and Kayla. I feel smarter already! I looked up at Alfonso in thanks; he winked and wagged his tail. Even when returning home Jlo and Tinker made more sense. I'm thankful for meeting Alfonso he was a very wise angel who gave me great strength and renewed hope. The overwhelming feeling of "Yep, I can do this mission with vim and vigor" as I said this out loud, I felt vibrant, alive, and spontaneous. I was proud to be an angel that day, even if I was in a purse at the mall.

Philippians 4:13 I can do this through him who gives me strength.

23

DOG TALK

The brown dog at home still tells me to call her "Your Majesty." I say "Hi your Majesty" when I want to get close to her. I really do like her even if she pretends I am not there. She is so smart and people love her voice. She talks in many levels, it probably sounds like a song to humans. What she is really saying is

"I am performing" and saying "Aren't I cute and please give me treats!" She also says "wa woouv wuuu" which in dog words are "I love you." It's pretty darn good. I can especially appreciate it since I don't even bark yet. I wish I knew how she did so many sounds and can immediately respond to the humans.

Either way she gets the treats and they all think she's cute. The little girls taught her to do a high-five paw thing. They say "Give me a high-five, Jlo! High-five!" and she puts her paw up in the air against their hand. Then they say "Two paws, Jadey!" and she sits up on her hind legs and puts both paws against their hands, she's so talented with her dog acts. Jlo told me that this home is the best home ever for dogs; she's just sorry that I can't stay. Thus far the angels think I am where I'm supposed to be. Otherwise I would believe her. She is smart. When or if, I grow up into an adult dog, I want to be as smart as her, you know, for a dog! But Seriously, It is good that I have Jlo to learn from. If it were not for her I do not think these dog things would make much sense. I have to quit analyzing things as if I were human and let the dog in me take over sometime. Or the human in me step aside. Either way, I need to get into the groove of this new peculiar life.

As I was tentatively watching Jlo perform one day it dawned on me that when she gets excited that she looks like something from the Wizard of OZ, or maybe a stuffed toy. As I sat turning my head trying to decide, I wondered Hmm what makes my memory race to think of such things from the past? But I still can't help to look at her and giggle to myself. Jlo definitely has a look of her own.

The maid takes more and more care of me daily. Since the tricycle accident she carries me around a lot. Jlo does not like it at all, but the maid actually explains to her that I was hurt and need to heal. I think she feels a little bad that she pays so much attention to me. I have learned to kind of fake it to Jlo, so it is justified, but she just rolls her eyes and sort of puts up with the extra attention I'm getting. Besides most days she is so busy, running around barking at anything that does not belong in our yard, just to be heard or maybe to let us know something is out of place. I just stay on the maids lap and wait for Jlo to tire out and soon she joins us and takes her place alongside of us in our chair. Some days I think about sharing her lap when she jumps up, but then I think again and say, nah maybe tomorrow.

The family is so busy. Jlo and I would be left alone a lot if it were not for the maid. She picks me up daily and tucks me right next to her; I ride on her arm and strategically place my paws on her wrist to balance myself. At other times I just nuzzle under her shirt and hide from everyone. This is the safest spot I've found on earth yet. I'm supposed to protect the family but in reality she protects me. I do get sick a lot and she cleans up after my sickness all the time. She never seems to gets mad. I wish my food would settle better sometimes, but I just don't feel very well after I eat on certain days. Oh well, this is nothing I can help or fix, I'm just thankful the maid is so understanding.

"We both get Ellie's attention, But I usually
score her warm lap" . . . Sof

Job 21:6   When I think about this, I am terrified; trembling seizes my body.

24

GETTING FIXED

Wait—where's my food, my bowl is empty? I'm actually hungry today, what's going on? I ran out to the maid and jumped up on her leg to tell her she forgot me. Then the oldest daughter, Tori, picked me up, "Oh mom, she's hungry and begging grandma for food," she said, looking at her mother, whom I recently figured out her name was Monica,

"She's getting fixed today and she can't eat this morning. We're taking her for her appointment in a little while," she said. Since I was so close and up high I heard it. I'm getting fixed. Yeah! I'm a sick dog and I'm getting fixed. It's about time. This will be good; I will be normal and have better health. Okay, I'm all for that!

Tori put me down and I ran right over to where Tinker and Jlo just finished their food.

"Hey guys, I'm getting fixed today, isn't that great?"

"Oh . . . yeah, it's not what you think" said Tinker,

"Yeah, besides Sof, there's no fixing what's in your head" murmured Jlo.

"No, no! I heard it they are taking me this morning. I'm going to be a new dog!" I chimed, Tinker just gave me a wink and Jlo scoffed,

"I doubt that," I paused for a moment before brushing off what those two were saying.

"Well, see ya later alligators, I'm getting fixed today!" I scampered off to find Tori and Monica, and as soon as I did, they scooped me up with my blanket I sleep with and off we went. As I rode along in the car I was anxiously anticipating my new health.

I wondered where they were going to fix me at, and then we pulled into the vet's office. Oh no I hate this place, I thought, but maybe they have a good pill or something new for me. I sat in my blanket or under it mostly and shook. I hate the pungent smell of the office and all these other dogs looking at me. I now weigh almost three pounds, they said that I was just big enough. Whew, I really want to be fixed up right . . . I'm glad I've grown.

Next we go into the room where I get those awful shots. Then Monica hands me to the doctors, and kisses my head, "Good bye, Sophie, see you tomorrow," she smiled. Oh no, don't leave me here, this wasn't what I wanted! At this point I hoped that maybe one of these people were angels, so I tried to stop the panic and started looking each of them in the eyes. But no response, no twinkle and my family were already gone. I began to pray, "Oh Patience, please help me, I'm alone and afraid." I could feel the trembling inside of me taking over, yet this time it's not a seizure.

Next thing I knew I was on a table and they were hooking needles and wires up to me. Oh no, I died the last time I did this and I'm not dying this time. No way! I need to stay here and finish my mission. I tried with all my might to break free, but I just slipped into a deep sleep. Patience came to me in my sleep and I begged her to not let me die quite yet, I was just getting used to my family and my mission can't be over now. She told me I was just having the operation so I could not have babies. Babies? Really, babies I thought, now that would be a trip. Can you imagine, a seventy-two year old man having puppies? Now that thought made me snicker at how ridiculous that would be. But I guess not out of the question if I'm a female dog. As disoriented and delirious as I was I chose to use those silly thoughts to entertain myself, during my slumber. I groggily thanked patience for her support and asked her to please stay close by.

I woke up and felt terrible. My tummy was all sewn up and I could hardly see I was so dizzy. It reminded me again of the breeders place . . . I hated it there. I whimpered and a lady came and gave me some water and food. I tried to eat but the food was cold and yucky, and it hurt to move. I fell back to sleep in my blanket and finally morning came.

Boy, it seemed like an eternity and I had never before been so glad to see my family. I could hardly move but I squirmed out of the nurse's arms and lunged towards Monica. She held me tight as the nurse gave her instructions for me to heal. The nurse also told Monica that while I was under they inspected my mouth and my front adult teeth aren't formed right and that is why my tongue hangs out sometimes. No wonder Jlo has said, "Hey if you make that face again you're in trouble." I didn't know I was making a face? Monica asked if it would be detrimental to my health and they said no but my tongue may protrude sometimes. Oh great, just another goofy dilemma for me to endure. Maybe I won't' need to stick out my tongue to bad guys if I run into any, it will probably be out already.

When reaching the car Monica gave me to Tori, and we began our ride home. Tori held me close to her chest and I could feel her heart beating and the warmth of her body. She sang songs to me and one I recognized, *"Hush little baby don't you cry, mama's going to sing you a lullaby,"* it was soothing and very sweet of her. When we got home, she put me in my blanket on the sofa, Tinker and Jlo came up to see me. They said they were sorry but as a female in this house everyone has to have this done. I shook my head and knew they were probably right, they both lay down next to me and Tinker licked me now and then to check on me. Then the maid came in and held me. This was good, I felt safe now, a bit sore but safe as I snuggled under the maids' shirt. My thoughts were thankful for being home and safe, and my wishes were that, I never go back there again. I was hoping Patience was listening.

Matthew 11:28 "Come to me, all you who are weary and burdened, and I will give you rest.

25

SPIT BATHS

To show Patience that I am always thinking about my mission I try to watch out for the cat, Tinker, and the other dog, Jlo, but they kind of tell me what to do. I try to explain to them that I'm on a mission and that I need to look out for them. Jlo doesn't even listen and Tinker squints her eyes at me and just shakes her head. I see them playing together, Jlo barks and growls and sort of nips at Tinker and she sits up on her hind legs and sort of boxes with her paws at Jlo when she comes by, then she flies at her with both paws going so fast, it's scary. Tinker is even bigger than Jlo and she has some speed. They seem to be having fun, but I want no part of this tormenting each other in fun or seriousness, it is definitely way out of my league as far as sticking up for myself. Jlo makes about three of me and Tinker probably four or five of me, *plus they got moves*. No thank you, I will stay back and watch them do their own thing.

Whenever I try to explain human things or words Tinker says I must be getting a fever. She tells me I'm talking "dog muck" and must be delirious or something. She sometimes just swiftly sneaks up when I'm talking and pins me down to give me a bath. A yucky spit bath, of course. If I say no or back away, Tinker chases me and bats me down and pins me until I can't move. I'm really scared because she's so huge, like four times my size, and she is very diligent about getting me cleaned up, I lie very still in any case and just let her finish. I'm afraid if I interrupt her she will bite me or it will take longer, I have seen her wash herself and she is very particular. Afterwards I quickly go rub off the wetness on a blanket or the nearest thing I can find. Of course, I don't let her see me, or the spit bath would start all over again. If she keeps this up I may need some serious therapy when I get back to heaven, I just wish there were sensible explanations now.

Once in a while Tinker pins me down and licks me what seems like to death. Or I should say, I seem to kind of wake up, and feel paralyzed and dizzy, and then I realize she is licking and licking me, "You need a bath. I will fix you, little one," she murmurs to me, sometimes she tells Jlo to go get the maid or the mom. Or I think that is what happens, I can't seem to move and it frightens me. I have these moments on occasion and I hate them. Then the bath begins. It reminds me of the puppy farm where I came from. Yuck, she means well, but I don't like it when she washes me.

Then one day the maid said "Good girl, Tinkerbell, you're helping her come out of her seizure," Oh my God, I'm having one of those seizures and she's trying to help me? I guess I'm thankful. Tinker is being a caregiver and seems to have a motherly spirit. Then the maid picks me up and holds me close and pets me until I really come fully aware of what's going on. This is a nuisance, but I guess its part of the assignment because, like I said, nothing is by accident when it comes to heaven. Being a little dog is hard enough . . . why do I have to have these horrible seizures?

Jlo, she is kind of accepting me in a way. I now sneak up and lie by her if she is sleeping. She is showing me how to protect the house when people come. It is our duty to let the household know when people come to the door or walk by. She barks and I just run behind her and pretend to look important. I have not yet mastered the "bark." I just want to scream out words but they are not coming. I can't remember if my other pets we had in my past life were this way, for some reason they all just seemed noisy to me.

Proverbs 31:12 She gives him good, not harm, all the days of her life.

26

SICK WITH THE MAID

The past few days have been terrible. I'm sick again and have to take these horrible eye drops every six hours. The maid is giving them to me. Everyone else is so busy and they don't have much time, but they still love me and pet me. Tonight the maid took me with her in the car and we went to another house. She kept on giving me the drops, I slept a lot and I slept with her. She put me in a towel from this house and I loved the smell. She put me right next to her and petted me to sleep. She even hummed a tune and I felt so drowsy it sounded like beautiful music to my disproportionate ears. Sick or not this was for sure the best night of sleep I've had since I came back to earth.

I really like her and she carries me everywhere. That tricycle accident actually worked out in my favor. The home I live in has steps which I still can't do. This house is small and does not have steps. I like this house, I wouldn't get lost here and it smells familiar. Maybe because it smells like her shirt I hide under. As I peeked around from room to room, I found a great place, it's a little stand. For some reason I just love the smell and it seems so inviting. I just walked underneath and curled up on the lower shelf this afternoon. The maid found me there and said, "That's a funny place for you to be . . . that belonged to my husband, it was his smoking stand," Funny, it felt like a place I *should* be. I wish it were at the other house, it smells great.

Then suddenly I remembered my mission and that I'm not at my family's house. I tried to tell her take me back, so I started pacing and whining. She looked down at me, "What's wrong little one?" concern showing in her voice as she scooped me up. I love that, and I licked her hand as a thank you. As I pawed at her she gave in and told me we will go home soon, and it wasn't long before we went back. She lets me ride on her lap in the car. She is good to me. I know very well that I am more work for her than Tinker and Jlo, she tends to my needs and I think she likes me almost as much as Jlo, at least this is what I tell myself.

Proverbs 22:6 Start children off on the way they should go, and even when they are told they will not turn from it.

27

GOING TO CHURCH

Today is Sunday; I know because everyone is home and they all get up at the same time on this day each week, everyone gets up to go to church. It is usually a busier than normal morning and every man, woman and child for themselves. Everyone is running around trying to put something good or suitable on for church, food is flying in the kitchen and someone is always lagging behind. I've seen this and Tinker has made sure to warn me, "Kid, just stay out of their way," So I listened and usually found myself under the table or in my little bed by the back door.

Today the maid came over and brought something that needed to be taken with them. She was going to church also so she just told them to" leave it in my car and I will meet you there." As they were leaving, Kayla paused,

"Wait, I have to go to the bathroom!" she said,

"Of course you do . . ." the maid muttered as she told the rest of the family to go ahead and she'd wait for her. I, on the other hand went into the bathroom to visit Kayla, she reached down and picked me up,

"Do you want to go to church, Sophie?" Of course I always want be with people so I wagged my tail. She had a little case-like pursc and she opened it up and took out a group of little stuffed animals, tossing them on the floor, and stuck me inside. To hide me she took some toilet paper and put it on top of me to fill in the top of the purse, "Okay!" she smiled, "Here we go, don't jump out or let anyone know you're here, it's our secret," I agreed in silence, though I hoped she wouldn't swing me around so fast,

"Hurry up girl, we're going to be late!" the maid called for Kayla, and in a few minutes I could tell we were in the car and I tried to peek out but she pushed my head back down. The car stopped soon enough and we did not go very far. I occasionally just put my nose up to sniff. This wasn't much different than the dog bag they take me shopping in, so I just settled in and decided this was good to be a part of this outing. I have no idea what church is but I was going to find out soon enough.

Once we stopped moving Kayla set down my bag and I peeked out. Wow, there are a lot of people here, I can't see them all but I sure can hear them. Kayla pushed my head down once again and began to pet me. Oh yeah, this feels good—right there, on my neck—oh, yeah . . . and there on my sides, Oh I'm so tired, just keep petting me, please!

I must have fallen asleep because I woke up and did not know where I was. Then I realized I'm in Kayla's bag—but where? There is so much noise and I realize everyone is singing. Pushing the toilet paper out of the way I peeked out. There are a lot of feet and legs in here, but more importantly I really need to pee. I tried to whine like I do when I'm in the other bag to let them know I need to go, but no one listened to me. I need to get out of here to find a place quick. Since Kayla wasn't around I jumped out and started to sniff and look around. I'm walking through lots of legs. Thank goodness they aren't moving around. I went through all the legs sniffing a few and there were some very odd smells on these people, one man smelled like a cow pasture and some woman had such a strong smell of medicine and perfume I thought I was going to toss my biscuits right there.

Ah, finally a clearing. I think my bladder is going to burst, come to think about it no one let me outside this morning. Where's a good place? I can't wait much longer. Where's that diaper pad thing when you need it? Then I saw some paper on the floor, great that will do. Ahhhh, I knew this was an emergency pee, sorry whoever owns this big house, but it was a real true emergency.

Okay, now I need to find Kayla or my bag. As I looked back to where I came from it seemed like a jungle of legs to go back through again. So I sat down and looked around and saw a doorway. It is quieter now and people are sitting down. I walked towards the door and realized suddenly that if I go out there it would be the opposite direction from which I came. As a human I was very good with directions as long as I got my bearings. So I stood for a minute and walked further and voila! There was a big long hall that went the direction I came from, so I started to walk up the carpeted hallway. Wow, there are rows and rows of people. This seems familiar; I'm mesmerized at how still everyone sat in their seats. I heard a consecutive "Amen" as I kept walking slowly and sniffing for my bag, Kayla or the rest of my family.

As I got a whiff of a new strange smell and as I stopped and tried to figure out what it was, I heard,

"Well, we have a visitor today," someone said as I looked ahead, and a man was pointing to me! "Either heaven sent us a dog or this little fella is lost,"

Man, you have no idea how true that is, I thought. At that time everyone turned to look at me. No one noticed me before, but now that they did people started laughing, oohing and calling me, at first I wagged my tail but then I was scared—where is my family? For a split second I heard the dad's voice yell,

"Sophie?!" then there were about five people coming at me from all different directions. I was so scared that I bolted into the people's legs, and they were reaching down trying to catch me. I was petrified of all the hands grabbing at me I just ran for my life.

The big man in the front who had initially spoke raised his voice once more, "Ladies and gentlemen, please calm down while Mr. Schultz tries to recover his dog," he said. I was safe for a moment behind a diaper bag and in front of a purse. My heart was pounding and I was just wishing I was home. Looking around it was then that I heard it, Kayla and Mr. Schultz calling me; I decided Mr. Schultz sounded closer so I darted out into the original hallway and there he was. I ran right up to him and he picked me up and scratched my head,

"There girl," he murmured, and Kayla came running up to hug me and her dad. He looked at the crowd,

"Well, I guess it's bring your dog to church day," he smiled and the crowd laughed he handed me to Kayla and shook his finger at her. She pretended not to notice but knew she was in trouble.

Well, I'm literally out of the bag and sitting like a person on the bench beside everyone like I should be, of course. After all, that's what the humans are doing. I was looking around and spotted the maid next to Tori and ran across their laps to sit with her. She just hugged me and put her sweater around me and I curled up. *This is a safe spot, thank heavens*, I thought with a sigh of relief. I'm not leaving her and getting lost again.

As we left, Mr. Schultz or Joe as he is known around here, was embarrassed but the girls were proud to show me off. Everyone wanted to pet me and they even let two people hold me. I wanted to protest but I saw the maid following close behind and keeping an eye on me. Then she finally took me and told the girls to go get cookies, she hugged and kissed me, "You little stinker, were you a stow-away?" she smiled, I wanted to say no, but then Kayla would get into trouble, so I just looked sheepish. She tapped my nose and I licked her fingers. On the way home, the maid turned to Kayla, "I think she stowed away in your bag," Kayla shrugged,

"Yep, must have," she said before running straight into the bathroom when she got home where the stuffed animals were on the floor. She quickly took care of the evidence and went along with the stow-away story.

I survived, but didn't want to go back anytime soon, just too many people for my taste. After dozing off that afternoon for a nap, the revelation came to me in my sleep. A man with a robe, singing, pews of people, yes-! I was at a place of worship. Oh goodness, I went pee in "God's" house. Then I thought, *But—maybe it's your fault*, I'm sorry Lord, but if I weren't here on a mission from heaven as a weird little dog, then this would not have happened. I told Patience I was sorry, it was an accident or should I say, emergency relief, and that I really am sorry, I just now realized where I was at. Then, probably from the stress, I fell into a deep slumber, safe in the sunshine coming through the window on the floor. This is heaven to feel so safe on earth, and in this home I do feel safe.

Romans 1:11 I long to see you so that I may impart to you some spiritual gift to make you strong—1:12 that is, that you and I may be mutually encouraged by each other's faith.

28

ALERT "DANGER"

The next evening we were out in the yard. We had just gotten back from a walk where the maid and Tori took turns carrying me. Tori set me down in the grass and I was doing my thing, and Jlo, was around but just pretends not to see me. She was trying to show me how thoroughly she sniffs for strange smells in our yard. As she was glancing my way to see if I was paying her any attention she suddenly was barking and running towards me, "Run! Brutus is coming!" Of course I knew nothing of Brutus, so I had no clue what she was talking about, as I was trying to process what she was telling me I asked,

"What?" and at that very moment an enormous tan and black ninety pound German Shepherd came running up, grabbed me up in his mouth and then dropped me and I rolled into the grass. Whew, what just happened? I lay there dazed and this Brutus was growling at me. I looked straight at him in fear, and it happened. *His eyes twinkled,*

"Sorry if I hurt you— I live down the street and I have an electric fence that keeps me in. I broke loose because I needed to let you know that I will be sending you messages so you need to learn to walk with a leash so you can come by and we can communicate!" he said. Stunned for a moment, I thought, Wow! Angels come in all different shapes and sizes. Brutus is an enormous German Sheppard. I'm pretty sure if he was not an angel I surely would have been dead.

"Where down the street?" I did not get to say much but I managed to ask this before his master came. His master was out of breath after chasing him, and was apologizing profusely and yanking Brutus's collar. He even tried spanking him even though it really didn't do much through his thick fur. He waited for the family to see I was alright, before he took him back home. Brutus was looking back, telling me,

"Be sure to come this way as often as possible and listen to the people's words!" he said, I was then scooped up by the maid and the kids. They were frantic and screaming

"Help her Grandma, help her Grandma!" I realized then that she must actually be their Grandmother. I did just as Brutus said and listened to the people's words. I must have missed this "Grandma" word since I was always so caught up in daily dog duties. Maybe I never listened very well; I will do better to pay close attention. Already I feel as if my ears are more alert to things.

Then Grandma wiped me off, I had Brutus spit on me and grass stain on my white fur. I was a bit dazed but I was okay. The Grandma sat me down and I toppled over on my side, not hurt but still a little out of it and wobbly. Jlo was licking me and saying "Get up, Sophie," it was the first time she ever said my name, "Get up and do something!" Instead I lied still and let her plead and lick me before I snuck a lick back and she wagged her tail. She does like me; she just doesn't want me to know. They all were scared for me. I guess Brutus is the biggest, meanest dog in the neighborhood. He doesn't have any dog friends because everyone is afraid of him, he has a reputation. They were all worried so they just held me all night and gave me treats galore. I don't need a concussion every day but the attention was great. Even Tinker slept next to me and licked me every so often to be sure I was okay. They all think I cheated death that I was brave to look at my attacker that way. I did lose a tooth in the mishap, but it was loose anyway. How could I tell them Brutus is an "Angel" they would never believe it. I guess I will let them think I was brave.

Today, we were going for a walk. I did pretty well, and I tried hard. Wow, I sure am out of shape. I wanted to go towards Brutus's house but of course Jlo wanted to go the other way. I pulled in the beginning but didn't have the strength to persuade their direction. Oh well "Rome wasn't built in a day" and I'm on a learning curve. Okay, I decided from now on I am going to get good at walking on a leash.

A few days went by and we finally went by Brutus's house. I went by before but never saw him. Today he was out. I ran as close by him as possible. After all we have to look at each other's eyes. Grandma was pulling me back but I did catch a glimpse, "Stay next to Grandma, she will need help," Brutus said. I asked him about the family and he said not to worry. By this time Grandma scooped me up and Jlo was praising me for my bravery. Jlo kept saying

"Stay away! He attacked you, remember?" I pretended to listen but knew what I was doing. I acted brave like I knew he could not hurt me or that I could hold my own, besides Grandma scoops me up into her arms whenever other dogs are around. I will have to figure out how to get a better glimpse of Brutus.

This friend "Malcom" who passes by our home shows the resemblance of our "Brutus." As you see Sophie is quite leary of him.

Job 37:2 Listen! Listen to the roar of his voice, to the rumbling that comes from his mouth.

29

NEW ENJOYMENT

As days come and go I am getting bigger. All kids like me because to them I am still so small. I like kids too but I'm afraid they are going to drop me whenever they pick me up. Jlo doesn't like to be picked up so she will only let the family hold her. She gets grouchy if people reach for her, you can only touch her if she wants you to. Now me I'll take a pet or a scratch from anyone. Also I learn more about people when they pet or hold me.

After the kids run off to school Grandma, Jlo, Tinker and I settle down about mid-morning and watch TV. I just yesterday realized she likes to watch a program that I loved. "The Price is Right!" I love it when I get these déjà vu moments, I remember watching this every day at 11:00a.m., when I was retired. This was my favorite daytime show. But now there is no Bob Barker, why is this name familiar? The man on the show now is unfamiliar to me, but I can't seem catch his name. We also watch the weather channel a lot and I like it when the kids watch a program called "Animal Planet." I listen to them as they plead, "Please, can we watch Animal Planet?!" and when this happens I just sit and watch with them. This is a new show about all different animals, like last week for instance, I think I saw two giraffes that looked like they were angels, and they seemed to be communicating special messages between them. It was a good show.

Then it happened; I finally got so excited about all the guests coming over to the house that I actually barked out loud! This is FANTASTIC!!! I finally have a voice. Yeah, now I can speak. Just this triumph alone makes me feel more important. It's not a big bark, kind of shrill and high but it is a bark! Even Jlo was surprised and excited, we sound so much more important when we run to the door with two of us barking. I'm proud to be heard, can't wait to show Blue and Brutus! I was not sure if Tinker had heard me so I ran right up to her and did my best to show her my new skill, "It's about time, but now we have to hear that for the rest of our lives," she said as she rolled her eyes. I could care less how good it sounds, it's a bark and nonetheless it's mine. I love my new voice even if it is shrill.

By now I am pretty much included on all the family activities these days. I go outside with them, ride to the store with them, and I even sleep with them; they put me in my bed and place it in their big people bed. The mom said it was necessary so the girls don't roll over on me, and I agree, besides, this is way better than that room where Grandma put the clothes. I never feel afraid or lonely anymore, they rarely make me stay in there unless a lot of people come over. When they do put me in there it's for my safety not to get stepped on. Yep, that being stepped on thing has happened once or twice and it almost broke my leg.

Also, Jlo has taught me how to beg for food at the perfect time. If you do it correctly they can't resist giving you a bite. I'm learning from "Jlo the Pro" on this task. Even if I am clumsy or not doing it right when they feed Jlo they have pity on me and give me a little bite too. I have learned to stand on my hind legs and they love that. The perfect barking thing like what Jlo does needs work but dancing around and bouncing up and down on my hind legs seems to get their attention every single time. I'm going to practice my outdoor bark on our walks maybe that will strengthen my voice.

How could you explain to a human you appreciate barking, but I do! Jlo and I sound like a small posse with our barking and the clicking of our nails on the wood floor when we go to the door. Not quite a stampede, but for all thirteen pounds of us combined we sound pretty good. We are probably not as impressive as Brutus, but maybe close. Of course I wouldn't want him to know I'm comparing my might with his. He might not be happy. But truly inside of me my mind is a strong agile man. I just wish my body would cooperate in the way my mind thinks.

Psalm 122:8   For the sake of my family and friends, I will say, "Peace be within you."

30

MY FAMILY

Daily I think about my luck, or dumb luck depending on the situation. I truly adore my family. Jlo and Tinker are right, this is a good home. The mom, Monica, is so fun; she is always happy and keeps the family organized. She calls the girls, Tori and Kayla, "Squirrel Girls." This is so cute, she says, "Baby squirrels, it's time to go," and they just scamper around preparing for their outing. Monica always has time to hold us pets and dole out her affection to us daily. I've noticed she must kiss everyone and say "I Love You" every day to all of us, on a seemingly constant basis. The girls mimic her happiness so this house is full of love and joy.

Hey, come to think about it my family and I used to call our girls squirrels . . . the name must have caught on! They were always scampering around and running to and fro, their long golden brown hair swinging, sometimes in ponytails or pigtails. I would laugh to myself, watching their antics; they were so precise and feminine. Growing up with all brothers my daughters were my first exposure to little girls. Oh the memories, I love these wonderful déjà vu moments that bless me now and then, they are past visions of love.

But now I have a new family and these little girls have very long blonde hair and each of them are uniquely different. Tori has a pink fetish and is kind of a Diva. Kayla has a purple flair and is very artistic. Since Tori is two years older she looks out for Kayla. She's sort of a self-appointed mentor to Kayla whom she nicknamed "Muffin." At first when Tori called "Muffin", I thought it was treat time. But it's just her *love name* for her sister. Kayla just absorbs the mothering and goes on her way, she is very much her own person, and busy and happy in her creative mind.

The father, Joe, has come to accept me. This is a relief, especially since I was not a favorite on his list when I arrived. He is a busy man and very protective of his family of women. I can relate to him, the only guy in a girls world, but now I have become one of his girl pets. As I say, just dumb luck. Oh well, I'll take it. This family is best. Since I had no control where I ended up on earth, this household is a true and complete blessing.

Then there is Grandma, she is such a lovely person. She spreads her attention around to everyone. It seems she has endless energy and love for each one of our individual needs. She is a senior citizen but an extremely active one. I seem to care for her more and more each day. Don't get me wrong there is a special place in my heart for all of them, but Grandma is definitely at the top. After all she feeds me, cleans up after me and soothes me when I have those awful seizures. Also this family wouldn't function well without her, that's for sure. I can see, as much love and adoration they have for Grandma, she gives back to them consistently every day.

The three of us make the family complete!
Sophie—Jlo—Tinker Bell

Ecclesiastes 7:8 The end of a matter is better than its beginning, and patience is better than pride.

31

DANCE RECITAL

I called on Patience the other day for clarification, "What exactly am I supposed to be doing?" I have been looking for clues and learning to be a real dog, "I try to watch the cat and dog, and I try to watch out for the family but they watch over me instead. I am still not 100% sure what my earthly mission is,"

"Just love them with all your ability," she told me,

"I do love them very much," I retorted, this is the best place ever for a little dog, I was put in a good home, but I'm just not sure how I can be of assistance to anyone yet. She reassured me everything is going according to plan. I just have to trust, believe and do my mission.

"It's not how you do the mission; it's how you see it through all the way to the end," she mentioned, and I agree but my efforts as Rob don't come through very well as "Sophie." It is quite a dilemma some days. I told her how everything is hard to explain and relate when you're a dog. I just want to scream what I'm thinking; I want to reason with the people and the animals and the only ones I can totally communicate with are the angels, and then the mental telepathy is easy. Again, she reassured me that progress is being made; I just need to relax and enjoy my family.

I honestly do think my family is the best on earth. They are laughable. I wish I could say "Good one!" or "Atta girl!" at times. They all seem to have a sense of humor, like the other night the girls were dancing and singing, it sounded good to my dog ears, and people were laughing at them and with them. Right when I was enjoying the show, the oldest daughter Tori, came and got me and the younger daughter Kayla, retrieved Jlo, they then they took us in tow with them to fetch Tinker. Tinker was asleep on a kitchen chair, but not for long. Tori picked her up in her other arm, legs dangling she peered out of one eye at me, "Hey kid, where we going?" she grumbled, just waking up from her nap. I shrugged,

"Not sure," At that time Kayla met Tori in the living room with a little blue suitcase. Tori sat Tinker on the sofa, and Kayla began to pull little clothes from the blue case. Jlo and I were perched upon the footstool watching. Out came glitter dresses, hats, and jewelry adornments, "Oh no, please no," I cried, this can't be happening, Jlo was just looking down and shaking her head as if to ignore them, yet disagreeing. Then the torture began, Jlo and I were soon fully dressed in girlie dresses, mine a little pink tutu and Jlo in red fluff. The girls were delighted once we were all adorned. "Oh I hate this," I complained. Tinker was watching and with a smirk on her face she began snickering,

"Better you than me. Before you two came along that was my job," she chortled, then the music started and they danced with us moving my paws to the music and holding us up like we were singing for Tinker. I looked at Jlo, as if to say,

"Help me".

"Just go along with it, they get tired pretty quick. Remember we could belong to bad humans and if this is the price to live with good humans then I'll cooperate, are you in, kid?" she asked,

"Yep," I replied, but I was just closing my eyes and trying not to toss my biscuits. Besides what else could I do? At this size when people pick you up it is like a tree bending down and scooping you into the sky. You don't move around because it is a long ways down to the floor. I was doing my best to be good sport and soon enough they put me down.

Thank heavens one more minute and my last doggie sausage treat was going to resurface again. But they forgot to take the outfit off. Oh for heaven sake here I am in a pink tutu, how embarrassing. I'm not connecting with my past life at all right now. I could never dream this situation up, not in a million years. So here I go to find someone to help me not look even more pitiful than I already am. You know this rings a bell; my children when they were little would dress our pets up. Hmm, maybe it has become a popular thing? Right then Tinker piped up, "Yeah, you best find someone to get you out of that or you could be stuck in it a while, the girls just went outside." Then she proceeded to tell me how she wore a bright green lace dress for a whole day once when the girls dressed her up before school then everyone left for the day. She told me wearing the green dress all day was pure torture. Well, that was enough for me to search for someone to save me from my fashion faux paux. As I passed by the big hallway mirror, there I was in full pink tutu garb with my tongue hanging out. Wow, now that's a sight that makes *my* eyes sore. This is really bad and with disbelief of my hideous looks, I needed to push on to find someone to rescue me.

Ah! The man, I see him. I waddled up to him and he laughed then picked me up and took the clothes off me. I'm glad I found him! He has been a whole lot nicer to me lately, but he said something very peculiar to me. "I'm going to miss you. But I'm sure you will visit." Wait a minute what does he mean? I just learned how to do the stair steps a month ago. What is this news? Does Grandma know? Do the girls know? Where I am going? Oh this is not good news at all. I need to find out what this means. Maybe this is a clue to my mission? I'm not going to panic yet, maybe he is going on a trip . . .

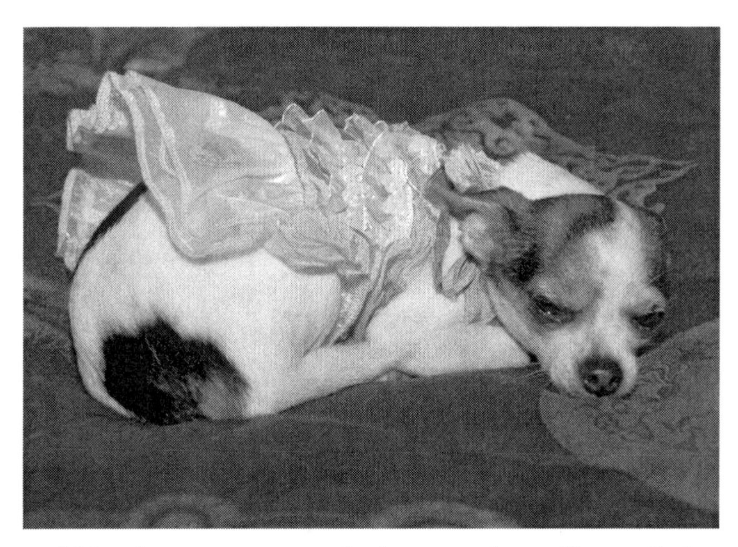

"Oh please someone help me, please!" . . . Sof

Psalm 115:13 He will bless those who fear The Lord— small and great alike.

32

ANIMAL KINGDOM

Well, my life seems to get better and better every day. Grandma carries me all over the place, and now because she says I mind well, she lets me walk off the leash alongside of her and Jlo. Jlo sometimes runs after squirrels and other animals even though she is on a leash and then is yanked back. I don't run after anything, after all I look like a squirrel on stilts with Jack rabbit ears. I don't want to try to scare anything; I just want to have a relaxing walk. When I get tired I walk slow or just stop and Grandma picks me up! It's a technique of walking slow and batting my eyes at her and it suckers her in every time, definitely fool proof. I don't ask to be picked up if we are going past Brutus's house. The last two times we went past his house he unfortunately was not outside. I hope he's okay; I slow down to linger to see if he is around but Grandma scoops me up into her arms to carry me past there quickly.

I did find out the other day that a lady bug was afraid of me she was yelling like I was going to eat her or something, also one day a toad was hopping as fast as he could from me. I have seen dogs bite at them—yuck, how awful.

So I guess my rule in the animal kingdom is pretty low on the list. But I have found out for sure that I absolutely hate flies and bees, I know it sounds crazy, but these things are huge to me and seem to buzz right at my face or my butt! How rude they can be, and scary! I duck or hide when they come near; they are the size of birds to humans, and when they dive bomb me! Oh, I just whimper or jump like a normal girl reaction when you're afraid, no mustering up courage when they are nearby.

Oh well, I just find all this pecking order in the animal kingdom very amusing and it gives me a lot to think about each day as I learn. I just want to communicate to the bees and flies that I'm an angel and they should leave me alone! So far, all of my attempts have only failed since I am usually in a panic when I'm addressing them. Maybe their ears are too little or maybe they are ignoring me altogether. Who knows I just wish they would take their interests elsewhere. Now I think about it I will take this concern up with Patience, if I can't seem to get this matter into control. Yep, maybe she will make them listen!

One day when Blue came to visit again we were all running around outside and I was so tired I laid down on the sidewalk to soak up the sun. I was almost asleep on the warm sidewalk and then a caterpillar walked by. I was getting up to get out of its way and as I looked at it. Then it happened! *The twinkling*, the tiny creature spoke "Hey sorry I'm in a hurry, but I have an ant war going on across the yard and I have to make peace," he said,

"Really? I can't believe you are an angel!" I piped,

"Yep" he said, "We come in all different sizes," since I was so much bigger than him I instinctively inquired,

"Can I do something for you?" I asked,

"Sure can you get me over by that bush ASAP?" he shouted with urgency in his voice, looking towards the bush I nodded,

"Okay, How?" He suggested that I lie down and he would get on my back. So I did and he crawled up on me and I scampered over to the bush, he slid off and I asked him if this was good,

"Yes, very good job, I made it just in time to stop the war," he said. Who would have known, I thought I was small, but he was minute. I sat for a few minutes and tried to watch what he was doing and finally went back to the side walk when both Blue and Jlo called me to come and smell something. I pretended to be interested and obliged them. Running towards them I was thankful for being a weird little dog angel and not a caterpillar angel. Another chalk up for better luck than what I originally thought.

Once inside Jlo and Blue run around to anyone who would pay attention to them. Jlo will accept whoever will feed her or pet her. She lives for any and all the attention. I on the other hand just prefer grandma; she's definitely the one for me. I will sit with someone for a minute just to say hello, but really if I'm going to sit with someone it has to be grandma. It may be her soft lap, maybe her finger nails, or just her smell, and I just like her more than the rest of the family. Well there I admit it; she's my favorite person I've met so far. In my mind I think of myself as her favorite pet, but I don't share these thoughts with others.

Proverbs 16:23 The heart of the wise make their mouths prudent, and their lips promote instruction.

33

VENTURING OUT

Today we are going for a ride in a different vehicle. Grandma the girls and I are going in a big black truck. This car is huge for a little Grandma, but she just hops in and drives like it is no big deal. She puts us dogs in and we take our place on the girls' laps. When we get to where we are going they let us out in a beautiful garden area. Jlo and I run around and Grandma and the girls are putting flowers in different places. It's really nice and quiet here.

I was minding my own business, and business is just what I was doing when a beautiful white bird flew down and stared right at me. "Oh great, couldn't you give me a minute before you pester me?" I asked, I looked right at her thinking, please give me a minute and then she started communicating telepathically. I must have missed *the twinkle;* this was an angel, for goodness sake! A flying angel! How amazing. She was so smart and she said she was a messenger from the angel of death, "What the angel of death! Who's dying?" I piped up in my head,

"No one you know," she said, "But we're in the cemetery,"

"What?" I said, "The cemetery, you mean where people are dead?" realizing this I wondered if I had just done my business in a bad spot. Oops . . . too late now.

"Why are you here?" she asked.

"I came with them," I told her, as I gestured to my family,

"Oh, I've seen them before! They are visiting the graves of their loved ones,"

"Really?" I said, genuinely surprised, "Who is here?"

"The mother of the Grandma, the grandma's only sister and brother, and her husband are buried here. Also a childhood friend of Monica's lost to cancer at an early age," she cooed,

"How sad . . ." I said, looking back at my people,

"Yes, but as humans you and I both know death is inevitable," she had a valid point there, but it was still a sad concept to me nonetheless,

"So why are you here" I asked, she told me that those people way down the road there were burying their pet, "Wow, people are crazy about their pets aren't they?"

"Yep, they wanted his ashes right near where they will be buried," I asked what kind of pet, and I was told it was a horse. Wow, that's a new twist. I asked this angel, what her name is,

"Dovie," she replied,

"Okay Dovie, can you tell me am I going to die or are any of my people?"

"Not in the near future, but some day, yes," she replied, this thought saddened me, but again like she said, death is inevitable. As we talked only a bit more she mentioned that she would have sooner or later met me on earth because she helps pets and humans cross over to angelhood. I didn't remember her when I died as a human but she said there are many mediators from life to death as she calls herself.

She told me to go home and pay special attention to the family today; sometimes they are sad when they leave here, "But please just stay here and bark for them so they clean up your mess, because Mr. Johnson," she paused as she read the headstone, "Would not appreciate your donation to his grave site," as she peered at me with raised eyebrows, she suggested I bark for them now. *Oh yeah,* I thought, *good idea.* I barked as she told me to, looking a little sheepish and feeling rather stupid that I initially didn't know where I was at, which ended up with me leaving a present for "Mr. Johnson."

Song of Solomon 1:2 Let him kiss me with the kisses of his mouth—for your love is more delightful than wine.

34

EXTRA KISSES

So on the way home I rode on Grandma's lap, even though she was driving she welcomed the company. I kissed her hand whenever possible. I wanted her to know I loved her and felt sorry for her loss whenever it had happened. She seemed to understand my sympathy. Oh, and as for the kisses, I want to tell you that licking someone is either great or just plain yuck. If you like someone you may do a quick lick to say you're accepted, I like you. When you kiss their face it is not by mistake. It is an intentional kiss type lick. Not all people are worthy of face licks only the ones you really, really like or the ones with barbecue sauce on them, that or excess ice cream is good too. I loved ice cream as a human but can't seem to convince them to give me it to me as "Sophie." This is something I really have to work on.

I kissed the girls a lot today too because of the chances that they may be sad also. They usually kiss me right back, but they always squeal, "You have bad breath!" What do they expect? I'm a puppy! Do any dogs have good breath, I want a good toothbrush and I'll show them. Not much longer after that though did they give

Jlo and I toothbrushes. Of course, what was good as a human is not always good as a dog. They are brushing me with beef flavored paste with something the size of a baseball bat. It hurts my mouth and it is nothing like the enjoyment I remember. Oh well, at now a whopping 3.2 lbs. I can't object very much. I just hope the girls think my breath is better.

Next we were all sitting around and I realized the girls were taking Jlo's and my collar off. It felt really good to be scratched where it had been. It seemed almost unusual to have it removed. With a bell on it and all, it becomes a part of you. Then I see Grandma doing something in the sink, as Tori was holding me I realize that she's putting me into the sink, Oh no! I'm in a bubble bath. I don't know why this is so awful, but I hate it and want out. It's warm and I want to like it but suddenly I'm afraid. I begin to whine uncontrollably and shake like I never have before. Grandma is scrubbing me and Tori is holding me firmly otherwise I would have jumped out. They are saying, "Shhh, calm down Sophie, its okay, we're giving you a bath, you're all right!" Sure, I'm alright for a drowned dog! I'm still whining, shaking and I absolutely loathe this. Next thing I was rinsed and Tori wrapped me up in a big towel. Boy, that's better! Next is Jlo's turn. Kayla puts her into the sink and the process starts again. Tori is drying me on the counter and as I look at Jlo, she is not happy but taking the scrubbing and rinsing like a pro. I peek out of my towel and admire her courage.

She tells me afterwards to quit being such a drama queen, good dogs get baths on a regular basis and it's so we can look like divas. She said that she doesn't care for it herself but it is totally necessary. Great, just what I always wanted to be, a Diva! But I guess I do get a little dramatic over the nails and bath thing. I'm just thankful it's not every day we have to do that. I'm trying to understand why some things that were pure joy for me as a human, are not very fun as a dog. I will have to think about this more and try to figure this out. I have resolved to try harder at being as good with new things as Jlo, even though I'm not quite as experienced. I've decided I need to quit comparing my dog activities with my human life. The parallel I'm looking for is definitely not there.

“It’s time for a Sophie kiss, ready or not
Grandma, here I come.” . . . Sof

Genesis 37:19 "Here comes that dreamer!" they said to each other.

35

CONFERENCE

The next day I decided to call a conference with Tinker and Jlo. I ran up to them after they ate their breakfast, which for them is the best meal of the day. They are starving after sleeping all night, and Grandma always makes us all this warm moist food in the microwave. They just thoroughly enjoy it. Sometimes I'm not hungry but I still sit and watch them eat, take a few nibbles and push my food around. If I have had a seizure or my teeth are bothering me my appetite is just not there.

"Hey, I really need to have a conference with you guys," I chimed,

"First off, I'm not a guy and what's a conference?" Jlo asked,

"Well it's a discussion, an important talk," I told them. They thought it over for only a few seconds before they both nodded, agreeing since they just wanted to lie down and let their food digest.

As they lay down on the rug by the glass slider door, I sat in front of them. First off, I asked Jlo if she ever wanted to be human. She looked at me with the strangest expression, thought for a moment then explained, "Of course, but I would want to be a human that can do all the things us dogs can do."

"What do you mean?" I asked,

"We are fed by the humans, they clean up our messes, we are held and petted by them, and we can sleep with all or any of them and all day long if we wish. They care for all of our needs and they think we are precious every day. Also we do not have to go work like they do, or do chores, and take responsibility for others, we can just have fun, play outside, sniff whoever we want and relax whenever we feel like it. If someone comes over that we don't like or are not treating our people with respect, we can annoy them and really make them upset. We can help take revenge whenever we want, and all of those good things," she said. Wow, I never thought about that, "Yeah, I learned that from Tinker, she says she can smell people who don't like cats. So then she just goes right up to them and rubs her fur all over their legs. It looks like she's loving them but she truly is getting them back for being cat haters. The humans all think it's sweet but she's really being a devil and enjoying every minute of it," Oh yeah I thought, I've seen her do that and then when she's told to stop she just keeps doing it until they pull her away. Then I've seen her lay as close to them as possible and make squinting eye contact with them as enough to tell them she knows they don't like her and she's just annoying them on purpose, she sometimes purrs so loud they really get annoyed or even sneaks a lick in with that rough tongue. I have seen that, and it's quite sly and vengeful of her but she does it well, "We should try this sometime, eh Sophie?" Jlo snorted,

"Well sure, but who hates us? I'm not sure I could get the hang of this,"

Next, I focused on Tinker and asked her the exact same thing. Would she want to be a human? Right off the bat, she said no and explained her life of leisure was all she wanted. I told her how great it is to be a human and how walking upright is grand, and how wonderful it is to pick a mate. Right about then she nailed me and pinned me down to give me a spit bath. She said that the pollen from the flowers has gotten into my brain and I needed to be washed off so I could think straight. I tried my best to tell her that I was actually a human before, but she just kept saying, "Sure you were, Sof, just don't tell that to animals outside this home. You will have no friends,"

"I have angel friends!" I piped up, but Tinker says I speak dog muck and don't make sense when I speak dog muck. Then she proceeded to ask me if I had been eating her catnip. This question was a test. First I'm not supposed to eat the catnip and she is very secretive about where she hides it. She wanted to know if I was high on something, "No—it's the truth!" I hollered, but she just pushed me over to my little bed after my yucky spit bath and told me to sleep it off. I was exhausted from the licking so I did end up taking a nap. As I was falling into slumber I wished they would listen to me, I know they would like to be human if they understood how wonderful it really is.

Genesis 11:2 As people moved eastward, they found a plain in Shinar and settled there.

36

BIG TRUCKS

Today something big is happening. There is not only a big, but a huge truck here, and a bunch of stuff is being moved outside and put into the truck. Grandma is here early and helping direct things but I don't understand what's happening. She just keeps me back out of the way and then picks me up. Tinker, Jlo and I are all concerned. The kids are at school, the Mom is working, and it is just the Dad and Grandma here with a few other men. I'm worried that this is not right. Now big furniture is going into the truck. There are too many big feet; I'm going upstairs where I can have a view of them going in and out without getting trampled. Upstairs I realized the man's closet is empty and not one pair of his smelly shoes that are always in the bathroom or bedroom are there. As a dog you actually like smelly things from people. You can actually tell a lot from their smells and they don't smell the same to dogs as they do to people. What people think is yuck we think is yum.

This is perplexing. I lay there and dozed off and finally they were gone. The door shut and it was quiet. Oh no! Grandma, where are you?! I ran downstairs and scratched at the door, I barked, and whimpered and realized she may be gone. What will I do?! I need her, and she needs me! I'm not sure for what, but she loves me I know she does! "Hey, hey!" I was yelling, "What about us?!" I was panicked, right about then; Tinker and Jlo found me and gave me the news. They figured out the man is moving out on his own to a new place, "Oh," I said, "Like a divorce?" They didn't know what that word was; they just said he would not live here anymore. I told them I knew that term from my human days but they didn't believe me. I asked them again if they heard the word divorce or what. They both just shrugged, they just figured if his office is gone so is he. I ran into his office and yep, it was empty.

"But where is Grandma?" I asked with fear. They looked concerned on that thought. We all know very well that the main reason we have such great lives is because of Grandma. Now they jumped up, Tinker into the window and Jlo on the sofa to look outside. They conveyed, she's in the driveway with a neighbor from across the street, Mr. Greene. This Mr. Greene seems awful nosy; he comes around all the time. Maybe he thinks he is the neighborhood watch guy or something. Any way, we were all relieved to find Grandma still there. We can't lose Grandma, now that would be a real tragedy.

That night it was pretty sad and quiet at the house. Grandma stayed overnight which she does on occasion. Monica, Tori and Kayla are sad and they all three slept together for a few days. Then Grandma kept staying over and the girls took turns, one of them sleeping with Grandma then switching and sleeping with their Mom. Jlo, Tinker and I all followed them and stayed close by to comfort them. The younger daughter, Kayla, stayed home from school. I think it was more from sorrow than it was sickness. I just stayed by her all day and gave her tons of dog kisses. That makes her smile and it makes Grandma happy that I'm so attentive.

I then remembered the Dad saying before that he would miss me. I now know what he was talking about. He still comes over and gets the girls to go with him. It has been hard but everyone is adjusting. I'm sad, I wonder if this was something I could have prevented? Maybe this was part of my mission I did not fulfill? I'm really not sure. I was just starting to really get along with him.

Since this move, Grandma is here more and more these days. I like that part. She is the most wonderful and loving human I've met yet. She is a saint . . . you know, in the action type of way. She takes care of everyone and is never selfish. She is there for everyone and has a seemingly endless amount of energy. I'm not sure how old she is but she's a spitfire for an older woman like herself. I'm not so sure she should be driving that great big truck though, it's so big she can barely see over the wheel, but she just jumps in and goes. Apparently, she uses whatever car available when she has to go somewhere. Whenever she drives in this big truck the girls call her their "Hummer Grammy," whatever that means. Anyway she really is "as cute as a bug's ear!" Hey, I just remembered that saying from my past! It's weird like déjà vu and suddenly a memory, word or something familiar comes to me. It's kind of cool when I remember small things from my human days. I definitely feel smarter at these moments.

Hosea 13:7 So I will be like a lion to them, like a leopard I will lurk by the path.

37

SENIORITAS

Yesterday, the oldest daughter, Tori, and the mom took us for a walk. Monica does so much for everyone. I love the name Monica, it's a beautiful name, but it's hard to remember because her only name seems like "Mom." Unfortunately, on this walk I was in a pink coat with beads on it. Tori thought I might get cold. Jlo wore a blue sweatshirt type top with a hood and didn't like it but Jlo is always ready to go on a walk to sniff. She sniffs every blade of grass that any dog has peed on. Yuck, I just sniff for angel tracks. It's a crisp sweet smell or just a glistening on the ground if an angel has been around recently. I realized that after meeting Dovie. She made me more aware of my senses as an angel and how to better use them.

Jlo has done her best to teach me how to sniff better or "Read the Newspaper" as she puts it. She can tell all the dogs that have been around and about. This is exciting for her. I pretend to be interested but I'm only trying to be more dog like for her. She said when I started walking on a leash, I had to grow up and act sophisticated if I want to hang with her. I'm truly doing my best.

On this particular walk I was tired and really wanted to just stay home and sit on the chaise with Grandma. So I was pulling against my leash not to go. Brutus was not outside at his house and that is the main reason I like to go on walks, to get any new info he may have. Then I heard these dogs yelling "Hey senioritas! We want to dance the Cha-cha with you!" Jlo was ignoring them and sniffing, I turned to look and they were walking our way. There was one that I had never seen before and the other was just a loud mouth bully who is always causing trouble with other dogs around the neighborhood. I guess today is our turn, "Look up," I told Jlo, and I barked to them, "Back off guys we are not senioritas, we are Sophie and Jlo," They laughed and threatened to come and retrieve us if we wouldn't come to them. I told them in my most lady like voice they need to speak politely or not at all. Boy, men sure need to learn manners. I hope they are not approaching us because we look so beautiful in our clothes.

At this time Monica scooped me up, "Calm down, Sophie," her voice was calm as she spoke, the bullies just watched us but did not come closer. We walked about one house further which is at a slow pace since Jlo is in sniff mode. Then I heard the bully growl,

"I'm gonna get her!" I barked and Tori suddenly realized that the dog was racing across the road. As she began to reach down to pick up Jlo that awful dog attacked her, it was too late.

Suddenly in a blink of the eye, he had his mouth right around Jlo's neck, "Let her go, let her go!" I barked, the Mom was holding me way up high, screaming hysterically and hitting the mean dog as Tori was trying to push him off and protect Jlo's face. I was closing my eyes in fear, simultaneously screaming out prayers for help from anyone, "Oh dear God, please help us and save Jlo!"

Then in seconds, everything changed. I saw Brutus running towards us dragging his master behind him on his leash, all ninety pounds of him. That black and tan terror was coming right at us. He barked commands to the mean misfit that was biting Jlo, "You let go of her now! Back off!" he growled ferociously. Right then the dog let go as he was told and ran off back in the direction he came from. Brutus stood back and asked if we were okay? We were all shook up and Jlo was in shock, she just laid there on the ground. For the first time ever, I cried actual tears as a dog.

"Jlo . . . Jlo!" I was screaming, then Brutus stepped forward and licked her neck, it was then that Jlo opened her eyes. This all happened in mere seconds, just like any other tragedy what seemed like hours was just seconds. Brutus sat down next to her and Jlo tried to get up. All the humans even Brutus's Master Ken was amazed. Brutus was a hero and such a gentleman. Jlo looked up and could hardly believe her eyes, the meanest dog in the neighborhood just saved her life and he is looking right at her. Monica gave me to Tori and then she bent over to pick up Jlo and she reached over to pet Brutus' head, and said, before turning towards home;

"Thank you, Ken, Brutus sure scared those mean dogs away, and thank you too, Brutus,"

"I can't believe it, he really seems to like your little dogs," Ken turned stroking Brutus and told him what a good boy he was and kept going forward on their walk. I looked at Brutus as they moved away from us,

"Thank you," I told him,

"No problem," he said, also mentioning that when he saved Jlo he gave her important information we both will be able to use. He told me to take care of Jlo and I thanked him again.

Upon arriving home, Grandma came running down the drive and brought a wash cloth and towel to wipe Jlo off. She heard the horrible barking and yelps from Jlo and I along with Monica and Tori screaming. Jlo had that horrible dog's spit all over her neck. Thank God she has a nice chubby neck along with that big sparkly collar and that dumb sweatshirt on or she might have died. I thought she was dead for a few minutes, which frightened me because I love her. Yeah, no matter what she says to me, she's the best dog sister I could ever ask for. Everyone was so upset we all just sat near Jlo. I let Grandma hold her all night; I didn't even try to take her place on Grandmas lap tonight. Monica and Tori were so surprised at Brutus they were constantly talking about how he saved Jlo. Yeah, I love happy endings. I knew Brutus was good I just had no way of telling them. Jlo slept all night and occasionally looked up, "Hey Sof," she said, I just walked over and licked her, she smiled and went back to sleep. We all slept soundly till morning came.

Jlo the next day was all achy and sore, but she was relieved and thankful for her save. She finally came to me and told me what Brutus conveyed to her. She said that Brutus will always be there for us and will protect us. He said because she did not tell on him to other animals when he attacked me he will always respect us. He will watch out for us and wants us to come see him down the street. Jlo was surprised and grateful, "We will go see him and thank him," she said. I know it is because we are angel encounters and he is just doing his job, but that is too deep for Jlo to understand.

The very next walk Jlo pulled to go towards Brutus house. He was in his electric fence. His master, Ken, was out in the yard with him, they both walked towards us to see how Jlo was. Grandma was apprehensive but she slowly approached with us. Brutus came right to the edge of the fence wagging his tail and sat down. I wiggled and squirmed until Grandma put me down and Jlo on her leash went right up to Brutus. Jlo thanked him profusely and then she did that friendly dog sniffing thing. How embarrassing, but she's just being a dog. Then Brutus gave me a message, "The dogs in the neighborhood will not bother you, but at home, soon things will change, be mindful of Grandma and her surroundings. Be on the lookout for anything that may be different. Be diligent and ready to take action if necessary," he told me,

"Okay," I replied, but wondered what exactly he meant by that. I wagged my tail and gave him a dog wink. We bid our farewells and went on our way. When we were nearing home that awful dog that bit Jlo was in a yard between us and our house. I barked as loud as I could to alert Jlo and Grandma but he just walked the other way and never said a word to us. He looked ashamed and just skedaddled away. Whatever Brutus meant about them not bothering us he was sure right! That guy didn't even come close to us when he saw us. Good, maybe it was Brutus or could my bark be getting scarier? Wishful thinking but, nah, probably not!

When I lay down to sleep that night I practiced removing bad thoughts and replacing them for good ones. This was something I did when work used to bother me and keep me up at night. I began to think about when I used to dance with my girl on date night, we used to square dance, it was something like, *swing your partner round and round, dosey doe and promenade,* yeah that was it, I think? Wow, I love it when my thoughts work in some sort of right direction. I'm going to keep thinking of that, it's a wonderful thought as I saw two people in my head swirling around, smiling and laughing. I was so engaged that in the morning I remembered my thoughts or dream, it was crystal clear. So I thought about telling Jlo and Tinker and just when I was calling them, I realized they won't believe me or understand me anyway, so I just laid down and closed my eyes for another glimpse of that happy promenading couple.

Psalm 86:7 When I am in distress, I call to you, because you answer me.

38

WEATHER CHANGING

It's been weeks and the weather has been getting colder. Maybe my pink coat I wore on walks was a little premature, but now maybe it's called for. I get so cold outside that I run out there and do my duty then right back in. I remember there were names for specific seasons back when I was human. They were, let me see, "Spring, Summer, Trip and Cold." Yeah, something like that! Well, wherever I am on this big planet, the environment I'm experiencing seems to mimic that type of weather. How am I going to see the angels if I'm too cold to go outside? I will have to ask Patience or maybe she will help me arrange something. Oh well, I guess that's what I will soon find out?

Weather is changing fast, it's not just cold, it's freezing and there is a lot of commotion in the house. When we go outside Monica and the girls are moving the ice chunks just so Jlo and I can go potty. Oh yeah . . . I remember snow. I didn't like it then and don't like it much now! Jlo and I watched as Kayla pushed the snow and I knew that was for us to do our duty. I hate the cold ice on my paws, can you believe it, I hated the crappy galoshes that I had as a kid but at least they were foot protection of some kind. Now I'm like an ice cube trying to go potty with damp feet. This part of being a dog stinks. The other day I was so cold I couldn't poop, I think it was frozen in my butt. I talked to it and asked it to please come out but it didn't work. I did the leg lift, the waddle walk and even prayed, but no way, it was as cold as I was and not moving. Then an hour later there was no stopping it and oops, I ran to that clothes room that I first spent the night in and out it came. I think it was just thawed. From then on grandma constantly kept a diaper pad on the floor for me. I appreciate it; I can do my duty there, no matter how cold it is outside. I hate to be so childish about the cold, but when you're less than four pounds, you don't have much fat to keep you warm.

I hope this doesn't last too long; I'm not a cold weather dog. Jlo has more beef on her and she seems to have a high tolerance for the cold. I hope I adapt or my poop unfreezes so I can get out and relieve myself quickly without turning into an ice cube. I say a little prayer to Patience to please, help me and my bowel habits to cooperate. I know to some individuals this is not a big request. But for me it's quite an ordeal, and unfortunately on a daily basis since it's been cold out. "So please Patience, give me some help, and thank you."

Job 12:12   Is not wisdom found among the aged? Does not long life bring understanding?

39

SOMETHINGS UP

Today something is happening. I can vaguely remember what is going on, but it seems familiar. The whole family, Mom, the kids and Grandma are bringing boxes upstairs and opening them and putting things all over the house. Tinker and Jlo seem unconcerned, so I call a conference. I was running around yelling "Conference time, you guys!" and Tinker and Jlo came into the hall to see what all the commotion was. Tinkerbell laid down first,

"What now, Sof?" Jlo had just woke up from a nap and stood there looking dazed,

"What do you want kid?" I was so inquisitive about all these things that I had to know the details of this undertaking. So I started rifling off questions and asking about what was happening,

"Well," Tinker began to speak as she was licking her fur, "This happens every year, they put up all this stuff and it gets real bright and it glows at night, then they put a tree up in the house which I find fun. I have to climb it at least once every year. Then their family comes over and they have fun. That's about it kid!" she summarized, Jlo piped up next,

"That's not all, they have lots and lots of food and everyone is in a good mood, and we get lots and lots of treats, but the price is wearing some kind of get up the kids put on us. It's worth it though, isn't it, Tinker?" As Jlo wagged her tail, I started getting excited at the sounds of this,

"So does that mean a party?!" I'm so glad when I can remember things correctly from my human days,

"I guess so if that's what a party is," said Jlo,

"Yep!" I chimed, "A party is when you get together with people you like and there is fun, food and laughter and lots of people doing goofy things," As I went into further detail, I turned to look at them and they both looked like they were sleeping. With a huff, I went scampering off to see what my family was doing.

They were busy, busy, busy and singing really good songs to the music on the stereo. The kids were helping the Mom erect a tree, wow, Tinker was right, and I sort of remember this. Grandma just kept unpacking things and putting them all over the house. I followed her as she arranged decorations from room to room. The house remained this way for weeks and I truly grew to love it. I was never afraid at night since the whole house was glowing.

I woke up one day and wow, the kids were crazy and screaming and people were knocking on the door very early. It was the daughter of Grandma, Kathy with her husband Steve and her kids with Blue, my buddy! There was also Kathy's son a nice looking man with his wife and her beautiful daughter with her husband. What a nice looking family grandma has! Oh, and Blue had a colorful collar of red and green on, he looked especially nice.

That day I had about every treat imaginable. Of course, I did not get to eat them all at once but I'm looking forward to trying each of them. I love the sausage treats, they are the best, they kind of taste like soft sausage steak but my size and easier for a small dog like me to chew.

Everyone was over and there was lots of laughter, food and fun, just like I said. Jlo, Tinker and I were all dressed up in hats and bell collars that were ruffled. Even Tinker didn't mind, she got a lot of treats as well. Hey, this is fun, I could get used to this. Then I remembered this was a "big holiday," Tinker said it happens every year when they put those lights up all over the house. What a day, I loved to see all the people together, they were a very loving family, a lot like I remember mine being.

I fell asleep with my ruffled collar on and dreamt about what it was like when I was a human when this holiday occurred. But when I woke up, poof! The picture was gone. Darn it, I want so badly to remember. Or maybe I was dreaming about today? Anyway it was a nice dream; I definitely woke up feeling the familiar love of a family.

Soon after that day the lights were put away. It was good to see everyone so joyous at this time of year. I loved my family and the joy they brought me, especially on those special days. After these fun days I get serious people envy. I want to join in as a human, and I do the best I can. But I have to remember that I am on a mission and there is a purpose for me to be here. I just wish it were more apparent what it is I'm supposed to do while I'm here. I don't think I've been of much use to Heaven thus far.

Psalm 44:26 Rise up and help us; rescue us because of your unfailing love.

40

ICY FALL

It was a very cold day and everyone was lazing around the house. I didn't even want to go outside for any reason. Grandma came over early and realized our bathroom spot that was cleared away had filled back up with snow. So worrying about us wading in the snow she went and got a shovel to clear it out again. I kept trying to tell her not to worry, I'll use the diaper pad on the floor, but Jlo had no inclination of being a baby and doing that. Tinker told us we could use her litter box but no thank you, her poop was gigantic and I would probably jump right into a pile of it when trying to get inside. After all, her litter box looks like a house and I'm not supposed to poop in the house.

So grandma put on her warm clothes and out the back door she went. Everything was fine but then as she was coming in she slipped on the icy steps and fell. She was half in and out of the house. Jlo just jumped to her and barked for her to get up, but I ran upstairs as fast as I could to get Monica and the kids. I was frantically barking and running back and forth. They were so shocked to see me so crazy they all followed me down to the back door where grandma laid. I was barking and jumping. When they saw her they screamed, "Grandma, grandma! Are you okay?!" Grandma was just then lifting herself up and she had a big bump on her head and a cut near her chin. Jlo was licking her and Tinker was standing watch over her, but I ran to get the family. I knew I could get them to follow me. I was as serious as I could and besides I am four pounds now and mightier than ever.

Maybe this is my mission to help alert my family when things happen. Yeah, I think this is it. All that day I stayed close to grandma to be sure she was alright and so did Tinker and Jlo. I was worried about her bump on her head and the cut on her chin. So I got up on her lap and put my paws on her chest and stood on her legs right in front of her to inspect her injuries, "What's this?" she said, and I wagged my tail and licked her sore chin. She laughed, "You little thing, you helped me by getting the family to come, now are you trying to lick my wounds?" I wagged my tail and was truly mesmerized, how beautiful this woman was, wounds and all. Looking square into her eyes I realized there was more to this wonderful person than I had seen before. I do need to watch out for her, she may need me more since she's hurt now. She spent the night so I cuddled her in the extra bedroom downstairs. I love her and I know in her own way she does love me. I want to protect her from any harm, and today was very scary. I'm glad I was here. I hope this may be one of the reasons I am here on a mission.

As I slept that night listening to Grandma's heartbeat, Patience came to me and said *"Job well done, Rob,"* In my mind I was pleased. I cuddled in closer to Grandma and dreamt she was a puppy I could talk to. It was a wonderful dream how we could communicate so perfectly.

Zechariah 2:3 While the angel who was speaking to me was leaving, another angel came to meet him.

41

GOING TO HEAVEN

It's Spring time now and Mom and the girls have been busy going back and forth to Grandma's house. This is many more trips than usual, and one day a big truck came again to our house again. Now what, I thought? There are a bunch of boxes and things coming into the house. It's confusing at first, and then I realized the stuff and boxes smell like Grandma. It is her belongings that are coming into our house. Oh boy, this could be good! The room in the basement that has a living room and a small kitchen area is where her things are going. A bed and other furniture are being moved there too. This is exciting and interesting; Tinker, Jlo and I are all watching. It's definitely a busy, worrisome, yet sort of interesting day. Grandma is exhausted so she goes to bed this particular evening upstairs in her normal guest bedroom; I am staying right by her. I don't want her to get away from me. The room in the basement is filled with boxes and furniture; tomorrow we will see what takes place.

The next day I watch her and the girls' work all day in the basement fixing up what looks like her old room at her house. Her bedspread is here, her favorite chair, her dresser, that smoking stand that I like so much and her clothes. Yup, this is good. I'm feeling great until I see Dovie fly by outside the window. It suddenly worries me because she works with the angel of death and she's at my house. Oh No, I thought, no one can be dying now, life is good, I don't even want to go back to Heaven, my dog life is in full swing and I've become a good little girl dog. Yeah, I know, the dresses, purses and all, but these people are worth every suffering minute of it. I see Dovie is in a tree by my yard. I begin to bark and she flies over to the window, "Hey Sophie, is this where you live?" she asks,

"Yeah, pretty great, huh?" I piped up with pride,

"Yes, I do think you are lucky," she cooed. Instantly and not on a funny note, for the first time, I thought, *Yeah, dumb luck, but truly lucky,*

"But why are you here?" I asked,

"The old Tom Cat next door is dying today and I am here to comfort him while he passes, and escort him to heaven."

"How do you do that?" tilting my head to the side curiously,

"Watch out this window and you will see," she told me. I asked with worry if anyone here at my home is in jeopardy and she confirmed we were safe, so watch I did.

When Frank the big old Tom cat went outside a few minutes later Dovie flew down to him. Instead of him trying to chase the bird he just seemed to communicate like I do with her. She actually rubbed his head with her wing as he sat in the sun warming himself. Then he slowly got up and went inside. She waited in the tree nearby. I barked, "Hey, he didn't die!"

"Wait," Dovie said. Within the hour I saw Dovie and Frank together they were both walking slowly up into the sky. He was youthful and healthy, not ragged, the way we were used to seeing him. Then I watched them slowly disappear into the clouds. They were smiling and talking all the way. Wow, that was quite amazing, I wonder when I pass as an animal will Dovie help me get to Heaven? I'm not going to think about that now. I have an important mission to complete.

Luke 19:6 So he came down at once and welcomed him gladly.

42

GRANDMA IS HERE TO STAY

It's official, Grandma moved in. It looks like she's staying since all her stuff is here and I over heard her say that her house was "sold." I remember that from my past it means she can't live there anymore. Yeah! It's a celebration; I have to tell Tinker and Jlo. I scurried through the house to find them and they didn't seem enthused about this. They were just like "Yeah, it's good," I was shaking my head at this,

"No, it's the best news ever, what would happen if she did not take care of us? No chicken treats, no walks every day and no being carried around!" They both gave me the evil eye because I am the only one who gets carried around all day, "Well anyway, let's go welcome her!" So they agreed to go downstairs with me and welcome her here officially. I lead the way and could not stop talking about how wonderful it is going to be. Don't get me wrong, the Mom and the girls are great but they are all very busy with their lives and they don't have the time to cater to us like Grandma.

We all went into her room. It was a huge mess with boxes and things all over the floor, "Well, look at here it's the pet parade!" she smiled. Yup, that's us! Jlo even did her special bark a few times and Tinker rubbed up against her legs, I just jumped up on her legs as to say pick me up, "You guys are something else, aren't you," she said, petting Jlo and Tinker then reaching down and picking me up, score! I knew she loved me the most, or at least that's what I tell myself. Soon she set me down and covered me up with a blanket, Jlo found a spot and Tinker lay down in a pile of clothes on the floor. We were all just happy watching her. I peeked out from under the blanket and wondered what really my mission here was? I decided today it was to watch Grandma unpack.

I woke up from my nap in the blanket and wondered where I was at. No one was in the room and things looked different. I bolted from my covers to run right into Grandma coming back into the room with yet another box. On my way out I recognized that little stand that was at her house, the one that belonged to her husband. I stopped to smell it and for some strange reason I love the smell of this stand. It makes me feel good and sort of euphoric. As strange as that sounds I just want to be near this small wooden stand. I wish I could explain that, but it's just a feeling that I can't shake. Mm, one more sniff and, ahh, it's a good smell.

What could possibly be in the box grandma is carrying? The room is full and looking pretty neat, what now? I decided to sit down on the shelf underneath the little stand where I felt safe and out of the way. Besides I like it here. I was interested but just waking up so I yawned as she began to unpack. She laid all the items which were pictures out on the floor one by one. They were in all different frames and sizes and she meticulously lined them all up on the floor along the wall. This was quite the process and obviously very important to her. I acted like I was interested and watched her closely. Some pictures she commented on and seemed extremely overjoyed about. She even talked to some of them and spoke about scenarios of the people at that time. One particular picture she held to her heart and said "I do still love you, I always have, and I miss you. You were my rock," Then she kissed it and set it down. Hey, what was that, she did not kiss any other picture . . . ? I have to check this one out. As soon as I went over to it, the doorbell rang and upstairs we went.

Proverbs 24:27 Put your outdoor work in order and get your fields ready; after that, build your house.

43

POOPY DANCE

It was a package delivery and Jlo and I had to protect Grandma from the delivery man, or at least let him know we are here. Then I felt a poop coming on. Grandma waited for the man to leave and let Jlo and I out to sniff and rummaged the yard. I try to look like I have to find the right place to go but really I'm just getting comfortable enough to poop outside in front of everyone and God himself.

In my earthly days that was a very private time. I got the bathroom all to myself for a few minutes, of peace and quiet. The rest of the family would not come in because it might stink. And since I was the *only* man I didn't have to share my time. That was a good thing, or at least most of the time. Otherwise with one bath I could be shaving and the girls would pop their head in or yell through the door and say, "Dad its an emergency and I really need to come in, can I?" Then knowing they only did this if it was an emergency, I would reply

"Yes" and let them know of my location and vacate if I could. Then at times they would need to come in while I was in the shower. They would say "stay there, don't look," because the toilet was tucked away in a corner and they would just come in and go. When I was showering and it was an emergency they would tell me "you stay in there till I'm done." It would make me laugh and I would tease them and say

"Whew, stinky girl, don't forget to flush." They would say

"Sorry Dad, or okay I won't." But with one bathroom these things are bound to happen. Oh, those were the days, my family was the best.

Well I found the spot. Grandma says I do the poopy dance. I turn at least three circles, that is to pack down the grass so it does not tickle my behind. Then I lift my hind leg up, the right one and try to stay low to the ground. Sometimes I need to start to walk, kind of bow legged before I'm finished, mostly because someone is watching me or I'm just not comfortable. Then I hop on three legs until it all falls out. Grandma says that's the poopy dance. She gets a laugh out of it. I just get relief. At least it's not frozen inside of me, thank goodness for that blessing.

Okay, it's starting to rain out here, let's go back inside. Jlo and I run inside to get our chicken or turkey treats. We are spoiled big time, but Tinker gets one also and she just uses the litter box. But she is smart enough to watch us go outside and wait by the refrigerator until we come in so she gets her treat along with us.

Our mom is holding a piece turkey so you can see how we wait so patiently for our reward.

Tinker–Jlo–Sof

Psalm 33:11 But the plans of The Lord stand firm forever, the purposes of his heart through all generations.

44

PICTURE PERFECT

Now back to her room. Jlo and I follow Grandma down to watch the events. She is making her bed and folding towels up. I was just about to lie down and I remembered that picture. So I jumped down to look for it, "What are you doing?" Jlo asked, giving me a strange look. I told her about Grandma kissing a picture and Jlo said it was probably the picture of her,

"I don't think so." I said sarcastically, she said some important words and was mumbling stuff that seemed important at the time . . ." So I began to look for it. There were lots of pictures, family and old people, but mostly the kids and grandchildren in different settings. Jlo saw how intent I was to find this particular picture and she jumped down to join me. She immediately pointed out her picture, she had a boa of ruffles on in pink and she sat and admired her photo.

"This is the one she probably kissed!" she said, I just told her that it was a very nice picture of her but that is not the one. I saw a picture of Tinker lying in the sun like a movie star, but I could not find that one she kissed. Then I saw the wood frame. I went over to it and there was Grandma with a man. I thought what a nice picture. I couldn't help but admire it.

Then I was mesmerized by the picture. I could not take my eyes off of it. I just stared and stared. There was something familiar about it, I loved this picture too. They looked so good together. She was in her new white dress and he in his best suit. It was like déjà vu. I thought I loved that white dress on her, and those were my new wire rimmed glasses! Suddenly, I was trying to recall my memory, "Oh my god!" I yipped when I realized that the man in the photo is me! Well . . . it *was* me! I'm in that picture it's me *Rob*, I'm in the picture with Grandma! I kept seeing me the man, then me the dog, Sophie, then Rob the man. I was so excited and bewildered that I began scratching the glass on the picture with my paw, and trying to remember more. My tail was wagging and I could not control myself, it was like an out of body experience. I was going crazy,

"Calm down, it's only a picture," Jlo muttered, then Grandma came over to us,

"Whoa, whoa, Sophie what are you doing? That is my favorite picture of my husband and me. It was our twenty-fifth wedding anniversary. You stinker quit scratching it!" She said before picking up the photo and holding it to her heart once again. I barked so loud and jumped around and turned circles. She knew something was up. She laughed, "Sof, it's only a picture!" I was still going crazy and she held it down to me again. I gently put my paw out to it and was barking,

"It's me, it's me!" I squealed enthusiastically,

"Wow," grandma said, "You must like pictures, huh," So she showed me another one of the kids. I ignored that and barked for her to bring down the previous one she put on the dresser. I was standing on my hind legs as upright as I could. I was trying to look as human as possible. Trying to be that man I recognized as me in the picture. It was that brief nostalgic moment swarmed over and around me and I felt intoxicated, but in a good way. Suddenly when the scene quit spinning I realized,

I was Grandma's husband!!! I, Rob, was married to Grandma that means I am here *with Ellie,* right now! Then I was so elated as I bounced on my hind legs and barked that I lost my balance in my excitement and toppled over and hit my head.

Apparently I was knocked out for a few minutes and I awoke in Grandma's arms. She was petting me and saying, "Don't get so excited and you won't go goofy, fall over and hit your head. You'll knock your brains out if you do that too often," I hit the leg of the table when I fell and all I saw was darkness after that. She was real concerned and she was hugging me and kissing me. I felt like I was in a dream and a dream come true, kind of. I'm here with, um? Oh shoot, what was her name? I remembered when I saw the picture and now I forgot. But she was my wife! I'm the guardian of my wife here on earth. I'm here with her. I can't believe it, I love her, I just wish I could remember more and could tell her who I am.

"Help me Patience!" I screamed. I can't remember what her first name is, but the important thing is I am here. I was sent here to be with her, my love.

Patience came to me, "Yes Rob you are *with Ellie*, now just compose yourself, your mission is very important and now you know why you are here," she said calmly. I was looking at Ellie and trying to process this. She thought I was still dazed and just held me tight to her chest. Oh, yeah this is why she feels so good, smells so good, and is so comfortable and I want to be with her every minute. She is the love of my life and I've been here for a few years and never knew. This is my mission; I am here to be with her. It all makes sense now. That means, those kids, Kayla and Tori, are my grandchildren and the mom, Monica, is my daughter. I started yelping and running to tell Jlo and Tinker. Before racing out the door, I went back to get on more lick-kiss in to Ellie and to let her know with a gentle bark that I'd be right back. Jlo had already given up on my hysterics and was gone out of her room already.

The real twenty-fifth wedding anniversary
picture "1974"

Psalm 30:11 You turned my wailing into dancing; you removed my sackcloth and clothed me with joy, 30:12 that my heart may sing your praises and not be silent. Lord my God, I will praise you forever.

45

ANNOUNCEMENT

"You guys, you guys, wherever you are, quick come here I have great news! I'm home, I'm Home, and this is where I belong! This is my mission!" I found Tinker and Jlo on the floor in the sun by the back door. I went skidding into them, "Hey did you hear me, did you?" I asked,

"Yeah we heard your delirious dog muck," Tinker said, licking her paw, "Can you let us nap now?"

"No, No, No!" I replied, "This is important we need a conference. I'm the grandfather of the kids and the father of the daughter, and I used to be married to Grandma. Hey you guys do you hear me. I'm so excited!!" I was screaming the news and looking for the kids.

"Sure Sof, could you just calm down and quit this crazy talk. You were never human and you never will be. Seriously, you are getting a little crazy in your years," Jlo said,

"Dammit you rascals, I want you to listen, this is my best day of my dog life," I piped,

"Oh boy, more dog muck," Tinker rolled her eyes,

"Ha, I just swore in human you crazy little varmints. Hey, my human memory is kicking in. Seriously, I will somehow prove to you this is true!"

"Okay kid, you just do that," said Tinker, "

"Oh sorry Patience for swearing, I'm a little over excited." I squealed as I ran away.

"Yep, we're waiting for the proof," Jlo murmured,

"I will prove it. Hey, I love you guys too!" I yelled as I was half delirious with joy, Tinker rolled her eyes and told Jlo she was truly not sure about me and Jlo just stretched out to soak up more sun. Together they decided I was seriously deranged or probably brain damaged since birth.

As I ran back downstairs to Grandma, *My Love,* I was thanking God, thanking Patience, and expressing my eternal gratitude over and over. As I was howling my prayers, Ellie was listening to my antics and she looked up from her task with a gleam in her eye. She was on the floor, folding some towels and I just jumped right on her and kept licking her until she pulled me off. I just wanted to say "I love you, I love you, I love you so much!" She sat me down and I pranced on my hind legs and tried to look tall and upright. She just laughed,

"You are so silly, did you knock yourself goofy?" I just jumped back onto her lap, wagging my tail as I kissed her arms. I wore myself out prancing around until she tucked me into a blanket on her bed. This was definitely one of the best days of my dog life; no it "*is* the best day." I snuggled in deciding, I should settle down and process this wonderful news, but I was sure to keep one eye on Ellie!

I awoke to hearing the girls come home from school. Oh boy! Not only are these my favorite girls, but they are my grandchildren. I ran up to them and jumped all over them until the youngest one, Kayla picked me up. Oh, I love you so much; I was crying dog tears and slurping kisses all over her. She was giggling and saying Sophie you are so excited. She was kissing me back and holding me up and making faces at me. Loving faces and making kissing noises. Then I looked across the counter and saw the older granddaughter, Tori, and jumped onto the counter and into her arms. She was so surprised and was laughing and cuddling me. She was petting me and giving me kisses on my head. My tail was going ninety miles an hour. Yep, this is my heaven on earth. Even if I am in the form of a weird little female dog, I'm just glad to be here. I jumped back onto the counter and stood on my hind legs and turned circles. I was so happy, the girls were clapping for me and giggling and fighting over who was going to hold me next. Wow, they really do love me!

Jlo walked in, "You have seriously flipped your lid," she said,

"No, I haven't, I'm here for the endurance!" I said, "I belong here and I know my mission!" Right then Grandma let us outside for our daily after school potty time. I was barking loudly, "I'm an angel from heaven and here with my earthly family! Can anybody hear me? Yipee Yahoo!" Jlo just hiked her leg at that,

"The fertilizer is really getting to you these days . . ." she mumbled.

Ephesians 1:16 I have not stopped giving thanks for you, remembering you in my prayers.

46

TRUE LOVE

Every day felt like Heaven from then on. I just wanted to stare at Grandma all the time. It's Ellie, but now that name seems kind of formal since she's my caregiver. I put up such a fuss over that picture that she put it on the low night stand that I love the smell of, next to her bed. When she hung it up high I just barked and whined until she took it down. Now she has everyone come see how I act when she puts it on the floor. I lick it and wag my tail and sing "I love you so much" in the best dog words I have, not as well as Jlo, but it makes my Ellie smile! Then I curl up next to it or on her lap. It's a ritual and people think it's cute. She thinks maybe something sweet or sticky must have gotten on it during the move and that's why I like it. She's not sure but she definitely knows I really react to that picture. She even tests me with other pictures and I do nothing. She loves my reaction. She even said

"Rob would have liked this little dog" *Heck ya*, I thought, *because he is this little dog!*

When Monica returned home I was even more excited, just to know Monica and Kathy, Blue's mom, are my daughters I couldn't be happier. I have been floating on a cloud and now know that this is why I am a silly little sick female dog. Monica always had to save the littlest or most ailing pet she found and obviously that was me. Also the Harper family never had a male dog, only females; there was no way I would have made it to Ellie as a male dog. Ha, like I said there are no mistakes in heaven. God, Patience, or whoever knew exactly where I was to be and I am so thankful for having and trusting my heavenly family. I would have done anything to be living with my beautiful family again and here I am.

Isaiah 46:8 "Remember this,
keep it in mind, take it to heart,
you rebels.

47

VALENTINE

The girls are coming home today from school and everyday seems like a celebration when they arrive. I'm watching out the window sitting on the footstool and it looks cold outside, and all of a sudden I hear the brakes of the school bus. I see them running up the driveway. Here, they are and they are giggling, and throwing their back packs down and skipping through the house with a bag and box of goodies. I follow them to their room and they dump out cards and candy and little trinkets, I was jumping up and begging to get on the bed with them, so Kayla reached down and picked me up. I ran to both of them across the bed and licked them and was intently watching the activity with what seemed fun and important.

They were trying to get things organized. Obviously they were making something and signing their creations together. Then Tori saw a tiny little red heart pillow, she grabbed it from Kayla's pile, "Who gave you this?" she asked, Kayla reached for it suddenly,

"Give it back to me, a friend gave it to me!" she frowned, Tori giggled,

"Look Sophie, it's a little *I love you* pillow and it's just your size!" she showed it to me, and looked at it; I found she was right, it would fit me perfectly. Then as I looked at it, I thought, *that's it! I need this to give to Ellie!* As she was showing me the pillow I grabbed it in my mouth and jumped off the bed and began to go down stairs to Ellie's room. Lucky I'm stronger now because two flights of stairs are a lot to do, especially when being chased by your granddaughters! I was so close! I almost got to Grandma's room when Kayla grabbed me with a laugh,

"You little thief, where were you going, silly!" she said,

"What's up girls?" Ellie asked, Kayla told her to come upstairs that they have a surprise for her. I was trying to give Ellie the little red heart, *I love you pillow* but my plan was foiled.

Tucked under Kayla's arm I went along with the crew upstairs. She tapped my nose and said "you little thief, you tried to steal my pillow, what were you going to do? Hide it in Grandma's room?" I wagged my tail, because she was right and she thought I was playing, but I have serious intentions that I won't forget.

Tori and she prepared a surprise for grandma on the kitchen counter. Grandma came in and there was a little box of chocolates and a big card that they made. Ellie was so delighted as she read the card and opened the gift, "Come on girls have some chocolate!" Kayla sat me down on a placemat on the countertop and I was watching them give each other hugs and kisses,

"Happy Valentine's Day Grandma," they both said, and it was then that it all made sense. I remember taking Ellie out to dinner for Valentine's Day. Oh, how I wish I could treat her again. Then Tori told Kayla to show grandma the heart pillow. Kayla pulled it out of her pocket and gave it to grandma. Grandma smiled and said

"How sweet!" I bolted across the counter to Grandma and tried to reach the pillow with my paw so grandma showed it to me. I pawed at it and tried to say

"I love you" but they just laughed and thought I wanted a pillow. Grandma scooped me up,

"Sof, if you want a pillow I will make you one, but this belongs to Kayla," I wagged my tail and licked her; I just seem to melt when she talks right to me. I couldn't love her more; I just want her to know it.

Not giving up on my plan, I followed Kayla to her room and saw her put the little red heart pillow up high on her big dresser. I sat looking up at it and thought this will be a task but I will figure it out. I will somehow show Ellie how much I love her and what she means to me. This tiny pillow has to be my voice, just how do I execute my plan? Darn, I almost made it to her room the first time. I guess more exercise is in order to be fit to outrun my darling granddaughters. I will have to work on this but now it's almost dinner time. I love the evenings, everyone is home and it's such a warm family time. I could just stare and listen to them talk all night about their events of the day. If I get tired early, I just cuddle up underneath Ellie's shirt. Here I feel safe and can feel our hearts beating in unison. I eventually drift to sleep, in my own little heaven on earth.

Proverbs 27:10 Do not forsake your friend or a friend of your family, and do not go to your relative's house when disaster strikes you—better a neighbor nearby than a relative far away.

48

NEW ANGEL

I met this new angel friend; she's an orange long haired tabby cat in the neighborhood. I think she lives at the angel lady neighbor's house and she has recently come around by our house. I heard Tinker when she was sitting in the window talking to her and whining about not getting to go outside. Then the tabby said, "Hey is there any other pets you live with?" Tinker told her about us and said to me,

"Hey kid look at this she lives a couple houses away, say hi to her," I jumped up on the chair by the window, looking out I saw the orange cat. I asked,

"Excuse me what's your name?" Right then *I saw the twinkle*, and at the same time she replied

"Kit," I did too. Tinker looked at me,

"Have you met already?"

"No, I just knew," I told her,

"Right," said Tinker, "Good guess . . ."

I asked what she was here to tell me about, and she said that there had been some break-ins in broad daylight close to our neighborhood. She is posted to help watch out for the neighborhood. She said the burglars are looking for large vacant homes that look empty during the day. I told her we are always here even when the kids are in school. She was just letting me know she's on the prowl for anything out of the ordinary.

I thanked Kit personally and said out loud, "How wonderful, heaven sent us a watch cat for the neighborhood,"

"Her?" Tinker asked, "She's just a ball of fluff . . . soaking wet she's probably only half my size," I then politely reminded her,

"Kit has all of her claws and can go outside," Tinker just rolled her eyes,

"Point made, but what good is she?" she asked,

"I don't know but I like her, and she thinks you're very pleasant also,"

"Oh," said Tinker "I guess I will try to get to know her,"

I now do not want my earthly days to end. I still wish I were human but I'll take this fate or should I say strange luck, to be with Ellie. Unfortunately, we are both getting older and my health is not the best. I now have seizures more often and require medication at times to get me out of them. I just freeze up stiffen my legs, I go numb and my eyes dilate, I can't seem to make sound so I just shake uncontrollably. When Ellie, Monica or the kids see me they rush over to pick me up and hold me tight. If it's bad enough she puts some awful drops into my mouth and massages my throat and then I start to come out of it. It's a bummer, not being healthy. As I always said, "If you have your health you have everything," while apparently Jlo says,

"If you have people snacks you have everything," but she could eat the cardboard off a box and be happy. I'm a little more particular.

Brutus always comes up into our yard if we are out, his owner Ken said he has never seen Brutus take to any animals like he has us two. My daughters and Ken, they joke that Jlo and Brutus have a thing for each other. Whatever? They have no clue it's the angel thing with us. He has been on earth for a while, and is very good at being a dog. He sniffs other dogs and just takes liberty in any yard he feels like; I always hold it for home in my favorite potty place unless it's an emergency. I got up the courage today to ask him what he did before, when he was human. He said he was a police officer, a male, he never asked me. I think he thinks I was a female in my earthly life. I don't know how to explain why I wasn't a female in my human days, but today is not the day to go into long details or explanations.

Proverbs 29:25 Fear of a man will prove to be a snare, but whoever trusts in The Lord is kept safe.

49

INTRUDERS

A few days ago, Brutus told me he was going to be boarded, for a short while, because his owner was going on vacation. I wished him good bye and I told him to let me know if there were other angels at the boarding kennel. He said "Saud right" and gave me his big Brutus grin.

It is almost time for the school year end, the days are getting longer and I love to be outside when it's pleasant. Jlo, Grandma and I have a ritual just before the girls come home in the afternoon; we go for a walk out back of our house on the private trails. We have been doing this for weeks now that it has been nice weather outside.

Today we take a little longer due to Jlo's extra sniffing. She said there were some new dogs here today and it was very interesting news. Yeah, yeah, yeah, same pee, different day. I wanted to go home and sit on grandma's lap on the swing, in the sunshine until the girls come home from school. I prefer snuggling to walking any day, besides I don't need exercise, I'm skinny enough. My outdoor time is for doing my duty or visiting with other angels, no need for sniffing.

Today was a beautiful day; we left the slider open and just shut the screen. Tinker was lying in the sun on the floor when we left. Since Grandma did not make me use a leash, when we approached our yard, I bolted for the door. Standing at the door, I could hear Tinker moaning. What would she be moaning about? Then I heard Kit talking, "Sophie, don't go in there!" I looked by the bush and she said an intruder opened the screen and kicked Tinker out of the way.

"What?!" I gasped, genuinely shocked,

"Yes," Kit said, "You have to stop your owner from going inside,"

"Oh no," I screamed, "I must stop Ellie!" I ran back barking and growling and biting her pant leg and trying to tug on her to stop. But she just said,

"You goofy thing, come here!" and scooped me up. I was wiggling and trying to tell her to stop, "What's got into you?" she questioned, she then opened the door and let Jlo in and put me down. I screamed to Kit,

"Go get Brutus!" *Oh please be back from the kennel!* I thought. As Kit went tearing down the street to get Brutus, I was still trying to wiggle to get down.

Finally, Ellie put me on the floor and I ran until I found Tinkerbell. Tink, crawled into the dining room and was hiding under the buffet, when I found her she was hurt bad and seriously worried for our safety. "There is a man and a woman with masks on that came in . . . I think they're upstairs," she murmured, "The man kicked me when they opened the door," Her cries for help made Kit come up to the house right before we came home.

Oh no, Grandma . . . where is she?! I can't let her go upstairs, so I found her on the other side of the house near the back steps; this house is so big that there are two staircases. I knew if I didn't do something she may be going up. So I told Jlo to quickly go to the dining room and talk to Tinker. I started to limp and whine and pretended to hobble into the lower bathroom, "What's wrong with you?" Ellie asked, she followed me into the bathroom. Good plan, she shut the door to use the toilet and picked me up. I was acting limp and wondered if the intruders were still here?

Then I heard Jlo barking, "Hey, whoever you are if you're in here I'm going to tear you apart!" she growled,

"Be careful, Jlo," Tinker warned,

"What's wrong with you now, Jlo?" Grandma asked, truly confused at this point, she then tried to open the door and I had no choice but to bite her a little to stop her and stun her, "You little squirt, what's got into you?" brow furrowed as she tapped me on the head, at this point she held me tight under her arm and went out,

"Oh no!" I screamed, "God in Heaven, help us!" I was wailing and Ellie thought I was really hurt. As she exited the washroom looking puzzled at me, we heard the front door open and Ellie and I went into the hall to see a man with a suitcase and the woman with a bag getting ready to go out. Then we heard Jlo running down the upstairs hall screaming in her angriest growling bark, "I'm going to tear you from limb to limb!"

Jeremiah 1:8 "Do not be afraid of them, for I am with you and will rescue you," declares the Lord.

50

CALLING ALL ANGELS

The intruders were so startled when someone returned home that they gathered their goods and just ran out the front door without looking back. Ellie was screaming and holding me tight. My adrenalin was so high I squirmed free and leapt out of her arms to the floor, and ran right out the front door the intruders had opened. I started screaming as loud as my little voice could, "Calling all angels, calling all angels! It's an emergency, please help us . . ." I screamed this over and over once I reached the sidewalk; I fell to the ground with my paws over my face praying for help! I'm sure the burglars didn't even see me dart past them out the door and into the yard.

Suddenly, Brutus came leaping past me like a rocket launching to the moon, and before the man could fully clear the door with the woman behind him Brutus was airborne and knocked the man down, attacking his sweatshirt and wrestling him on the ground. I stood frozen wide eyed and afraid to move. The woman following behind tried to jump over the man's feet as he kicked while being swung about by Brutus. She was running with her bag and Jlo followed her out narrowly escaping the door slamming on her. Jlo, ran so fast and grabbed the woman's pant leg with her teeth and was trying to shake her down, then at once here came Kit with the most horrible cat screams I have ever heard! She was screaming explanatives I won't repeat. That cat jumped right onto her thigh and sunk all her claws into her skin. Jlo was biting and tugging, Kit was clawing and scratching, holding onto her leg tight, and the darn woman was still going. It was within a second that Dovie came screeching in with a dive bomb of poop right in her face, and then kept diving at her head. The woman then quickly fell to the ground.

Little did we know but the angel maid up the street called the police when she heard, my plea in the yard. I heard sirens, "Thank God for angels," I sighed, and when I looked back, I couldn't believe my eyes, Ellie came out of the house with a gun. Shaking and crying she was in no mood to mess around. The bad robbers were both face down and Brutus had the man worn out and pretty beaten up. He was going nowhere, but grandma was making sure.

I felt like I was in a nightmare, what took five minutes seemed like years. I ran over to Ellie and she scooped me up. She walked closer to the man and said "You move and I'll shoot you, I swear to God I will," Wow, I don't think I've ever seen her so mad and shook up, she wasn't kidding in the least. The woman in the driveway never made a move and the man said,

"I'm not moving." I thought you bet you're not moving Brutus has a paw on your back, he's growling and his teeth are real close to your neck. Jlo is still shaking the woman's pant leg and Kit is sitting at her face ready to claw.

I was so scared and saw this was the gun I gave her thirty years ago, having told her then, "If anyone ever tried to hurt you, then use it to protect yourself," I reached my paw out in a frail attempt to motion her to put it down. The police were entering the driveway and had their guns drawn. Ellie, shaking lowered the gun and called Jlo and sat down on the steps. Stunned and relieved she began to cry. I stood on her lap and licked her face, Jlo paced with her hair raised on her back barking frantic commands.

Once the police apprehended the man and woman, it seemed the whole neighborhood was there and the kids were just coming off the bus. Jlo was so excited and was running up to Brutus, "We did it, we did it! We got the bad guys Brutus!" she boasted. Ken, Brutus's owner came down and he was checking him over as he was in quite a tussle with this intruder man. But he was praising him all the time on how good he was to help save our home and Grandma. Grandma bent down and was petting Brutus and he licked her. Then Brutus called Kit over and she came up to join the group. Dovie settled down on the small tree by the front porch to watch. Everyone, all the angels, were smiling and then Kit just said,

"It was Tinker who alerted me about the intruders," we all looked over at Tinker who was in the front living room window. She was just purring and asking if everyone was okay.

Just then Dovie landed on the lever of the screen door and let her out. She carefully jumped right into the center of all of us. Tinker at that moment knew something special had happened, she was in the presence of angels. She had heard me yelling "Calling all angels!" and it was then, of course, that all hell broke loose in the front yard.

Ellie was petting Tinker and holding her ribs gently and just so glad none of us were hurt. She just couldn't imagine what would have happened if we all hadn't helped out. When Tinker was finally at peace in Grandmas arms, it was then Dovie spoke up to her. Looking her in the eye she conveyed to Tinker, "You will be richly rewarded in Heaven," Tinker just nodded and snuggled in tighter.

Suddenly, my daughter came screaming up into the driveway with the girls in the big truck. She was headed home and heard the sirens, and picked the girls up as they were nearing the house. They all bolted up to Grandma and all of us. We were all hugging, crying and there was a lot of love and petting going on, we all were a family.

Proverbs 3:24 When you lie down, you will not be afraid; when you lie down, your sleep will be sweet.

51

FAMILY PRAYERS

My daughter's ex-husband, Joe came over and the girls were still afraid and they asked him to stay and protect them. After all, he is a police officer for the city, and fights crime and protects people every day. He tried to tell them that the bad people were in jail, but they were still nervous. As they begged he offered to take them to his house and they wanted no part of leaving their mom and grandma. So Monica told him that he could stay in the kid's room since we all were sleeping together in the master bedroom. He agreed and the kids began to set up camp in Monica's bedroom. The kids put their little play tent up in her room, and Ellie slept in the king size bed with Monica. This means I got to sleep with the both of them. Even Jlo was on the bed and Tinker was planning to sleep with the girls in the tent.

When it was time to shut off the lights, Joe came in and everyone was on the floor with the kids. They all held hands and we pets were on their laps. Each one said a little prayer of thanks. When the girls were saying their prayers, I seemed to remember that was the same prayer my girls said,

"Now I lay me down to sleep, I pray the lord my soul to keep. If I should die before I wake. I pray the lord my soul to take. God bless Mommy, Daddy, Grandma, Tori, Kayla, Tinker, Jlo, and Sophie," Yep, yep that's right I'm included! Oh, there was one more thing, Tori added,

"And thank you for watching out for everyone today!"

Then Kayla, chirped,

"And all the animals for helping keep Grandma and our house be safe, Amen."

Oh, I was so touched, I know they said prayers but this just touches my heart. My eyes were welling up and I was licking them both. I even gave Tinker a lick, and she responded with, "Kid, you're alright in my book, you can really scream when push comes to shove, Thanks,"

"You're welcome, and thanks Tink, you're a Hero for telling Kit," I said, and she just smiled.

Jlo just jumped up on the big bed and said "Get up here," I tried but it was way too tall, then Monica reached down and scooped me up. She snuggled me,

"I hear you were quite the little helper today," I wagged my tail and kissed her right in the nose. I love my daughter for being so strong. Now back to Ellie I go. It's time to do what I do best; curl into her and love her with all 4lbs. 2oz of me.

I kissed her hands and walked up to kiss her face. She smiled and told me she forgave me for biting her today. I felt bad but I had no choice but to try and protect her. I looked a little sheepish when she said this, but she grabbed me and rubbed my head and said "it's okay, I know you were upset." Now I can sleep after making the rounds with my family. I love them all so much I wish we could sleep all together in the same room every night.

Oh wait—"Good night Patience, and all angels, Thanks for being there for us," I was almost asleep when Patience replied,

"You're welcome and good job." I just tried to put all the bad thoughts of the day out of my head and go to sleep.

Proverbs 2:2 turning your ear to wisdom and applying your heart to understanding—

52

OUTSIDE SUPPORT

After yesterday's insanity, everyone was a little jumpy around our house, but lots of friends and neighbors stopped by frequently to check on us. The good thing is that the robbers had been put into jail, so they were off the streets. I couldn't stop thinking, Thank Heaven, and thank Angels. I now realize that earthly angels are put here to balance out the bad in the world and to protect good people from bad. Yep, that's what I will do to the best of my ability. I know that these things are not by accident, that angels are present when needed.

One of the neighbor's uncles came over today. He is an elderly Englishman "Mr. Greene," and he seemed very concerned about our mishap. I had seen him visit before but now this is the third time he has stopped by and always to talk to Ellie. I have decided he is a bit too friendly with her and he seems lonely. I've decided, I don't like him, Ellie is mine and he needs to go home. I growl a little if he reaches to pet me. Ellie just says "Relax Sophie, he's a nice man!" *Relax nothing* . . . I thought, *I want him gone!*

Tinker has a whole new respect for me now, she even told Jlo "We need to pay more attention to the little fruit cake that somehow she has some serious connections,"

I just rolled my eyes and nodded with a smile,

"That's what I've been trying to tell you guys," I muttered,

"Oh, of course you have," Jlo said, then trotted off to look for food.

Lots of neighbors and friends have stopped by with food and support, all of them concerned for our safety. Monica, Grandma, the girls and all of us pets are so grateful for the overwhelming attention. They all said they would watch out for our house and that they were all beginning a neighborhood watch program soon. This is a wonderful place to live.

Also, since that day Ken has been stopping by just to talk to Monica. She seems to like it and welcomes him into the house. Once in a while Brutus comes along; he even comes into the house now, and lies by Ken. When this happens, Tinker, well, she goes a little crazy and hisses at him and tells him to quit looking at her that way. Of course he's not really looking at her, but this is the first time he's gotten close to her on her territory. Tinker is just afraid of his size, which I can tell you, is understandable after all he is mighty. We were all witnesses of how he wrestled a grown man to the ground.

Brutus and I think Ken likes Monica and I think it's because we were here to help them get to know each other. We were discussing our ventures one evening at my house and I became so tired I fell asleep propped up by Brutus. He just let me sleep and I guess it was a picture frenzy event. I slept and Brutus laid still. No one could believe he was so loving and gentle with me. Of course I could, an angel never hurts another angel.

2 Corinthians 2:4 For I wrote you out of great distress and anguish of heart and with many tears, not to grieve you but to let you know the depth of my love for you.

53

PET STORE

This week has been different. Grandma, my Ellie, is gone to Texas because our Grandson is having a baby that makes it our Great Grandson. I wish I could have gone with her there, but she didn't even think of it, of course because she's flying. So I am very sad and lonely without her.

The kids seem to know I'm depressed they even tell me that Grandma will be back in seven days. That's seven days too long for me. Then each day they keep telling me how many days are left before she returns home. So to cheer me up they and my daughter Monica, took Jlo and I to the pet store. I was of course in that hideous pink tutu and Jlo was wearing a huge ruffled collar, sort of like a tutu on her neck. It was a bummer to be dressed up, but then again Jlo was just happy to be going away in the car.

When we got there they put us down on our leashes and I looked at everything. This store was like a huge JC Penney's or the SEARS store but all for pets. I have never been here. We walked around and it was amazing. Jlo was in heaven, sniffing all the animal smells, she was so excited that she just stopped and raised her tail and took a dump right then and there. Oh my, Oh no, how embarrassing. I was trying to hide my face as to not look upon her act of shame but she just kicked her hind legs as if to say "Look what I did!" and pranced away happily. How disgusting right in a public place, in a human, or should I say dog store? It was awful as Monica apologized and cleaned up her poo.

Even though I'm sure that I looked a bit ridiculous in my pink tutu. I tried to talk to the animals that were in the cages. As we strolled by and the girls were ooh-ing and ahh-ing at the baby animals, I was telling them that angels were looking out for them and to say their prayers to go to a good home. Some of them paid attention and thanked me and others just slept or ignored me. Oh well, I was trying to help them and give them hope. I remembered those days of longing at the puppy farm, and waiting to be picked.

Then Kayla stopped and found a collar for me. It was a little pink kitten collar with a bell. She tried it on me and ran up to Monica. She just laughed and said "Perfect, we can get that, it fits her well." Victoria found a cloth harness in purple and pink and tried it on. I do have to say that they are softer and more comfortable than what I have had. I wagged my tail and did my best bark, to thank them for considering my comfort.

It was a good day until we were riding home and I was worrying about Ellie and how she was doing in the heat, and what was happening with her. Suddenly it happened. I stiffened out and couldn't move and was just paralyzed, I just kept hearing their muffled voices and they were fading in and out of my vision. The girls were telling their mother to get home quick and something about helping "her get her drops." They raced home and

Monica ran in and got the drops, she squirted them in my mouth, and slowly I started to come to consciousness. I hate how this just happens without any notice; I do wish I could control this seizure mishap.

When Ellie called that night, they told her of my seizure and how bad it was. Then she told them about the same time of day she fell on the step and banged her knee. I just knew something was wrong with her. As an angel you just get those feelings that are *right on* and you just know they are real. We are both getting older, as a dog you age fast, and Ellie is almost thirty years older than when I died. We both need to take care of ourselves, because I want to be here on earth for the duration of her life. I try to do my best just for her.

I miss her so much, just being in Monica's arms when she was talking to her, I pawed at the phone and whined, Monica held the phone to me and told Ellie to "say hi" to me. She said "Hi Sophie, I'm coming home in two days, rest up little baby and don't have another seizure, I love you Sophie!" I just howled as loud as I could and wagged my tail ferociously. Monica laughed and told Ellie, how happy I was. She also told her she would sleep with me so she could watch over me.

Jlo, Tinker and I agree. It's just not the same with grandma gone. No warm food, no special sneak food at the dinner table and no long lap naps with her wonderful fingernails petting us. We all miss her terribly. My heart was aching so much for her presence. Then I began to recall the love letter I wrote to Ellie in my head when I was leaving heaven. I decided I would revise or add on to it since I could not stop thinking about her.

To the End of Time, I will Love You,

To my Beautiful Wife Ellie Marie Harper,

It has been decades since we have looked into each other's eyes.
I remember the very last touch and glance you gave me at the hospital.
Your love and concern has never been forgotten.

I have been with you in spirit every day since my passing and have watched over you daily with love and pride. You have been so strong with our family and children, I realize more every day why God allowed me to have you as my mate.

When we see each other again in heaven I can hardly wait to embrace you and hold you in my arms once more

Ellie, I have been with you for the past years and even though you have not recognized me, I was with you as Sophie, your tiny side kick. I now have even greater appreciation for your enduring kindness, love and care you bless everyone with on a daily basis. Your ongoing generosity and love is so apparent, even for the pets like I was. God did not want you to be alone in your later years, and that's why he sent me to you as your little companion.

You are the love of my life and until the end of time,
I will always love and adore you . . . Rob

“Jlo please, can you just get me out of this?” . . . Sophie

Proverbs 31:28 Her children arise and call her blessed; her husband also, and he praises her;

54

COMING HOME

Today is the day Ellie comes home from Texas. I'm so thankful; it's felt like months since she's held me in her arms. Jlo and I went to the airport with Monica and the girls; my daughter arranges everything so that the family can be together as often as possible. She is so thoughtful. I can hardly wait to see Ellie; I couldn't eat all day because my excitement and anticipation took over. Jlo's excitement took over too, and ate everything I couldn't. On the ride there, I sat on Kayla's lap fidgeting nervously counting every second until I greet Ellie again.

Then I saw her, I had my sundress on looking quite silly, and at once I jumped from Kayla's arms and ran right across the airport and through the people to her. I couldn't wait any more. She yelled to me, "Sophie, you little stinker, you could have gotten stepped on!" She knelt down and I jumped into her arms, then I was licking her face so fast she was laughing and telling me she missed me too and tucked me into my favorite spot on her arm alongside her. Yep, this is right where I belong, safe in the arms of my beloved Ellie. I can't help but stare at her and think how beautiful she still is. She is wearing a beautiful orange and yellow outfit with a cute hat and flower earrings. I seem to notice her beauty more when I haven't seen her for so long. Taking in her aroma and watching her hug and kiss her children and petting Jlo, I swear she's like fine wine she gets better with age!

She bought everyone a gift, even Jlo and I got a dog cookie and Tinker got new catnip. "There's nothing better than catnip," Tinker says. I have to believe her, because it's not dog nip. I just don't know why it affects her that way. But I like it; she will answer anything and even pretend to listen to me when she's rolling on that stuff.

Proverbs 31:29 "Many women do noble things, but you surpass them all."

55

ON THE ROOF

Ever since the break in, Tinker has been a little rambunctious. She has snuck outside a few times before, or should I say every chance she gets, pushing the screen out in the kitchen windows. Today we were going outside for our morning duty time and stroll down the street. Monica was home doing some paperwork, and as we entered the front yard a group of preschoolers were walking past our house all attached to a leash like rope. I acted like I was protecting our yard but really just wanted them to know I bark like all the other big dogs. Jlo, of course was going a little crazy, running circles barking commands like "Don't even think about stepping one of your little toes on my yard!" She ran to and fro looking like a Tasmanian devil in a gremlin form. Ellie scolded her and put her inside to calm down and not scare the children.

Then as Ellie was scooping me up to let the kids pet me, a little boy pointed to what looked like into the air, but was really pointing at the window over the garage. Saying "Hey look at the kitty," Ellie turned around to see Tinker sitting outside the window on the roof over the garage.

"Oh no," she said, "This is not good," As she told Tinker to stay there and she would come get her, Tinker sauntered over to thc corner of the roof. Oh brother . . . she could fall off she has no nails. Unconcerned, Tinker just ignored us and enjoyed the breeze from the rooftop. She seemed to sniff the fresh air and look upon us all as if we were pawns.

Ellie set me down and called for Monica inside the house. Then she went into the garage and got a ladder out. Jlo was barking from the entryway, and the kids looked on like they were watching a movie, but Grandma was on a mission. I knew Ellie handling a big ladder like that was not a good idea, as I began to panic watching her from the full screen door in the entryway. I darted through the house until I found Monica and barked and barked until she followed me. When getting to the door we went outside and Ellie was half up the ladder and Tinker just watching. Monica yelled, "Mom, come down from there, let me help!" Ellie backed up and said

"We need to get Tinker off of the roof." Monica sighed,

"Good grief, Tinker . . . what will you think of next?" With her hand on her head she instructed Ellie to go inside to the upstairs window and take out the screen. She then said she would go up the ladder to try and get Tinky to go inside to meet Ellie at the window she escaped from.

Ellie complied and Monica went up the ladder and Tinker backed up from Monica. Grandma went inside and said, "Jlo come with me," I stayed in the yard with Monica watching Tinker. I yelled up to her,

"Please Tinker go back inside, they could get hurt!" Tinker replied that she can get back in by herself. But I told her they would not stop until she was safe, and remember they might get hurt trying to save you.

Ellie now had her head out the window and was calling for her,

"Tinky, Tinky! Come here, kitty kitty!" Jlo was barking still in a panic but this time for everyone's safety. Finally, thank God, Tinker just gave in and jumped back in through the open window. For the mean time we had forgotten about the little kids on the leash, but they all clapped once Tinker was safe back inside.

As Ellie and I went back outside to help Monica that "Old English Monkey's Uncle" or whoever he is was there. Boy, I wish he would mind his own business. But he was chatting with Monica and was telling her he could fix the lawn mower as he was helping her put away the ladder. I was barking and even gave him a little growl but Grandma being Grandma had come out with cookies for all the little kids. I followed her to greet them. We handed out cookies and I ate the crumbs falling to the ground, kids are sure messy and that's good for little dogs. They all waved goodbye and were on their way. I found the last few crumbs and when I turned around, Ellie was talking to that old fart. I barked and growled and when Ellie picked me up I even showed my teeth, as sad as they were, I was trying to let him know she's mine, all mine. I've come a long way to be in her arms again and I'm not sharing one moment with you.

When we went inside, I was pacing back and forth so upset about this nosy old geezer. I told Tinker that this man from across the street should stay his distance. Tinky informed me that Mr. Greene was harmless and matter of fact, he was quite the fix it man and that he has been around for years. *Oh, this is not good, not good at all,* I thought, "I don't care if he is the Easter Bunny, he should stay away from Ellie!" I grumbled,

"Boy you have some real issues with some things; you just can't let them go," she murmured,

"You're right, and I won't let Ellie go, especially to an old fart like that!" My jealousy was at an all-time high, and this man was just paying too much attention to my Ellie. It was more than I could comprehend, I can't let him come between me and my girl. I began ranting "I'll fight tooth and nail for her because I'm not sharing her, not now not ever!" Tinker knew I was irritated but just nudged me,

"Calm down fruit cake, Grandma is going nowhere," she reassured me,

I watched out the front screen door as he came back across the street with some tools and Monica showed him into the garage, where he worked on the lawn mower. Ellie was busy, but soon she went out to see what was happening, and without me! I was so nervous, I was pacing and whining. Later she came back inside, "Oh silly girl, I wasn't going away, calm down," she smiled, and soon I saw him go back across the street where he belongs. That old geezer better look out or next time I'm going to bite him, even if it means losing a tooth.

I watched and watched from the doorway for him to cross my path again, but I became weary, and fell asleep on the rug. Not a bad place in the cool spring breeze. I dreamt of being Ellie's Knight in Shining Armor and protecting her from possible suitors' like that dumb old fart.

Ecclesiastes 3:12 I know that there is nothing better for people than to be happy and to do good while they live.

56

BIKE FOR GRAMMY

It's Ellie's birthday. I really can never keep track of the days or months. In dog years I'm totally confused and in heaven days are like years, and years are like days. But in any case it's May tenth; she was born on Mother's day. Everyone was saying Happy Birthday this morning and they all had some special favor they did for her that day. Monica took her to get a manicure and pedicure, her hair done, the works. The girls each made her something at school and cleaned their rooms after school without her having to tell them to. That was a gift in itself! I watched the girls do their cleaning task because their grandma was quite particular. If they left something on the floor I would bark and paw at it. As they giggled and followed my gestures, I was thoroughly enjoying them and trying to find more for them to do. It was so fun to participate with my Granddaughters to make Ellie happy. The more I look at them the more they remind me of Monica and Kathy when they were little girls. Their love for one another and their playful attitude is a delight.

When they were done we were all waiting for grandma to get home, and the girls decided us dogs needed to have a special treat. So into the bathroom closet they went and then calling us, Jlo and I came running. Of course, the trusting girls us dogs are, we ran right up to them and then we saw it . . . oh no, fingernail polish. Tori grabbed Jlo and Kayla grabbed me, then they proceeded to sit on the bed holding us and polishing our nails. I think they thought it would be special for their Grandma. I think this is insane, and Jlo is less than happy.

As I was closing my eyes, and getting asphyxiated from the smells, Jlo was trying to lick off the polish as fast as Tori was putting it on, Tinker sauntered in jumping up on the bed, watching the mayhem, then she smartly said, "I guess no nails are good nails," Then she just sat amused with a snicker and a smile on her face watching the torture. Finally the painting was over and they held us for quite a while to let them dry. Afterwards we did get a turkey treat, which was the only good part of this. I looked down at my nails and oh my goodness, I have bright pink toenails, Jlo has bright red. We both feel hideous and Jlo goes to hide behind the sofa. I just try to not look. Besides I'm too preoccupied with Ellie coming home. As I wait watching for Ellie, I recall Monica and Kathy playing beauty shop as kids and I was a customer. They had clips on my hair, spray and even some powder on my face, but I drew the line at the fingernail polish. I remember I let them paint my one big toenail, figuring no one would see it. Today I have all my toes painted by my grandchildren, and there is *no* hiding them now.

I wish I could go buy Ellie something wonderful, but of course that's out of the question. I just hope I don't have a seizure today that would spoil her day, because she worries about me when that happens. Then I heard the car pull into the drive. I went running, through the house, yelling "She's home, she's home!" I couldn't wait to see how beautiful she looked. When she came in she was gorgeous, I ran straight up to her prancing on my hind legs, and telling her the best I can, which sounds like an off tune song, "You look beautiful, I love you!" She grabbed me up and asked me,

"Who beautified you?" I wanted to point to the kids running up to her and say those smart alec little grandchildren we have, but I kept the thought to myself. Then she saw Jlo and just laughed, "Not you too?" Then Tori and Kayla ran up hugged her so tight I almost fell off her arm on the floor and said,

"Happy Birthday, Grandma! We love you!"

It was then that Monica suggested we show Grandma her gift, so the girls lowered me to the floor. Each of them helped cover her eyes, one on each side, and held her hand and walked her through the house to the garage. On the other side of the garage there was an adult size three wheeled bike for her. Up till now she still rode the old one speed bike from forty years ago. This is much better and safer. She doesn't seem to fall or be unsteady riding the two-wheeler, but I'm sure happy this is her new ride.

There was a big pink bow on it and the bike itself was a turquoise blue color, and on the back there was a big basket with a blue pad in it. Grandma said, "Oh you shouldn't have, I have a bike already!" But you could see she was delighted. When she was reaching over to try it out Tori helped her and then noticed the seat was too high. So she adjusted it to fit her legs perfectly to the ground. Monica showed her it was a three speed and had hand breaks so she was explaining it to her. Now Grammy was on the seat and they gave her another gift, a new helmet. This was a turquoise helmet that matched the bike. She laughed and put it on and said

"There, now I'm ready," Right then Kayla picked Jlo up and put her into the basket, and then she reached back for me. I was just so happy to see her joy that I never thought about riding with her.

So they launched the bike onto the street with us in the basket behind her and off we went down the street. We passed Brutus house on our way.

"Hey Brutus, look at us!" I barked, I stood up with my paws on the side of the basket, "Pretty good, huh? I can come see you and not have to walk!" He just shook his head,

"Way to go, Sof!" I was so happy and Ellie was in her moment. She loved the bike. We rode around the neighborhood with the greatest of ease. Even Jlo noticed how much Grandma liked her new ride. We smiled at each other knowing this is a new outing event all three of us could enjoy and do together. Ellie liked the exercise, outdoors and sunshine, Jlo loved all the smells and being up so high when we passed by other dogs, and I loved not having to stop and sniff dog pee every three seconds.

When we returned from the maiden voyage on our new bike and we all went inside and had a special dinner. Ellie's only living sibling, her brother, came. He's a few years older than she, and her friend Maxine stopped in when we're having cake. I say we, because Ellie was sneaking Jo and I little bites of everything. Yeah, birthdays are always so good. I was sneakily tucked under her shirt under the table and Jlo was under her chair, we didn't miss a bite. Maybe everyone knew but it was Grandma's day and nobody cared.

When they were singing Happy Birthday and she was blowing out the candles, I realized they said she was going to be ninety in a few more years. I was stunned. I just sat there trying to do math and that's not easy for a dog, because our years are seven to one of every human year. But I guess that would be correct she was near sixty when I passed and it's around thirty years now. Yep, that's about right. Wow, she's even more amazing than I gave her credit for. But her sister Irene passed when she was ninety-six and her brother is I think they said ninety-eight. Oh, well, she's the most beautiful senior citizen alive on earth both inside and out and she's mine, or I'm hers or something like that! Anyway, she has me and I have her and that's what I live for, I just feel blessed that I'm here for her as she ages. She should get a gold star for being so awesome and active at her age. I've realized that active senior citizens don't kick the bucket early, they live life, not watch it go by.

That night I gave her extra special kisses, "Stop licking me, kissy poo!" she laughed, and I just wagged my tail and jumped up on her chest and licked her nose, she giggled, "Stop you silly thing, you'll give me dog germs!" *Right,* I thought, As *if I haven't kissed her teeth, lips, up her nose, and everywhere else I could sneak a lick in.* I'll lick her into eternity, and that's the truth. I will be there with Ellie forever and ever. I gave a couple more tiny barks to tell her happy birthday and that I love her more now than ever and she just said, "Sleep little baby, I love you too," I wagged my tail and I heard her laugh and say "Oh Sophie, you're the best," I just smiled and thought, *Yes, dear, I am.*

Proverbs 31:27 She watches over the affairs of her household and does not eat the bread of idleness.

57

SPA DAY

Even though yesterday was a big day, today is back to normal, and grandma was back into the routine. We got to the laundry room which I now know was my first room when I was brought home. Ellie gets all the laundry out through a huge hole in the wall and she puts it in piles sorts it and then washes it. After losing me a few times previously in the piles of clothes she started putting my little bed, on top of the dryer and I get covered up with the warm towels or clothes from the dryer. It is warm and wonderful like a sauna. She always asks us, "Hey girls, you want a sauna? It's a spa day on the dryer," Sometimes Jlo joins me and we share and snuggle in the bed, but then Jlo soon gets too warm and woofs, then Grandma puts her down on the floor. I just lay there until she comes and gets me down; I pretend I'm in the warm sun, in the safe and warmth of my beloveds care. I tend to daydream about Ellie and me walking hand in hand instead of paw in hand.

Of course, Tinkers toilet and her water and extra bed has always been in here so she thinks we are crazy for wanting to lie in warm clothes on the dryer, "Are you guys' nuts? Just go lay in the sun somewhere, I know all the best spots in the house," she implores, but I tell her the view from up here is great and if by chance someone comcs to the back door I jump up to protect the house and alert Ellie. I love it that she thinks of giving us a spa day even if it is on top of the dryer, our comfort usually comes first on every level. She's the best.

I only wish there were some way to repay her for the constant attention and kindness she shares. I hardly think getting her to join me on the dryer will do and I know she isn't one to pamper herself. Maybe someday when we are old and in heaven, I can arrange something nice for her. Yeah, I'll think about that.

Job 4:12 "A word was secretly brought to me, my ears caught a whisper of it.

58

ANGEL SECRETS

This afternoon, Grandma, Tinker, Jlo and I sat down together, on the family room sofa and started to watch "Dog Whisperer." I finally understand why he is so good. That dog whisper guy is an angel, when he was trying to communicate with one of the wild dogs and *I saw the twinkle.* I couldn't believe it; I didn't know I could see other angels communicating like that. He has been sent here to earth to help dark pets to become good. Some pets are born with a mean streak, or have been so abused that they turn out angry and frustrated just like people. This angel dog whisperer can talk to their soul and help them understand that these people want the best for them and to let go of the past. He helps them become well behaved dogs and to be thankful for their masters.

I was trying to explain this to Tinker and Jlo and could tell them the outcome of the bad dog's situation before it happened. That's only because I could read the mental talk the whisperer was doing and the reply from the bad dog. I told them that he's like a counselor on a dog mentality level. Jlo was interested and watching intently she asked "So how is this dude going to stop biting his people?" Feeling kind of smug, I wagged my tail,

"That's for me to know and you to find out, just keep watching!" Hey, I even sound smart to myself today. My wisdom goes from not knowing basic things to remembering stuff that just comes to me from the past. Tinker was listening in and said,

"Sophie, you're so full of dog muck, but I do like your silly sayings, wherever you get them," Then she smiled and curled into her sleep position and shut her eyes. She thinks all dogs are a little messed up and need the dog whisperer. Her saying is "dogs drool and cats rule"! I just laugh; she's a real "cool" cat.

Next we were watching some weird show about people and I could not concentrate. So I did what I do best, I snuck underneath of Ellie's shirt and was just getting comfortable and starting to doze off. Then it happened again, Oh poop, I hate this, please stop this I pleaded, then Ellie picked me up onto her chest for the hundredth time, "Shhh, Sophie, shhh, grandma's here, shhh, don't be afraid, I got you," speaking softly to me she stroked my fur from head to toe and just kept repeating this until I slowly started to come out of it. I have no idea if she needed the drops in my mouth or not. I just become clueless and paralyzed until I regain a conscious state, even though I know this is going on. I do thank God that this never happened to me or the members of my family when I was human.

Finally, I can focus and I look into her eyes which are full of concern and love and she is now telling Monica who is now sitting beside her. "If anything happens to me, please have her put down and let her go with me, no one will take this kind of care of her. She has good days and bad days and I don't want her to suffer alone, these seizures are more frequent, longer and more difficult for her all the time and I don't want her to suffer if I'm not here to take care of her,"

"We all love Sophie to; she would be well taken care of," Monica said, Ellie smiled a half smile while holding me in front of her and said,

"You're a lot of work you little bird turd, but I love you," With all my might after a big seizure, I did my best to wag my tail and try to reach out at her with my paw. She drew me close to her face before she wrapped me up in a blanket and petted me to sleep. There is nothing like her fingers stroking me and soothing me after those awful seizures. Drifting off I listened to her heart beating like the hum of an angel choir comforting me.

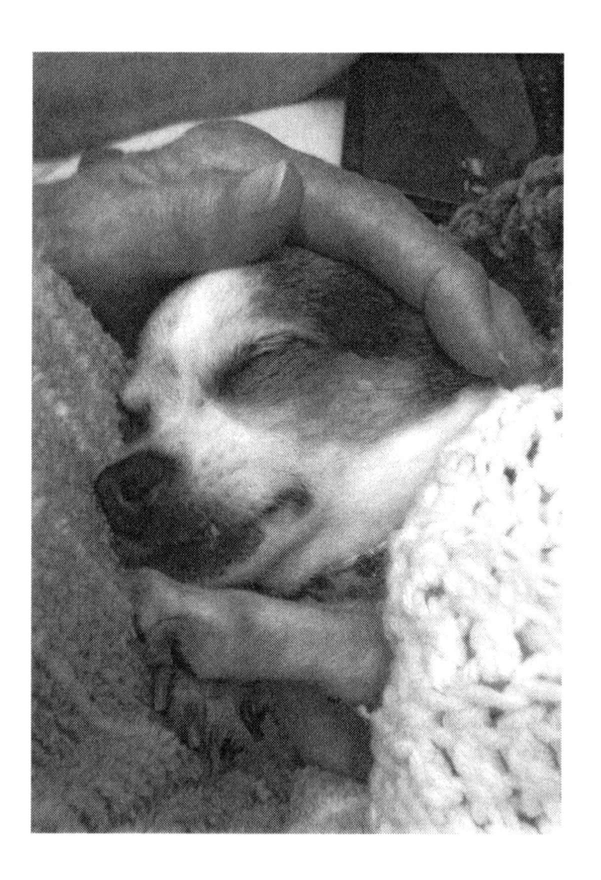

"No matter what, I'm always safe on Ellie's lap
with her hands caressing me." . . . Sof

Job 36:29 Who can understand how he spreads out the clouds, how he thunders from his pavilion?

59

THUNDER DOWN UNDER

Today seemed unusually dark outside. The girls even had some extra gear on when going off to school. I sat by the back door and the rain just kept coming down. I tried to quickly dart outside to go potty, but I felt like I was being drowned while I peed. Jlo just said "Hurry and get it over with and you won't be so wet," Again Tinker saw the humor in us both scurrying to do our duty, when she never got wet when trying to go to her potty room.

After breakfast, the skies became increasingly darker and the wind started to pick up, I sat in the slider window to watch the events. I knew something was going on in heaven. I always enjoyed storms when I was human. They fascinated and intrigued me when they were brewing and taking place. I still like them because I know heaven is up to something whenever it storms. Ellie has always been the opposite she watches the skies and worries on how bad the storm could become, and where the family is and if they could be in any danger from it.

Soon I wanted to curl up with Ellie, and she was nowhere to be found. As I went from room to room, she was upstairs in Kayla's room and heading into Tori's, "Jlo come here baby, its okay, come here and I will hold you," she hollered, upon seeing me she said, "Sophie, help me find Jlo, she's hiding." *Okay,* I thought, *this is like the hide and go seek game the kids play,* and began looking with Ellie. She opened closets and looked under and behind all the furniture. I thought, *Wow, Jlo is good at this game.* Ellie kept calling her and encouraging her to come out. As we were leaving Monica's room, I heard a sigh. I started to call to Jlo myself and wait for her response. Then I heard the deep sigh again. I went over to the bed you can only go under it in the middle because there are drawers on the sides. I peeked underneath and there she was,

"Hey Jlo, we are looking for you," I told her, she only blinked at me, remaining quiet, "Are you okay?" She just shook her head no. I walked underneath the bed which was easy for me because of my size, but a little of a squeeze for her. Once I reached her I realized she was shaking and had quite a gathering of family items. I sat down looking at her, "Can I help you?" I asked,

"No," she replied in a faint voice. Boy, I had never seen her like this. I asked her what was wrong and she said "That noise, I want it to go away,"

"The Thunder?" She looked at me,

"The what?"

"You know the Thunder from the storm," I told her. She tilted her head just a bit,

"How do you know its thunder and what's that? It may be guns or firecrackers!" she exaggerated,

"No no," I said, "In heaven, God and the angels have to rearrange things and use their power and sometimes it is noisy even here on earth,"

"Really?" Jlo asked,

"Yep, it has to happen sometimes, there is a whole other world up there and they can't be quiet all the time," Jlo paused before she asked,

"So you aren't afraid?"

"Nope" I said, "It's a good thing, sort of like cleaning the house, but with angels moving clouds around,"

Jlo loosened up a bit and as she listened she was watching me. I went over next to her and told her I would stay here with her. Right then Grandma came in the room, "I'll be right back," I told Jlo and I came out wagging my tail,

"What are you doing here?" Then she looked under the bed and saw a pair of big brown eyes, "Good dog, Sophie. You can stay with her, she's afraid," she just petted my head and I then went back to Jlo.

As I approached Jlo I saw she had a slipper from Grandma, underwear from Kayla, a sock from Monica and a bandana from Tori all gathered together and she was curled up on top of it. I asked her why she took all those things from the family, "They make me feel safe and I want to hide from the noise," I lay down beside her,

"Next time just say these words and you will feel safe," I began,

"What words?" she asked, so I said,

"Repeat after me, Angels in heaven take my fear of Thunder away," She said the exact same words. Then in a few minutes later she was sitting up and talking with me in pretty normal fashion.

I asked her how she felt, "Okay, I guess," she said, from there I asked her if we should return these items back to the family, "Nah," she peeped, but I encouraged her to at least help me bring them out into the open. So we dragged the items out to the end of the bed and went on our way. She turned to me a few minutes later and said "That's a funny saying, but I'll use it next time," I winked at her and said,

"I promise it will work every time!" Ha, I think I just taught a dog to pray. Yep, and it worked! I was proud of myself to help Jlo, she has helped me so much, I never want to see her weak or afraid again.

I now know prayer helps no matter what, even if animals give them up to the heavens. I've always known they work for me. But this is proof no matter how small the request, it is answered. I'll have to teach Tinker to pray. But knowing her she will pray for her nails to grow back, and then next she would request to be able to go outside. On second thought, unless she needs it maybe I won't tell her right now. If she asks for things that can't happen she will be convinced I'm even more off my rocker than she thinks. I wouldn't want to disappoint her, or lead her in the wrong direction with prayer.

Numbers 11:17   I will come down and speak with you there, and I will take some of the power of the Spirit that is on you and put it on them. They will share the burden of the people with you so that you will not have to carry it alone.

60

WORRIES ADDRESSED

"Hey guys it's time for a conference," I shouted,

"Conference, Shmonference, what on earth do you want?" Jlo sneered. I had been thinking to myself, on earth I wish I could get what I want, and that would make me a man again with Ellie. Oh well, I just needed some questions answered,

"Where's Tink?" I asked, Jlo shrugged with a sigh,

"Nothing else to do, let's go find her," So we went off to scavenge the house and found her in Monica's bedroom laying in the sunshine on a big rug in the middle of the floor. She was purring and when we arrived she barely opened an eye,

"You're interrupting my beauty nap," she murmured,

"I know," Jlo said, "But the kid said we need a conference, It's important,"

"Really," said Tink.

"Yep, I need to get some information" I told her,

"Like what?" she asked, "You know I won't be nearly as beautiful when the kids come home from school without this nap," I jumped forward,

"Sure you will be, they always adore you, no matter what!" I piped, opening one eye Tink sighed,

"You're probably right, so what's on your mind?"

"I wanted to know how long you have both been a part of the family," Tinker was looking around as if she were counting the years,

"I'm not sure but Kayla was pretty little, maybe before she went to school, I was here for a while and then they brought Jlo home maybe when Kayla was in school for a while but not grown real big. Why do you ask?"

"Well, how long before I came here then?" Jlo smirked and said,

"Not long enough," but then she rubs up against me as we sat in our circle. I knew she was just teasing. I wanted to know if they knew of animals before them, or were told from animals before them about the man who used to live with Grandma or Monica and Kathy's dad. They both said, they had no idea, that Grandma had just been Grandma and they did not know of any man. They asked me why I was asking,

"Well I know you guys think I'm crazy," I said,

"You can say that again," said Jlo, but Tinker nodded her head for me to proceed.

"Go on," she said softly,

"I just wanted you to understand that us, we, you are here for a purpose and we are probably grandmas last set of pets," I told them,

"Why do you say that" Jlo asked,

"Well, since her birthday I realized she is almost ninety, in human years that's a lot. I want you to know, that someday, we all will be in heaven together and be a family together again,"

"Whoa, Whoa, Whoa, I ain't going anywhere, nuh uh!" Jlo stated firmly,

"I know, not now!" I reassured her, "But when we die, we will all be together again, and if grandma dies before me, I want you both to help me die to," They both eyed me suspiciously,

"Why would we do that?" they asked,

"Because she was my wife and I have to go back to heaven and be with her when she goes there someday," I stated,

"Sof we know how much you love her, but we couldn't kill you so you can die with her," Tinker replied, now fully awake and looking overly concerned. With the most convincing face I had I told them both,

"But you have to understand, I'm only here for her, I used to be in heaven as her guardian and I'm on a mission now and don't want her to leave Earth without me,"

"That bird friend who helped with the robbers said I would be richly rewarded in heaven, what did she mean?" Tink asked,

"That's what I'm talking about you guys, she's an angel who is here to look out for us," I said, "Really you have to believe me!" Jlo was just looking at me and said,

"You sure have a big imagination in that tiny little beady brain of yours, I'll give you that . . ." Tinker now interested wanted to know more,

"So kid if you know so much about this stuff why don't you explain it to us?"

More than happy to share my wisdom I began. Now our circle was more of them sitting in front of me like I was teaching a class. I told them "When we are conceived and in our mother's womb, we are in what we think is a luxury water suite which is warm, dark and cozy. Then when it is time to be born we are disrupted from this comfy place and are pushed out to a new world.

Once we are born then we are in an air atmosphere, this world is half sunlit days and half night time. We adapt and start our lives with our family. When we die from our earthly life, again we have been comfortable and do not want to leave, but this is a whole new spiritual world of the soul. Then we go into a peaceful world of total light and love. Death is not to be afraid of but to be looked at as a whole new life of love and light that goes on forever and ever with our loved ones who have lead good lives. Therefore we all have to be the best we can be during our time on earth."

Tinker seemed amazed and with her paws tucked under her and her head held high she said, "Sophie that is a wonderful story. Jlo, what do you think?" Jlo nodding because she was dozing off and said,

"Oh yeah, sounds great," trying to please me as if she listened,

"If this were true, what do you expect us to do?" Tinkerbell asked,

"I don't know, but please believe me, and if this day ever comes you have to promise with all your heart you will help me, okay?" I pleaded to them, but was quickly interrupted by Jlo,

"It's too sad to think about and I am never going to die, so can we go look for a treat or something?"

"Sure, but before we do can we shake on it?" I asked, and they agreed and Jlo stood up and did her best shake as if she was shaking off the water from a bath. I just shook my head and said,

"No, just put your paw on top of mine and say 'I will',"

"What does it matter?" Jlo asked, I told her how this is the way people give their word to keep their promise and do what they said. So they both put their paws over mine and they said they would,

"Great, I just want back up from you guys in case I need it in the future, thanks. "You're both true friends," I chimed happily while Jlo trotted off to look for a treat or just food on the floor and Tinker laid still and winked at me in assurance. I think she liked my explanation of life and death. In any case I felt better about them understanding my place here and exactly what my wishes were.

1 Kings 20:38 Then the prophet went and stood by the road waiting for the king. He disguised himself with his headband down over his eyes.

61

HALLOWEEN

It's school time and the kids are so busy again. Ellie is getting them off to school and waiting each day for them to get home. I love this time of year, the trees are so pretty and it smells so good outside. Kayla and Tori are getting ready for a party and they are so excited. Monica has taken them shopping to get outfits and special things for this event.

Yesterday I was in their room and there were so many things laid out on the bed and they were putting lots of decorations on themselves. They seemed to be having so much fun. Then Tori picked me up, "Do you want to go trick or treating with us?" she asked, of course I was wagging my tail off, I love my granddaughter so much and she was so full of enthusiasm. She went running down the hall calling Kayla. Suddenly Kayla was laughing and jumping up and down and clapping her hands. This was fun they are so cute, probably the cutest grandchildren ever. I just wagged my tail more watching their delight.

Once they started giggling they carried me as we went on a hunt for Jlo. Once finding her they scooped her up and sat us on their laps. Me on Tori's lap and Jlo on Kayla's lap, then they started to discuss what was going to be our demise. I was just glad they weren't painting our nails again. They were bantering and giggling and I was watching their expressions on their cherub like faces and soon they said, "Yes that will be perfect!"

"I'll work on that as soon as we get home!" Kayla mentioned, whatever that means, I was just glad to please them so much. After that discussion Monica came in and off they went out the door with her, probably to a practice of some kind.

A few days later they were full of giddiness and laughter. It was the day of the party. I realized all that stuff they had in their room was for a costume party, that's the word, "costume." Yeah, I love it when my memory works! They dressed up in their costumes and put their special color on their face and I could hardly recognize them. Ellie and Monica helped them the whole time, all of us animals sat watching and I was admiring how involved the whole family was in this fun for the girls. Tori, she was a green Witch and Kayla was a Chinese Princess, they looked spectacular and very real. They went off to their party and we watched out the window as they happily jumped into the car, with Monica.

That afternoon was pretty uneventful until they arrived home from the party. The girls came in and a few friends came with them. A few of them were scary; Jlo and I did our best protection bark. We were just warning them we really are tough. Soon the door opened up and in came my daughter Kathy; I love seeing her and so does Jlo. Also my buddy Blue is here and he's wearing a blue and gold shirt with an "M" on it, I heard Kathy say "Blue is dressed up like a Michigan Fan," Oh! That's right, we live in Michigan, and either my hearing is better or I'm just remembering more things lately! I always loved Michigan and here I am again. Oh, I love it when my thoughts make sense, I don't feel so dog like at those moments. Then Kayla and Tori took us upstairs and her friends were watching. Ellie and Monica seemed busy with getting some things ready and Kathy and Blue stayed there helping out. Besides Tinker greeted Blue and she was having a welcoming conversation when he came in. Blue always listens to Tinker, he thinks she's wise. Some days Tinker just ignores us all until she feels like talking, so to welcome him first thing means she's made an effort.

When we reached the girls room, they sat us on the bed and out came costumes for us. Tori opened a bag and pulled out a white gown with a veil, and necklace, then a tuxedo with a bow tie and a little boutonniere. I was thinking, *Oh no, really?* As I looked at Jlo she was squinting her eyes and pretending not to look, "I think we are going to be a bride and groom," I murmured, Jlo just huffed,

"I'm the bride," she said,

"I really do hate this," I grumbled, and then she reminded me that this is what we put up with to have a good home. So I thought about it and, knew putting up a fuss would only render more struggles in putting these contraptions on. Kayla picked me up and started to put the white gown on me and Tori was busy outfitting Jlo in the tux,

"Hey, I'm supposed to wear the gown!" she protested,

"It barely fits me; I don't think it would fit you," I told her,

"Oh well," she said, "Grandma will get us out of it soon, just cooperate," Of course I have to, there is no other choice when your only 4 lbs. what else can you do? Once Jlo saw me she was glad that I had to wear the veil and not her.

I just realized in a déjà vu moment that Jlo reminds me of those flying monkeys from the wizard of OZ, or maybe those silly gremlin creatures. The faces she makes and her chubbiness, it's just too funny. Just something amusing that comes to mind. Don't you think my human memory of things could serve me better than remembering kid's movie characters? Oh well, I guess it's not a bad thing, just sort of goofy to remember this after this much time. At least the thought entertains me during my unnecessary ball gown fitting.

Their friends were giggling and I thought I couldn't get any more embarrassed, but this takes the cake. I'm now dressed up like a bride by my granddaughters. Jlo is just as embarrassed, mostly because she's dressed as a groom, and is waiting to be released. Once downstairs they showed Monica, Kathy and Ellie, they just laughed and said "Oh you poor babies, what did they do to you?" I wanted to protest but I just wagged my tail instead. Jlo looked the other way pretending not to notice and had her tail between her legs.

"They can't stay that way," Ellie shook her head, and I thought *Amen to that!* But then Tori announced,

"I borrowed the stroller from the neighbor and we want to take them up the street to show everyone how cute they are; besides they agreed to!" Monica chuckled, thinking, oh, I bet they did alright,

"But girls, they can't go very long," she said,

"Please just up the block and back?" Kayla pleaded, so Monica agreed,

"Okay, I will walk along with you to push them and bring them back soon," She asked Kathy if she wanted to walk up the street with her. Kathy agreed to go, and called Blue to come along. The girls were so glad and they took us out and put us into a stroller that smelt like sour milk and diaper wipes. Monica grabbed a sweater and off we went. Kathy grabbed Blue and put him in the stroller with us. He couldn't stop laughing and he thought his sweatshirt was a great outfit, especially after seeing ours! Ellie sat at the door with bright orange lights on and waved goodbye. As I looked back I could see how beautiful she was, I'm glad she doesn't have a costume on, she's too beautiful to cover up.

As we rolled down the street Jlo was disgusted yet had a little fun with Blue barking now and then at the kids. People seemed to want to stop and see us and ask to pet us. My veil kept sliding off, and needed a lot of adjustment. At a few houses they gave Jlo, Blue and I dog biscuits. My teeth are so bad so I told Jlo and Blue they could have mine. This of course Jlo loved. Once we got to Ken and Brutus' house the kids yelled, "trick or treat." Now I was looking out for Brutus and he came to the door with a police hat on and what looked like a holster and badge around his neck. I jumped up and said "Hey big guy, you're dressed up too!" Once Brutus saw me he was just laughing and said,

"Fit's you, kid. How does Jlo like being the groom?" Jlo smirked and said

"As much as you like your getup" Brutus laughed,

"Touché," Then our group of girls were leaving and they thanked Ken for the treats. Another group of kids were coming to the door, Monica and Kathy lingered for a while with us in the stroller. Ken and they were laughing and Ken even got the camera out and took a picture of Brutus, Jlo, Blue and I.

Monica set Jlo and I on the porch with Brutus, Kathy set Blue next to his leg, he was behind us and you could still see him perfectly. Ken, Kathy, and Monica were laughing a lot and then as Kathy was reloading us into the stroller, Monica said "Happy Halloween Ken, stop down later if the trick or treating slows down," I jumped up and barked,

"Brutus come to our house with Ken if he comes by later!" He nodded in reply.

Since the girls had gone ahead, Monica and Kathy strolled home with us. I loved watching my daughters having so much fun together. We got close to home and Jlo was saying "Grandma, Grandma, save us please!" and right before we stopped she jumped out of the stroller and ran up to Ellie, she looked like a runaway groom. That was quite a site, even Blue was laughing.

"Come here, I'll help you," she said as she started to undress her. Jlo was so happy to be home and free of those clothes. Monica parked the stroller and carried me up and I jumped onto Ellie. She laughed and gave me a kiss. She said "You girls were good babies." You bet your boots we were, but really it wasn't all that bad. A little hurtful of our pride but I felt better when I saw Brutus was dressed up too. Kathy was going to wait for the girls to come home and visit with Ellie and allow Blue to have fun with us. She had to work in the morning so soon after the kids returned back to the house, she gathered up Blue to return home.

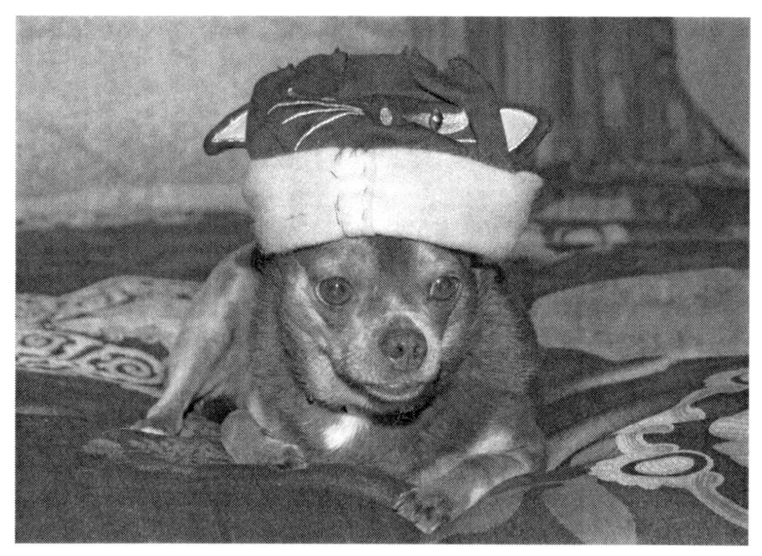

“This I can do and I get a turkey treat taboot!” . . . Jlo

“Tinker you look so much better in the hat than I. Do you like my Tutu? Smile Tink and we get a treat!” . . . Jlo

Ephesians 1:18 I pray that the eyes of your heart may be enlightened in order that you may know the hope to which he has called you, the riches of his glorious inheritance in his holy people,

62

THE VISIT

The Trick or Treating commotion slowed down and no more kids were coming to our house. The girls had taken off their face color and we were all watching them sort through their treats. It was a fun night and both Ellie and Monica seemed tired. Right about that time Monica was going to open a bottle of wine. The doorbell rang. Kayla ran to the door, and Monica peered down the hall. I of course was curled up under Ellie's shirt right where I belong. Jlo went barking but I was too comfortable to move. Then I heard Ken's voice and I could tell by the way Jlo was acting that Brutus was here.

I peeked out to see them coming down the hall from the front door and Brutus was walking like a gentleman with Ken holding his collar, "Sorry, I tried to leave him home and he was going to have no part of it. He scratched and jumped upon the door so I gave in. We won't stay long," he stated,

"Nonsense, replied Monica, he seems to like the girls, it's just Tinker who's a little cautious," Tinker was perched upon the counter top on a piece of newspaper, peering down at Brutus who is as tall as the counter.

She thinks if her feet are not on the counter top then its okay to be there, Since Monica senses Tinkers fear she allows her to stay in her safety spot. Normally the counter is off limits to Tinker.

"I was just opening a bottle of wine, would you like white or red?" she inquired,

"Red would be great, thank you. How are you Mrs. Harper?" he asked thoughtfully,

"Fine" Ellie said "Did you have a lot of kids tonight?"

"Yes quite a few, especially from 6:30-8:00pm," Ken said.

"Us too, but then it really died down after that," she mentioned,

The kids came running over, "Come look at our haul, we have a ton of candy!" they squealed, as he thanked Monica for the glass of wine he took it over to the table to inspect their goodies,

"You kids sure did well," Ken said with a smile.

"That's for sure" said Monica. The girls offered them a treat, but Monica and Ken declined. Brutus was just taking the whole scene in and was happy to be around us all. Brutus was to follow Ken and stay where he could see him. He plopped down on the floor over by the fireplace near the TV.

I decided I better go see my friend, so much to Ellie's surprise I jumped off her lap and started to make my way into the living room. Tinker watching me said, "I know he likes us but be careful he's so big,"

"I know Tinker, thanks," I nodded, Jlo was passed out already on the sofa; this was an exciting night for her. I sat down by Brutus and he winked at me, then our mental dialog started. I told him that the dress even though it was hideous was okay for a while. He laughed and agreed that we have to put up with goofy things for our people. I then asked him if he knew my role in this family. He told me yes,

"You're the littlest angel here to watch out for them and we, your angel friends are here to help," I agreed but decided to tell him that I used to be Ellie's husband before I died. He looked at me and said "Really-" Then let out a howl, "And you came back as this!?"

"I know our family has never had a male dog before and I guess my daughter Monica and the girls are into Chihuahuas," I reasoned,

"Oh, that explains it," he said, still laughing, "I thought just being a dog was bad, but a little female dog is hilarious!" I assured him I would be a fish if it brought me back to my beloved Ellie! After thinking about it, he agreed, "You're a good man,"

"Thanks, and I just recently remembered that my earthly name was Rob, short for Robert, Not that it matters, it really doesn't apply much as being Sophie," I said,

"No, but its good information to have," he said laying down on his side. I laid down next to him; it felt good to have an angel friend like Brutus.

Then he rose up and looked concerned, he said, "I was put here to be with Ken to help him find a life partner or wife. He is so busy with work, and he is not a guy's guy. The only women in his life that come around are when he is with me, at the boarding house, on walks, and when we go to the vet. Also the nanny angel up the street always stops and pets me, she has told me a woman will soon come into Ken's life and for a good reason. Do you think it's your daughter, Monica?" I sat up and started to watch Monica and Ken talking on the sofa, I'm now eyeing a potential suitor for my daughter,

"Maybe so . . ." I said, "Can you tell me about him?" Brutus told me about his engineering background and how he is contracted out through a major corporation to do special field assignments, and how he works real hard and is a very good man. He said that he has always been a gentle soul and has pretty much been into cycling and skiing. He has lots of friends and just hasn't taken time for dating due to his extensive work travel and since his wife passed away four years ago.

I asked him what was that about, what did she die of? He told me she had ovarian cancer and it was a very sad death, Ken loved her very much. They were married seven years and he just couldn't think of anyone else. Basically since then Ken had increased his workload since her passing to occupy his time and keep him busy, that's why I have to go to the kennel. I was already a part of the family for two years before she passed. I loved her also, she was kind. But maybe now it's time for him to move on.

Brutus assured me that there wasn't a nicer man and if he had a daughter he would want her to meet him. Whew, that's a relief. I sat watching them and processing this information until Ellie came over and scooped me up. She said "Time for bed little one, we have to go outside one last time," I looked back to Brutus,

"Thanks for the information, I have to go, this is my job!" Brutus smiled,

"You're good at it too!" he barked. I was happy to retire with Ellie; it's the time of day I get her all to myself.

Genesis 31:14 Then Rachel and Leah replied, "Do we still have any share in the inheritance of our father's estate?"

63

THE STAND

Every night we retire, I watch Ellie do her routine and just before she climbs into bed she kneels on the floor with her elbows on the bed. When she does this I lie down right in front of her on the bed and put my head on my paws and watch her intently. Ellie says her prayers to our Lord and asks blessings upon her family. On occasion she talks to Rob and tells him of achievements or her dilemmas; this has been her way to stay connected. Little did she know that I always heard these concerns and paid attention to her every word very closely. Tonight Ellie prayed for Monica to be happy and move forward. What do you know, that thought crossed my mind tonight also.

As she said, Rob I hope you can hear me and know the family is doing well. I jumped up and licked her face. She laughed and said "Oh, Sof, you're so cute," Jlo was on the chair almost asleep and with a sigh rolled over and began to snore; Ellie went over to cover her with a blanket.

I decided I wanted to try and get her to notice me as Rob, so I stepped over to my favorite night stand that our picture is on and waited for Ellie to come back by the bed. As she turned around she paused, "Sophie what are you doing standing on my nightstand?" I was getting ready to lick her face in the picture when she said, "You know Sof, that was Rob's smoking stand and it was always by his chair, he loved that piece of furniture because only his things belonged there. After he was gone, I have used it as mine every day since then." Her words stopped me in my tracks, and then she scooped me up, and rubbed my head. I suddenly remembered she had said this before, but now knowing it was *my stand* I need to inspect it more thoroughly.

I was so excited; when she sat me down on the bed, I bounded right back over to the stand to look over every inch of it very carefully. This time I was sniffing it all over and really looking at it as if it were the first time I had seen it. Oh yeah, I remember, my papers went here, my glasses were in that drawer and this drawer was my pipes, I only smoked a pipe, and that door held my tobacco. I was delighted Ellie still had it and it was in such good shape. She was right; this was my favorite piece of furniture. I was sniffing it from end to end while walking on top. Ellie was so taken back at my interest in it she said, "Well, aren't we the little investigator tonight?" Then she said "look Sof" and opened the top drawer where my pipes used to lay. I can see it now, I remember it perfectly; I would open this drawer and carefully select my pipe of the day.

Then Ellie said "I keep nothing in this drawer because it still smells like Rob's pipes," and as she lowered her head to smell the aroma that still lingered in the wood inside this drawer, I stepped down right into the drawer and sniffed and sniffed. Wow, now that's a déjà vu moment! Standing in the drawer, I took a whiff, Mmm . . . . could smell it plain as day, the smell never went away! I was picturing myself in my gold lazy boy chair with my pipe, relaxed and enjoying my smoke and the aroma. Oh my, this is surreal, I can't get my nose out of this drawer, and this is like a moment of heaven on earth. I was wagging my tail as I sniffed and Ellie just laughed, "Boy, you sure like the smell, don't you Sof!" she exclaimed. I wanted to tell her *"You bet more than you can even imagine . . ."*

From then on, I would occasionally climb over there and paw at that drawer and she would open it and let me sniff, but not for too long. Ellie didn't want the scent escaping. After all I quit smoking thirteen years before I passed, so that scent has been there a long time. She relates to me "Rob" through this favorite piece of both of ours. No wonder I liked this stand from the beginning and it's smell. Hmm, I wonder what else may be here that was a part of our life together that I just haven't discovered or recognized yet. I think I will do some thorough investigation of the whole house. Who knows what I may find? This could actually be fun and interesting.

Upon retiring my thoughts went dreamily into fond memories of watching my family while sitting in my gold recliner chair with my pipe.

Proverbs 17:6   Children's children are a crown to the aged, and parents are the pride of their children.

64

HOLIDAYS ARE COMING

Again lights and decorations were coming out and going up all over the house. Oh boy, I love, love, love this time of year. It means my entire family is coming here. I wish years earlier I knew what was happening, but like life, with this mission there is a learning curve. I'm so excited that I find myself daydreaming about the past years with my children and grandchildren. I heard that my new grand baby is coming from Texas that would be my great grand baby, he's a boy. I wish I could tell him about his dad and I when J.R. my grandson was small.

We used to play Bill and Joe, I was Bill and he was Joe and he would take my finger and lead me downstairs where my workshop and gun collection was. We pretended we were going off to work and fiddled around with all kinds of things. He could spend hours playing there, gluing wood, polishing metal, and doing anything from useful to creative tasks, he never tired of the workshop, and I could get a lot of work done on my gun collection. It was a fun and bonding time for both of us. I'll never forget that little face saying "Come on Bill, it's time for work," he was only three when we started this routine. I died before he was ten, but we still went down there and he did his projects. The last few years my granddaughter Courtney joined us when she was three or four years old. Again unfortunately, I never saw her fifth birthday. Anyway, I can't wait to see those kids, or I should say adults now but, in my mind they will always be my little grandchildren.

It is so exciting to have the whole family around. Just to watch Tori and Kayla each day with the excitement and anticipation. They are constantly having parties at school and at church they are having a special nighttime concert that the girls are singing in. Ellie seems to never leave the kitchen. She's so busy making food for the kid's parties and different events. Jlo, Tinker and I sit at her feet and watch her waiting for the occasional drop of food to the floor. Actually Jlo sits at her feet and Tinker and I wait till we hear her licking her lips, then we come over and beg to!

Monica is planning a fun open house type party at her home with Ellie and Kathy's help. Kathy is a massage therapist and she has lots of clients, who she invites to the party. Her home is a smaller condo, so she and her husband Steve helped out with moving things around and picking up supplies that day, to make the party a success. My granddaughter Courtney, who is now a famous hair designer, comes with her husband Ron and they bring all kinds of lavish desserts and set up an impressive bar. Oh she's so ultra-creative, I'm proud of how successful my entire family is.

Monica is seeing more of Ken and it seems they are doing well together. Ever since my talk with Brutus, I'm still protective of her but feel like this guy is a good man. She seems happy and that's what I want for her. Also she is still very much in contact weekly with the girl's father, Joe. They get along and share in parenting the girls and making important decisions for their schooling and their future. They work very hard on making things work for the best of everyone involved, especially the girls. This is admirable. I didn't spend a lot of time with him, but I could tell he is a good man.

Tonight is the big open house. The good thing about this is I know that after this party then Christmas will be here soon. I don't know when, but not long after. It is busy with food and music and tons of people coming in. Blue is here with us and they put him, Jlo and I in a bedroom for a while until the party gets into full swing. They let Tinker stay out because she won't bark. But she has the biggest red bow on, Jlo was jealous that she couldn't bark at everyone coming into the party, so as they were shutting us in the bedroom Jlo stuck her tongue out at Tink, "I'll trade you, you can wear the bow and I'll go in there to sleep," Tinker said,

"Deal!" Jlo replied, but only right when they shut the door, but our opinion didn't matter; we were sequestered to the bedroom for now.

We heard all the voices and Jlo and Blue were on the bench looking out the window. I was curled up on the bean bag chair and just listened to their chatter about the guest coming and going. They had opinions about everyone. Jlo was saying how that lady always smelled like old stale perfume and Blue was saying that some woman smells like the massage balm Kathy uses every time he sees her, he wondered if she bathed in it? They were laughing and then talking about how they didn't like that a certain man and how they may bite him if given a chance. Then they said that old Mr. Greene was coming in. I jumped up and was looking out the window with them; darn I really dislike that man. I wish he would just stay away from my Ellie, that old fart, I wonder if it's time for him to die? Maybe I should talk to Patience about an opening in heaven or even a few floors down where it may be warmer? I didn't see him coming in, but I went to the bedroom door and was whining and scratching to get out. I was just missing Ellie, and wanted to see my family with their friends and most of all protect Ellie from that googly eyed old fart.

Soon Tinker came to the door, "Hey guys, Kayla's coming up soon to let you out, but you get a surprise," They were both so excited for the surprise, but I just wanted to find Ellie. The door opened and in came Kayla with three huge bows,

"Hi babies, it's time to join the party, come here," Blue ran right up and she snagged him with a big green bow, then Jlo was next with a big silver bow, and then she put the gold one on me. It was bigger than my head but as usual, here we go looking silly, well at least it's not a wedding dress. Then she opened the door and we scampered downstairs. I worked my way through the house and all the legs and feet of the strangers. Jlo and Blue did a little woofing and that's how I found Ellie. She came out and said you silly girls and Blue and Jlo wagged their tails. She saw me and scooped me up to my favorite place on her left arm. I rode through the crowd with the greatest of ease. I love being up here I can hear thing clearly and kiss her whenever I want to. I saw Mc Geezer but he seemed busy talking to another neighbor, whew, I may have had to bite him if he was pestering Ellie. Besides I'm here now and that's what's important.

I was just taking in the sights and an older man and woman were talking to her, when they asked, "Ellie, how many years has it been since Rob passed away?"

"Let me see, it was twenty-nine years just a few months ago," I was surprised but I knew that was right. Then the man said,

"He was a good man, I still miss him," I perked right up and stared at this man in the eyes, nothing was coming to me. Then the woman said,

"Wasn't it only a week before his surgery that you two went to that big gun show in town?" Suddenly it came to me, this was

"Little George, my old gun buddy he was just a kid then but now he must be almost seventy." I started to bark my "hello" bark and reached my paw out to him,

"She must like you," Ellie smiled, he reached out and said,

"Well come here little fella," and took me in his hands, when I got closer I could smell his smell. He's still wearing Old Spice, yep, its little George! I licked and licked him. He asked why my tongue sticks out and Ellie, explained I had lost teeth due to ill health. As I licked him George said, "I must have cookies or something still on my hands."

They all laughed and Ellie couldn't believe it, she had never seen me act this way. I was just trying to say Hi, haven't seen you in decades. This guy was a real friend to me and we had so much in common with our gun hobby. I wish I could tell him who I was. Oh well, he knows I like him, and it pleased me he kept in touch with my family. It warmed my heart.

Romans 12:19 Do not take revenge, my dear friends, but leave room for God's wrath, for it is written: "It is mine to avenge; I will repay," says the Lord.

65

UP TO NO GOOD

They set me down and I heard the pets and they were snickering, definitely up to no good. I found them contemplating a devious plan in the dining room. There was a next door neighbor sitting on our living room sofa, and he does not like animals. One day when Tinker got outside from the kitchen window he kicked at her as she was just peeking through the bushes. Then another day Rambo, that funny little Jack Russell terrier who is harmless went by ahead of his master and he swatted at him when his master wasn't looking. This man is definitely an animal hater.

So the posse was sending Tinker in to tantalize him into a frenzy. He was paying no attention at all and the room was filled with people, so it was then Tinker made her move, she rubbed up on his pant legs which were black corduroy, he brushed her away but she came back and a few more swipes and he had almost as much hair on his pant legs as she had on her legs. Jlo, Blue and I were peering out from under the Christmas tree which was in the same room, snickering at her antics. Next she jumped up on the back of the sofa, and sat right behind him and purred her loudest. Everyone was surprised at her friendly demeanor saying how cute she was. He was trying to tolerate it but he was very annoyed. He whooshed his hand to get her away but she just licked it with her rough tongue, and he almost died. We were laughing so hard and having such a fun time watching. Then Tinker signaled Jlo that she was leaving and right then Jlo walked by and passed the worst gas right in front of him, making it look like it may have come from him. After all the treats Jlo ate today preparing for this party she was filled with all kinds of rotten smells. We were all trying to plug our nose and couldn't believe how good our tantalizing plan was going.

Next Jlo motioned us over and we all went into the coat room we rummaged through the coats until we found this mean neighbors, Tinker jumped up and knocked it off the hanger to the floor. It was black wool and Tinker, Blue with his long hair, Jlo and I all took turns rubbing our fur on his coat. I have white fur so they laughed as I rolled around leaving my white fur on his coat. I felt good to aggravate someone who is mean to animals. We finished our task and then all went off into the kitchen to find crumbs on the floor, this was fun and they were my pet family. I felt like a true part of the gang, "The fuzzy fur ball gang!" that is.

After the party, the whole family cleaned up and Ken stayed to help out. Ellie was tired but so elated with the wonderful turnout of friends and family. It was a successful evening. I told the animals this is almost as good as Christmas except there are too many other people here to enjoy the family. They don't understand my infatuation with them even though I have tried to tell them my past life experience.

Psalm 98:4 Shout for joy to the Lord, all the earth, burst into jubilant song with music;

66

SONGS OF JOY

Tonight the girls were getting ready for something special, they had beautiful dresses on and they were spending a lot of time on their hair. Ellie was asking them if they knew all the songs. That's when I realized their concert was tonight. Yippee, that means Christmas is tomorrow! I can't wait to tell Jlo and Tink.

I ran, yelling, "Conference, conference", Jlo and Tinker was sitting on the loveseat in the Christmas tree room. It is such a glowing pretty place in the house. I jumped up on the loveseat and excitedly said "its tomorrow, its tomorrow!" I rolled on my back and kicked my legs in the air, I was chanting, "I'm going to see my whole family soon, I'm going to see them all, Isn't that exciting? Aren't you guys thrilled," Jlo stood up and said

"I'm excited for the treats," and Tinker said,

"Yep tomorrow is special." I asked them to help me give Ellie a gift. They said sure, but what? So we went into a plan, with full detail and mapped out my idea. They thought it was crazy but they went along with it. I think they wanted to not only to shut me up, but also make me happy on Christmas too. These are the best pets ever; they are great friends, my friends.

Everyone was gone to the concert and I was so excited that I was pacing around thinking how wonderful it was going to be to see my great grandson for the first time and to give Ellie a gift. I kept asking Jlo and Tinker how much longer until they come back? Tinker keeps saying, “Ten minutes sooner than you asked me last time,” Finally the car door opened and I heard them. They all came into the house, Ellie, Tori, Kayla, Monica, Ken and following in another car was Joe, the girl’s dad, and another lady with him. They all came in and had dessert, and drinks. I do not know who this lady is but if she if with Joe she must be ok. Monica and Ken welcomed them in and it was a great atmosphere, I jumped up onto Ellie and she picked me up. She held me all during dessert and I and kissed her hands when I could. I can’t wait to go to bed and wake up to see everyone tomorrow.

Once in bed I could hardly lay still, the excitement was just too much. Even Ellie said “Calm down Sophie you’re a wiggle worm tonight, go to sleep.”

I wanted to but my adrenaline was pumping with excitement to see my whole family together again. Oh how I love these holidays and my surprise for Ellie was just too important. I went over the detailed plan I created in my head for Ellie. It just had to work, and tomorrow is the day!

Acts 5:20 "Go, stand in the temple courts," he said, "and tell the people all about this new life."

67

CHRISTMAS DAY

The doorbell rang and it was Ken he was here with Brutus. Yeah, the special day begins. I ran right up to Brutus and told him with excitement that he had to help us with a grand plan and he assured me he would. I rubbed up against him to show my appreciation. Ken came in to greet Monica and she was on her way to let us outside so he took Jlo and I out to the shoveled area to pee, I hurried because it was cold, but I did stand there for a second as the snow fell slowly and I thanked God, Patience or whoever let me be here today. With that I ran inside and the front door opened and Courtney and Ron were here! They had big packages and were singing songs. Oh how I love their joy and enthusiasm!

I was so excited, I could hardly stand it. Tori came downstairs with the big bows and even had one for Brutus. I laughed and said "You're a part of the family now." He smiled and donned his colorful bow. No one even protested the bows, it was a symbol of love and affection and we knew it. The door opened again and my daughter Kathy and her husband Steve were here. She had all kinds of bags and Blue came racing in with a red and green shirt on, he was happy to see us and said

"Wait to see what my mom brought us its way cool!" He was leery of Brutus but Brutus said,

"Hey Blue good to see you," Blue wagged his tail and even Tinker walked calmly past Brutus. She's given in to the probability that he may be hanging around.

Kayla was coming downstairs with a wild hairdo; she looked so cute, kind of wild eyed with wild hair. It was hug and kiss time with everyone and Cousin Courtney came to the rescue, she whipped out a brush and helped Kayla look tamer. Kayla just lay in her lap letting her fix up her long blond hair. Of course Tori being a little older was busy fixing herself up with trinkets to be as adorable as she could.

Everyone was buzzing around and Tinker being the watch cat said, "Sof, here they come," She knew my excitement for the new baby. I ran to the door and Kathy and Steve went to meet them and Steve helped them empty their car. There is so much stuff with a baby. Kathy took the baby seat and set it on the floor in the Christmas room. I ran to get Ellie so we could see the baby together. Barking and dancing on my hind legs, she noticed me. Then I ran into the living room where the baby seat sat. Ellie followed me and we went right over to the seat and as she lifted the cover that was over the baby, I felt my eyes welling up. I put my paws upon the side and as I peeked over the blanket, I saw him. I was crying dog tears and couldn't believe this was my great grandson. I get to see my great grandson in the flesh as an infant. I missed so much of my Grandchildren's lives that this was a very precious, special moment.

Ellie was knelt down by the baby seat and we were looking upon him together. I felt we were sharing the joy together of new life in our family. It was truly a magic moment, then Ellie said "Sof, this is baby Jack,"

Oh, I loved this name. I was so happy she wanted me to know! I just stared at him then crawled up onto Ellie's lap to get a better look.

Everyone is here, J.R.'s wife Becky, Courtney, Ron, Kayla and Tori are all around the kitchen table laughing and making fun at each other. There are my grandchildren all together and I just love them all so much. I paw at Tori and she picks me up to see the festivities. Kathy is holding baby Jack, after all this is her first grandchild. Ellie and Monica are getting the kitchen picked up. The men, Ken and Steve are talking sports or some sort of thing like that. Normally I would want to hear about those things, but what my grandchildren are chattering about is the music I live for.

Acts 20:34 You yourselves know that these hands of mine have supplied my own needs and the needs of my companions.

68

PRESENTS

Soon we are all crowding into the Christmas tree room and everyone is making room for each other. I rest on Ellie's lap finally under her big Christmas sweatshirt; I'm a little worn out after hardly sleeping last night. There are tons of presents, and I hear laughing and screaming. The opening of presents goes on for what seems like quite a while. Then I hear Ellie saying, "Monica get me that bag over there." I peek my head out looking around, Ellie said "come here all you furry kids," then called their names, "Tinker, Jlo, Blue, Brutus, and of course here is Sophie," as she uncovers me from her shirt I peek out looking sleepy eyed.

She reached into the bag and had a different present for each of us, they weren't wrapped, but she handed out a crochet blanket for each of us to fit our size and a crochet pillow for Tinker. Brutus's was the biggest in a brown and tan color, Jlo's was red and white, Blues was blue and white, Tinkers pillow was purple and pink, then she showed me mine, it was multicolored soft baby colors out of a softer fine yarn and it was like a sleeping bag for me, I even had a little "S" on it that she embroidered. We all were wagging our tails and I was kissing her hands as she was passing them out. This was so thoughtful; we all fight over and hog the big afghan that she made which is on the sofa. Now we all have our very own, and I don't even have to try and cover up my head and get tangled up, I can just crawl inside. Oh, I love her, she's absolutely perfect!

Now I'm hearing Blue say, "Guys, guys, come around; my mom has something for all of us too!" I sat up watching as we all were gathered. Kathy pulled out these special pet Christmas stockings one for each of us. Tinker, of course, got a cat one, Blue and Jlo got identical ones and Brutus got a huge one, he had a bone in his that was as big around as my whole body. As he was salivating, I was asking him,

"Dude, are you really going to eat that huge thing?"

"You bet, I love them," he replied, that sort of put a lump in my throat and a knot in my stomach.

I watched as Kayla and Tori were opening up Blue and Jlo's treats and Tinker was already pawing at the new catnip that was inside hers, "I told you guys my mom had the best treats!" Blue said. As I was admiring their joy, Kathy came over to me and sitting on the floor so her face was level to mine. She had a special little stocking unlike the other pets. It has soft sausage treats and she bought me some special soft cat food that she thinks I will like, it's for growing kittens. Maybe I will meow after eating it. She also got me special booties, teeny weeny bright green ones because my feet are always so cold and I don't want to walk on the snow. I pawed at her and went close to her and licked her face. She picked me up and said "Sophie you're so cute, and special too, that's why Grandma has to take special care of you. We think you're a few French Fries short of a happy meal, but she thinks you're perfect the way you are," I didn't understand the French fry part but I know Ellie thinks I'm just right, bad health and all!

Proverbs 3:3 Let love and faithfulness never leave you; bind them around your neck, write them on the tablet of your heart.

69

THE GIFT

Soon my daughters Kathy and Monica are now holding me and putting my new booties on me. Oh boy, these may work but what a pain to get on! I look back at Ellie and she just asks, "What are they doing to you, Sophie?" As they are wrestling me around I realize the presents are done and this is when I wanted to give Ellie her surprise gift from me.

I start to call the pets with my whimpering, Tinker is already loopy from her new catnip and she has a big part in this plan, so I have to rely on Brutus. With one look into his eyes we communicate and he knows the plan and nudges Tinker to her feet. She wobbles up stairs to Kayla's room and Jlo follows. Halfway up the staircase Tinker decides it's time for a bath, but Brutus and Jlo encourage her to keep moving

"We have business to do." Jlo barks! Tinker replies with a slur,

"I can't do business looking like this!" Jlo closes her eyes and asks her,

"Please Tinker, can you take your bath later?" Ignoring Jlo, Tinker just shakes her head and continues to lick her paws. Brutus sighs and in a gentle voice tells

Tinker if she helps them that there is more catnip for her afterwards. Lifting one eyebrow up Tink eyes him carefully,

"Really?" she asks,

"Yes really, but we have to go now if you want it," he says, Tinker rolled to her feet, crawling the next few stairs and into Kayla's room.

Brutus was telling her to "go get it."

Tinker looking surprised said, "Get what?" Jlo losing her patience barked,

"The little red heart pillow that we came for, on top of the big dresser!" Tinker sits there, looking dizzy and then gets a cheesy cat grin on her face,

"Oh yeah, that," she murmurs, then she jumps up onto the chair then to the top of the dresser. Once upon the dresser she lays down and looking around saying she already forgot what she is up there for, and Brutus reminds her, she looks around and finds the little red heart pillow with "I Love You" stitched on it. Along with a few other knick knacks, she knocks it to the ground and Jlo picks up the little heart pillow and Brutus follows. Tinker was looking at the floor spinning, lies down on top of the dresser again to stablize before coming down. As Brutus and Jlo were making their way out of the room, Tinker was mumbling,

"Hey, I may be a damsel in distress, how do I get down from here?" Brutus stopping for a moment listening, he looks at Jlo,

"No time, come on don't worry Brutus, cat's always land on their feet!" Jlo piped,

"Oh, right," Brutus said, and downstairs bound they went.

Now Jlo puts the little pillow down by the downstairs staircase and leads Brutus down the steps to Ellie's room. Jlo jumps up onto her bed and told Brutus to get that picture off from Grandmas night stand. Brutus gently put his paws upon the dresser and picked the picture up in his mouth, "Great, be careful with it and follow me!" Jlo said. And they ran upstairs as fast as they could with the picture in Brutus mouth. Jlo went to pick up the little heart pillow on the main floor landing. Running up to the hall Steve was passing them to refill his coffee not paying attention. Tinker was wobbling downstairs, and I was barely standing now with my new bright neon green booties. Blue was barking to help hold everyone's attention in the Christmas room as the plan came together. I truly wish I did not have these booties on but I can't remove them now. As all the pets got a good look at me they were snickering and Tinker just fell over laughing.

"Oh well, guys please help me do this?" I pleaded,

"Alright," Brutus said, so Brutus, Jlo, and Blue came in next to me, and Tinker did the belly crawl in her ecstasy or maybe even misery, with her eyes dilated and rolling back into her head at this point I wasn't sure if she could move. We all barked and howled in our best voices,

"We love you, we love you, we love you, we do!" Jlo did a few extra woo woos as usual, and Tinker just rolled around on the floor. Everyone was so delighted which was my plan to keep them seated. They were all taking pictures and laughing so hard. I started my trek over to where the little red "I Love You" pillow was and I was nearly falling over and having a hard time lifting my feet. But my determination to get the pillow was way beyond anything stopping me. I got to the pillow and I thought the whole family was going to explode from laughter watching me walk. I told Brutus,

"Now it's time," and he came around to the hall and grabbed the picture. The picture was Ellie and I on our Twenty-Fifth Anniversary, I grabbed the pillow in my mouth and off we went across the room to Ellie. She looked stunned and said

"Brutus, where did you get that?" Brutus laid the picture at her feet and she said, "What is this doing here?" Then she looked up and here I was trying to come to her with the heart pillow in my mouth and the clumsiest walk ever, "Sophie, what are you doing?"

"Hey that's my little valentine pillow, how did she get it?" Kayla asked,

I delivered the pillow next to the picture and pawed at the photo of us. I was trying to point to me, but the booties were impairing my aim. Ellie was speechless and had tears in her eyes, "Sophie if I didn't know I would think you're sending me a message about Rob," I just jumped up and down, stood on my hind legs, wagging my tail and even fell over trying to convince her she's right. She scooped me up and set me on her lap I put my booted paws on her chest standing up and did my best "I Love you, Ellie!" She pulled me to her face and said,

"I don't know exactly what this means, but I sure love you little Sof," Everyone knew this was a magic moment, for some reason, time stopped when we were looking in each other's eyes and she knew for one tiny second that I "Rob" was there with her. She shook her head and got up to go to the washroom. Of course taking me with her, she said, "I don't know how you did that, you sure are something else. But, I loved it, and you have to know that I know, somehow you've always liked that picture so I'm sure it's no mistake you put that I Love You heart with that picture. Anyway, thank you, it was one of the nicest gestures, I love you too Sophie, and you're one of a kind."

Rob & Ellie's Twenty-Fifth Wedding
Anniversary Picture

"Sophie you're the best!" . . . Ellie

2 Corinthians 7:16 I am glad I can have complete confidence in you.

70

PET JOY

As we came out the whole family was moving around and they came up hugging Ellie and said how special that was. I did my best to walk with my new boots on down the hall to the Christmas room where the pets were enjoying their treats and Tinker was almost passed out purring some kind of lulling motor rhythm. They said "Merry Christmas Sophie, we hope your surprise went the way you wanted," I told them,

"Other than the new booties slowing me down it was perfect," We all hugged dog style which is putting your head next to each other's head. I was so thankful for these great friends and my stoned friend Tinker; I walked over and said, "Tink, thanks for your effort, no one else could get up that high,"

"Sure anything for our little angel," she said, I looked at her and it dawned on me, maybe she kind of knows. I licked her,

"You're the best cat sister, a puppy could have," She just rolled on her back and said,

"I know."

The whole day was a complete and total joy. Everyone conversed, opened presents, played games and ate all of Ellie's wonderful food and treats. Now it was nighttime and Monica and Ken were still trying to figure out how Brutus and Sophie pulled off the gift to Grandma. Kathy and Steve were heading home soon with Blue. Steve owns his own business and has work tomorrow. Courtney and Ron are staying overnight which means fun, fun, and more fun till the late hours with Tori and Kayla. J.R. and Becky have just come downstairs after packing up little Jack, they are heading to Becky's parents who are celebrating the next day. Ellie is reading a new book, and guess what it's about, Heaven, angels and why the world needs them. Go figure, maybe someone is trying to help me with this, thanks to whoever gave her this book.

Hebrews 1:7   In speaking of the angels he says, "He makes his angels spirits, and his servants flames of fire."

71

DOBERMAN MANIA

It was still Christmas vacation. Tori and Kayla were having friends over and Tori's girlfriend stopped by and happened to have her family dog with her in the car when her mom was dropping her off. Tori loved this dog, it was an eighteen month old black Doberman, and she wanted Monica and Ellie to see him. She convinced Laura to bring him in so they could see how big he had grown. Laura's mom had to get gas for the car, so she said she'd be back in ten minutes. She confirmed it would be okay for Louie to visit for a quick minute.

When Laura and Tori came in with Louie, Jlo and I did the Chi-Chi stampede like usual to greet them at the door. Whoa, this is a huge intruder, let's slow down this race. We barked furiously and stayed our distance. This dog was as big as Brutus and looks like a devil dog to us, or at least to me. Tori told us to calm down and called for her Mom and Grandma. When they came I was backed up to the end of the entryway hall, still barking my biggest, meanest bark. Then I thought, could it be a possibility this is an angel? So I slowly took a few steps ahead and I stared into his eyes and I swear he was just licking his lips to eat me. Nope, he's definitely not an angel.

Ellie scooped me up and took me onto her lap. I don't know who this ugly black dog is but I don't want him anywhere near my Ellie. Tori and Laura were sitting on the floor calling this massive black monster "Louie." Jlo was barking and running around trying to get as close as possible to sniff this big creature. Then he would turn and she would back up. Ellie was saying, "Watch her, Tori, Jlo thinks she's as big as he is," Well I know I'm not that big, but I would bite him with what little teeth I have in order to protect my Ellie.

I watched this clumsy big dog try to play with Jlo. It was worrying me, he was so big and he has no idea of how small Jlo is. She's just trying to sniff him but his private stuff is up so high she can't even get her nose close, but being the sniffer dog she is, she's going to try. Now "big ugly" came over to look at me or check out Ellie. I about lost my mind, I have never been so scared and felt I needed to protect her more. I barked, growled, showed my not so good teeth and was frothing at the mouth, I was so mad. Ellie, tried to hold me close as he just kept poking his head at me and barked on occasion. She was shushing me and kept telling me to calm down. Tori and Laura laughed. Monica was trying to protect Jlo and watch over the situation.

Little did I know but Tinker was listening and knew this was upsetting me terribly. Before anyone could react, Tinker came in and was hissing and spitting like mad, and when Louie moved one inch closer to her, she turned into a screaming Tasmanian devil. Legs were flying every direction she was a flying fur ball of fury just swirling like a tornado across the room right at this Louie dog, she sounded like she was possessed. She was screaming cat obscenities that I could never repeat and even without claws she was a force to be reckoned with. She was as mighty as she could be and totally fearless. Talk about being on a mission, whew! That cat had spunk I'd never seen before.

Monica jumped up and tried to catch her but she was moving so fast and Louie was running and whining as he bolted to the door. Tinker stopped, staring at him and was hissing and growling with her back arched, and tail swaying as if to say, "Don't even think about it," Laura then jumped up and was hooking Louie up to his leash. Tori said

"Calm down you crazy thing, he's not going to hurt you," Still hissing Tinker backed up and jumped up to join Ellie and I on the loveseat, still giving him the evil eye as Laura was putting on her boots. Louie's tail was down, if it were long enough it would be between his legs and I'm sure he had no idea what just took place,

"Bye Laura, sorry he was so afraid, see you soon!" Tori said, Jlo looked a little miffed as if we took an overgrown toy away from her. Tori sat by Tinker and began to pet her saying, "You sure were crazy and protective, and you never act like that, what's wrong with you?" Monica said she wasn't sure if Tinker has ever seen a dog that big other than Brutus. Ellie was just shaking her head saying

"Mercy, mercy, that was more than exciting," while holding me tight and petting me.

I looked at Tinker, "What got into you, Tink?" She was licking her fur back into place and replied,

"I couldn't stand to see you so upset, Sof, you can't do that to yourself. I needed to step in to make this guy back off. Your health is not good and I don't want you to lose it over that ugly visitor."

"Oh Thanks, Tinker, I appreciate your love and protection, but what would you have done if he attacked you?"

"Well, she said, he could have, but I told him in no uncertain terms if he move any closer he'd be missing some important parts of his manhood," This made me laugh, I went over to her and licked her,

"You're the best, thanks," Jlo was listening and butted in curiously,

"Hey how would you have done that, Tinker?" She snickered and said,

"It's for me to know and you to find out," she winked at me. I was so tired after all of that, I just laid down next to her and took a nap, curling into her soft fur.

Tori with Louie, he's really just a big baby.

Psalm 31:9 Be merciful to me, Lord, for I am in distress; my eyes grow weak with sorrow, my soul and body with grief.

72

NO-NO-NO

It was a brisk winter day and I was not feeling well. I had a bad seizure the night before so my appetite was weak this morning. Tinker lay in the sun after breakfast and watched the beautiful white snowflakes slowly fall on this beautiful winter day. I can't wait till Spring, Ellie, Jlo and I take our walks outside and even though I've gotten used to them I don't have to wear my booties.

The kids are off to school and Ellie is going to run some errands, this morning. Monica has a longer than usual drive so she took the big truck in case it snows more later on today. She left bright and early with the girls. Ellie is so cute, she puts her boots on, her pink hat with a pin, pink gloves and her new coat she got for Christmas. She's quite a sight to see. Since I was not feeling well she wrapped me in my little blanket she made for me this Christmas and put me in the sunshine kissing me and telling me to rest, and that she'd be home soon.

As the day went on I was feeling nauseated and got up to see if Ellie had returned, I was weak and probably needed food. It seemed like a long time had passed, but I wasn't sure, only my bladder was telling me, it was time to pee. I paced for a while and tried to hold it but soon realized I better use the diaper pad Ellie puts out for me when she leaves. She probably is visiting her brother, she enjoys him so much and there is only the two of them left.

After a while longer I became concerned, I found Tinker on the sofa in the living room and asked her, "Shouldn't Grandma be back by now?"

"She's probably shopping for our turkey treats, don't worry, come up here and rest by me," she offered, but I shook my head,

"No thanks," and went to look for Jlo, she was on Ellie's bed, I asked her if she thought it was time for Grandma to be home and she said she had no idea, so I walked away and back to my little blanket. Soon I heard the door open and ran to meet Ellie. But it was Joe, Monica's ex-husband, he came in and said

"Come here girls," and I ran straight to him. I always liked him and he was good to me after he got to know me. We just didn't have enough time together.

He said let's go outside, and we rushed out to do our duty, while he was shoveling our pee patch in the snow, and then when we all went inside, he was taking off his coat and started to make us our food. This seemed strange but we all were hungry and sat at his feet as he warmed up our soft food.

As he sat Tinker, Jlo's and my plate on the floor, they dove into it, I could tell it was getting late and they were famished. I was hungry, my appetite was just returning. Soon the girls came home. They ran in and said, "Hi Dad, love you, is it our night to go to your house?" *Hey, where's Ellie,* I wondered? Maybe she's out with Monica or Kathy? Then I saw Joe take the girls hands and set them down. I realized that his eyes were welling up and he could not stop the tears from coming,

"Girls grandma has been in a car accident today," he said, and those words pierced my soul. I was stunned for a second; I went running over to him and scratched his leg to pick me up. Unconsciously he reached down scooping me up and caressed my head. He continued and said "She's in the hospital and the doctors are doing all they can for her,"

The girls burst into tears and I was whining and crying. No, no this can't be happening! Now Jlo and Tinker are by the girls, they know something is wrong. Through my choked tears, I tell them what I just heard. Jlo lies down and covers her face and Tinker jumps upon Kayla's lap. Joe goes on to explain, that they will wait until tomorrow to go see her and maybe things will get better. He tells them their Mom and Kathy are at the hospital with her now. They are crying and protesting that they want to see her tonight. I was so distraught that I could feel it happening, my legs stiffening out; my sight blurring and I could barely hear them. Joe was holding me, "Oh no, she's having a seizure, can one of you girls get her medicine?" He was petting me, "its okay Sophie," Tori jumped up and ran to Grandma's room and got the drops that helped me come out of these tremors. She squirted them in my mouth as Joe held me tight. Slowly I started to come out and was wishing this was a bad dream and I would wake up. But with all the tears flowing I knew this was real.

Suddenly I found myself in my half aware state praying to Patience. Asking her how I could fix this, "What do I do? How do I fix this, Ellie needs me?" Patience spoke to me in the most soothing voice saying

"Rob, this is all a part of your mission, take it in stride and remember your angel friends are close by to help you through this time. Do your best, this is life on earth, there is pain on earth. You of all angels can handle this. Be strong,"

I was waking up and processing what I should do, and trying to regain my focus. Joe had called Monica and she agreed that they should come up to the hospital. The girls were twelve and fourteen years old and Monica knew they had to see their Grandma, "Here, Sophie is better now, put her down on her blanket and we will get going," Joe said, Tori and Kayla protested saying Grandma would never leave her after a seizure and Grandma needs to see Sophie, it will make her feel better. Joe not wanting to argue settled and said "grab her blanket, and bag." Kayla ran to get her doggie tote and Tori to get her blanket. They wrapped her up and off they went to the hospital. Joe reminded them on the way there that dogs were not allowed in the hospital to keep her hidden. They agreed and I was just thankful to be going,

"Thanks Patience," I murmured.

Once arriving, we exited the car and went inside to an elevator. On the fifth floor we got off and I was nauseated. The girls were sniveling and Joe was silent as he held their hands on each side. Tori carried me in the bag over her shoulder; I laid still to not be seen. Monica was in the hall when we turned the corner and the girls ran directly to her and threw their arms around her. She explained that Grandma was severely hurt and they were doing their best for her, not to be loud and try not to scare her, she looks bad. The girls shook their head and I peeked out. Monica just smiled when she saw Sophie peek out of the bag, and said "that may help." As the girls and Joe came into the room, Grandma was hooked up to lots of things. She looked okay but she had a broken arm, the one I ride on, a broken pelvis and they said she had a head injury. She was coming in and out of consciousness.

I was wiggling to see her and once close to the hospital bed I leapt out of the bag and onto the bed and ran right up on her chest. It startled Kathy and they were all amazed because a second later, Grandma made a noise and I licked and licked her chin and neck. I knew not to get into the hoses and contraptions on her face. Everyone was crying and I stood staring at my beautiful beloved Ellie, I pleaded to God, Patience or anyone, "Please, Please, give me one last moment with her let her know I'm here, Please I beg you." In that very moment she opened her eyes and looked at me and then around to the family. I sat on her chest and stared at her, I knew at that very second that this may be the last time I may see her eyes. She tried to smile at them and was weakly trying to lift her left arm. She knew they were all there. Monica helped her kissing her hand and the girls leaned over and kissed her cheeks and told her how much they loved her. I told her by looking into her eyes, "Ellie this is Rob, and I'm here with you, and God and the angels in heaven are here too, if it is your time, don't be afraid," I knew she heard me because *I could see a twinkling in her eyes.* She then put her left hand on me and I lied down over her heart and closed my eyes as she did hers. She slipped back under and we all were frozen during the next while. Everyone was caressing her and praying.

In a while we heard a nurse coming and Tori quickly scooped me up and into the bag. I was so upset that I didn't care. I don't know what to do. If she dies and goes to heaven, she can't go there and arrive without me being there to meet her. I have to know what's going on. I have to be with Ellie, Oh, this is the worst ever, I thought I would never experience these feelings, but I can barely think. Joe took me and the girl's home; he was going to stay with us tonight. Ken was on his way to the hospital as we were leaving. How could I tell Jlo and Tinker? Oh this is the worst day ever, "Patience, please help me."

Lamentations 3:49 My eyes will flow unceasingly, without relief,

73

BAD NEWS

Once home, Jlo and Tinker were sitting at the back door waiting. Tori took me out of the bag and they knew by looking at me that it was bad. I told them I was not sure if Grandma was going to make it. They fell apart, I just put my head upon them, and we were a mess. I told them that I had a moment of communication and she was coherent, I told them she knew how much they loved her. All of us pets slept together that night, Monica stayed at the hospital and Joe slept in her room on a pull out cot and Tori and Kayla slept in her bed. Tori and Kayla cried off and on and hugged each other and Jlo and I tried to comfort them with kisses and snuggles. All of us animals were curled up together with our little blankets on top of the bed with the girls.

During the night everyone was fitful and not sleeping much. I just lay there worrying about what I was to do. Then I could feel it, another seizure. I felt my body growing tenser and I began to shake. I didn't fight it; I just lay there not to disturb them. Then Jlo realized I was shaking and went up to nudge the kids. Tori turned on the light and saw me stretched out and my eyes dilated, "Dad, Dad, help me, Sophie is having another seizure," She picked me up and he went to get the drops. I did not want them. If I had to stay here on earth when Ellie was not going to be here, I wanted no such thing. But something inside of me told me that she was not gone. They were all trying to help me and I appreciated their love. It's the love they learned from Ellie. I came out of it and then curled back up in my soft little sleeping bag Ellie made for me.

It was morning and Joe let the girls stay home from school. I heard the door open and Jlo and I jumped off the bed, almost expecting it would be Grandma. It was Monica and Ken coming in. We ran up to them and they both reached down and picked us up. Monica was holding Jlo and she looked the worst I'd ever seen her look. Ken was petting my head and holding me close. Monica reached over to pet me and said "You guys were the sunshine in Mom's day," at that time Tinker had joined us and she was rubbing on her leg, "You too Tink, Grandma thought you all were special, especially you, Sof." She was trying to smile and then the girls came in and Joe followed.

Monica and Ken sat us down and hugged Tori and Kayla; they were all a sniveling mess. I just wanted to hug them all. Joe came in and automatically took us outside for our morning potty. I hurried because they were all sitting down and discussing my Ellie. It felt like a nightmare, I would rather have the robbers back, I thought that was a bad day, but nothing could be as bad as this. Jlo and I came inside and I was pawing at Monica, she picked me up and Joe went to make us pets our food. This used to be his house and he was right at home. Monica was thankful for him, he was a wonderful father and very good to her. Monica proceeded to tell us that Grandma has been in a coma since last night. With tears flowing down her face she looked at Ken and he continued. He told us that there was not a lot of hope right now, that Kathy and Steve were staying at the hospital and Courtney was on her way there. I just buried my head and felt sicker and sicker.

As the moments ticked by Monica said she was going to clean up and try to sleep a few hours then return to the hospital. Ken was going home to let Brutus out and Joe and Monica decided that the girls should go to school for a few hours this afternoon. Joe was going to work a few hours after getting the girls to school and then he would pick them up and go to the hospital. Monica kissed the girls and Ken and went off to her bedroom walking like a zombie. In her room she was sobbing and blaming herself for not leaving the big truck for Grandma that day. She had the truck and maybe if Grandma had been driving it she would be okay. She was distraught, and I knew she did not know what to do. I prayed to help her rest and take this burden of guilt off of her soul. I begged to help her make it through this awful situation. She laid down and pulled me right next to her. The covers were still disheveled from the girls sleeping there the night before and my blanket was by her knees. She pulled out my blanket and snuggled me inside right next to her. I licked her hands and tried to rest.

Not able to rest I slowly walked up to her face; gazing upon my beautiful daughter and mother of my grandchildren I felt her pain. My soul was burdened and felt we were alone and I had no relief to offer. I could only love her; I hope she knew I always have with all my heart. She opened her eyes and said, "Sof, you have been the constant companion, we all love you so much especially Mom." Then she scooped me into her chest holding me as she cried, and I wailed right along with her in my whimpering voice.

Psalm 4:1 Answer me when I call to you my righteous God. Give me relief from my distress; have mercy on me and hear my prayer,

74

HUMAN ANGEL HELP

Ken had arranged for the nanny Darlene who was a great friend of the families and also an angel to come to our house that afternoon to get the girls from the bus and help out that evening. Monica was showered and still looking stressed was gathering her things and met Ken and Darlene coming into the house with Brutus. Monica embraced Darlene and thanked her for showing up on such short notice. Darlene ensured her it was no problem and told Monica she was praying for Ellie. Ken was driving her back to the hospital and Darlene knew the drill to get the girls fed and send them on their way with their dad later on after school.

Once the girls came home, they were glad to see Darlene. She had taken care of them numerous times to fill in when schedules got overwhelmingly busy or just to help out on occasions. The girls were not hungry but Darlene made them some soup and cupcakes. They picked at their food and were lying around on the sofa until their Dad came to take them to see Grandma. All of us pets were together in the family room, even Blue, Kathy had dropped him off since Darlene was going to be here to let us all out and take care of us. We were all silent lying still, and no one could say anything without all of us just crying, we just looked at each other. Darlene had gotten all of our blankets and had put on a fire in the fireplace. On a normal day this would be a good setting but today was a different story. My heart ached so much I wanted to die.

It was about seven o'clock and Darlene said, "Come on, guys. You have to go outside, the fresh air will be good for you," We all just looked at each other and Brutus got up first and nudged Jlo, Blue started to follow and then Brutus came to me. I looked at him and he spoke to me mentally. He told me he wished he could do something, and he wanted to help me in any way possible. I understood but was lost for words or even thoughts, I just needed strength. He got down and told me to get on his back and he carried me to the door and outside. It probably looked like a circus act but it was an act of kindness. He waited for me to do my duty and followed me inside. Kit was in the yard, meowing to the pets, and telling Brutus and I how sorry she was about Grandma. Darlene knowing she was an angel and it was bitter cold outside invited her inside to warm up. Upon us all coming inside Darlene was making us a little turkey treat with gravy warmed up in the microwave, it was all our favorite dish.

Dividing the warm treat up onto little plates and one big one for Brutus, she set them down one by one. There was no pushing, or stepping in front of each other, and even Kit got a plate of warm turkey. I took one bite and just couldn't eat it, "Jlo, your Majesty, you can have mine," She looked at me and said,

"Sof you never have to call me that, you're my sister now," I went over to her and put my head upon her, "I love you kid" she said,

"Thanks, I know" I squeaked out. As I was walking away I decided to look outside the sliding door, sitting down and looking up to heaven, I asked "What do I do now?"

Then as I was watching the snowflakes fall, I saw a big snow flake coming right at the window. As I leaned forward to see what that was, I realized it was Dovie. She was coming to visit. I looked at her and immediately she knew the torment I was in. She told me how sorry she was and this time she was here for me. I looked at her, "Am I going to die?" nodding she replied,

"Yes Sophie, or should I say Rob, it's time for you to go. Ellie won't last long and you have to go back now to meet her in heaven," Oh for a moment my heart leapt and I was filled with anticipation of our meeting face to face as human angels in heaven. Then I thought of my children and grandchildren and how sad it will be not to share in their daily lives. Then I thought of my furry friends, they have been a real joy and a true pet family to me.

I was reminiscing and thinking of all the good times I had here at this house and how fortunate I was to share in the lives of my family almost twenty-five years after my death as Rob. Then I started to shake and felt dizzy, I knew that it was a seizure and just laid down on the little rug by the door that Tinker always claims. As I lay there, Dovie summoned Brutus and he came walking over. He was taken back as he had never seen me have a seizure, he barked and Darlene came to see what he wanted. She knew and knelt on the floor by me. Everyone followed even though their treat was not quite finished. Tinker screamed, "No Sophie! Grandma may come home, just calm down!" and Jlo once seeing me ran as fast as she could to go get the drops upstairs on the bed from the night before. Blue was sobbing,

"Little runt cakes, I love you," Kit was consoling them and Brutus was crying huge dog tears,

"Sof you're the best angel friend I ever had, I will always be here to look after your family, don't you worry little buddy," he sobbed, Jlo screeched into the circle of pets and Tinker said,

"No Jlo, we promised we would help her die if Grandma wasn't here . . ." Jlo dropped the bottle and just let out the loudest,

"I love you, Sophie, I hope you know we are doing this for you, please remember me!" And proceeded to whine and cry.

Darlene was teary and was petting me but leaving me on the rug. She knew not to give me the drops and Dovie was confirming that this was the proper time. Tinker looked up to see Dovie outside the window and could see her beauty of light glowing around her and knew she was here for a purpose and that this was supposed to happen. Darlene began a prayer and as my tremors increased and the shaking became scary, I looked one last time into each of their eyes. Tinker, Jlo and Blue knew how much I appreciated them and loved them. I told Brutus and Kit to please explain to them that this is my time and I will always look out for them in heaven and that you are here for them now. I thanked them for protecting my family and being so good to me and that I loved them too.

I was actually suffering; my earthly form was in pain. I was used to being consoled when I had these tremors and my soul was yearning for a reprieve from the sorrow, bodily pain and separation from Ellie. Darlene, put a hand on my tiny body and here came

Jlo with my blanket in tow, Darlene smiled at Jlo's gesture and through her tears she covered me with my special Ellie blanket. To escape my pain and suffering I thought of the love letter I want to recite to Ellie when I see her.

To the End of Time, I will Love You,

To my Beautiful Wife Ellie Marie Harper,

It has been decades since we have looked into each other's eyes.
I remember the very last touch and glance you gave me at the hospital.
Your love and concern has never been forgotten.

I have been with you in spirit every day since my passing and have watched over you daily with love and pride. You have been so strong with our family and children, I realize more every day why God allowed me to have you as my mate.

When we see each other again in heaven I can hardly wait to embrace you and hold you in my arms once more.

Ellie, I have been with you for the past years and even though you have not recognized me, I was with you as Sophie, your tiny side kick. I now have even greater appreciation for your enduring kindness, love and care you bless everyone with on a daily basis. Your ongoing generosity and love is so apparent, even for the pets like I was. God did not want you to be alone in your later years, and that's why he sent me to you as your little companion

Ellie, I am on my way to greet you and pass into Heaven with you, I will truly hold you forever and ever. I pray with all my Love and Strength, will our Lord and Heavenly Father be with you and I will soon be at your side,

You are the love of my life and until the end of time,
I will always love and adore you.

Forever your Loving Husband (and pet Sophie),
Robert George Harper

As I finished the letter in my head I could see my human hand signing it. Then I felt that warm feeling, that fading feeling and I looked at Dovie, "Come on now, Sophie. Let's take a walk," she said. I got right up and just walked through the door and outside there was sunshine coming right through the nightfall. I felt relieved and terrific!

"Dovie where is my Ellie?" I asked, Dovie pointed her wing,

"Look over there, Sophie or should I say Rob," as I glanced across the sky there was another beam of sunlight leading into the clouds. It was hard to see but there she was, my Ellie, she was wearing a hospital gown and she didn't look hurt or like she had a broken anything, she was holding onto two beautiful white and golden clad angels hands and walking towards heaven. I yelled to her,

"Ellie! I'm here, look this way; I'm coming to meet you!" Dovie explained to me that she couldn't see or hear me right now, that she's on her ascent and needs to be processed as I was when I passed as a human, "Okay, but when will I see her?" I asked, and Dovie promised me it would be soon.

Lamentations 5:15 Joy is gone from our hearts; our dancing has turned to mourning.

75

NOT A COINCIDENCE

At that time, all the pets were mourning and the phone rang at Monica's home. Darlene had just finished her prayers as she felt Sophie take her last breath. She reached down and tucked little Sophie's limp body inside the blanket so she was wrapped in Grandmas love. As she answered the phone in tears, she had heard the news that Ellie had passed just moments earlier. As she held little Sophie in her arms in the tiny blanket, she knelt on the floor again and shared the heartache with the pets. As they were all depressed and broken hearted, Brutus took it upon himself to help explain the coincidences of events. As he cleared his throat from the huge lump that he was choking back, he began to explain.

First he told them they will not remember all of this because he is giving this message as an angel. He told them to stare into his eyes and they will understand. As an angel you are given special powers to communicate when necessary. This was the first time Brutus had this power. He began to tell them that this was all timed perfectly for Ellie and Sophie, that they were truly husband and wife on earth years ago until

"Rob" died and was sent back to earth to be with Ellie for her final years. He came back as Sophie, because Monica had a soft spot for sick animals and Sophie had been sick since the beginning, and the girls obviously like Chihuahuas.

Heaven always knows how to place angels in the right place at the right time. I am an angel and even though you will not remember that, I will be here to protect you and the family. I know now that is part of my duty while I am here for my earthly mission.

Darlene was listening also, being a human angel herself she knew her part was of no coincidence. So today we have to start new and fill in large gaps. We have to love our family even more and try not to mope around but be uplifting and show them our support. There will never be another Ellie or Sophie, but for us, when we go to heaven, we will be with them forever and ever. So when I finish talking, you will only remember parts and your burden of loss will be lifted off your souls and you will be able to rejoice for our true friends and loved ones Ellie and Rob.

As he said "Amen", the phone rang. It was Monica and she talked it over with the family, and the Avink Funeral Home was just fine with burying Sophie with Grandma together. The Avinks were personal family friends of the family and happy to fulfill their wishes. Monica asked Darlene if she could deliver Sophie's body to the Funeral Home so this could be done.

James 1:4 Let perseverance finish its work so that you may be mature and complete, not lacking anything.

76

FINAL ARRANGEMENTS

Darlene of course, accepted the task of taking Sophie to the funeral home. As she was leaving, she explained to the pets the wishes of the family and they all agreed this was best. She told the animal crew that she would be back soon. So off she went with tiny little Sophie wrapped in her baby blanket that Ellie made for her with such care.

Within two days all arrangements had been made and the family was preparing for an open house and funeral. Ellie being older, there weren't many friends her age around but the families' friends and relatives just kept coming for the viewings. Once everyone saw little Sophie in the casket with Ellie lying on her baby blanket tucked in Ellie's left arm next to her heart, it was unanimous that they were meant for each other. For the past five years they were inseparable and quite a pair. Before the funeral home opened for visitation, Kayla made Sophie little tiny white felt angel wings she attached to her collar. Everyone thought it was very fitting, on the day of the service; she even put a little crown of tinsel on her head like a halo. Kayla knew grandma always thought Sophie was a little angel.

The morning of the funeral Darlene was at the house helping out family and friends who came together with the preparation for an open house with food afterward. Monica and Kathy were busy with details and the arrival of the families. Ken and Darlene were in charge of bringing Jlo and Blue to the funeral home. Of course they got special permission, but knowing Grandma she would not want her beloved pets to not be included, after all they were a part of the family. Once leaving, Ken told Brutus that he had to stay in the back screened porch until the service was over. Brutus planted his feet in displeasure but had no choice. He howled and howled because he wanted to go to see his little friend one last time.

Brutus was in distress, remembering Sophie's angel contact, he cried out for Patience, *"Patience, I know you were Sophie's guardian, but please help me and allow me one more moment of reverence to a very special wise angel, Please!"* he howled, Patience's voice came to him,

"Brutus, I will see you through this one last task, be careful and be wise." Brutus looking around, slightly surprised yet thankful thought

"Excellent, but how?"

Soon Dovie came to his call, and was outside the screened porch. She began instructing him, "Brutus use your nose and push up the window," Brutus following her instructions pushed it up far enough and in came Dovie. She told him her little feet and beak was useful with levers and buttons, and soon she had unlocked the door, Brutus and she opened it up. Brutus still had to break through the electric fence, but it was worth it he thought. Once outside he asked Dovie, "But how do I get there?" she assured him to follow her flight pattern and she would lead the way to the funeral home. He winced as he jumped through the electric current that connected to his collar. As he began to follow Dovie down the street he yelled, "Wait Dovie! Tinker must feel like I do, left out, let's go see it she wants to go,"

Without hesitation they went directly to their home. Tinker was in the front window with a forlorn look on her face. She brightened up when seeing Brutus and Dovie arrive. Soon Kit joined them in the yard and they were asking Tinker if she wanted to go to the funeral, "Yes, of course, but how do we get there?" she asked,

"We follow Dovie, she knows the way and said it's not far," Brutus said,

"How do I get out," she asked, and Kit piped up immediately,

"Leave it to me!"

Soon enough she was at the back patio door and meowing as loud as she could, Tinker was watching from inside. Then a hired worker preparing for the open house, who was wearing an apron preparing food, came to look at what was going on. As soon as the woman reached the door Kit laid down and did a fainting type act on the step, the woman opened the door to see how she could help her. Kit laying still, gestured at Tinker who was creeping closer, and closer. They just waited until the woman was taking her apron off and went over to the sink to stop some running water. Kit raised her head and said, "Now!" Tinker leapt through the opening outside and when the lady returned Kit was gone. Looking outside she saw nothing and turned back around and shut the door.

Tinker was free and the posse began their trip to the funeral home. Brutus, being protective, said, "Kit, you follow Dovie and I will follow Tinker so she stays with us,"

Dovie leading the way through yards and fields they all were on a run. Tinker was so delighted to not only be outside but to be able to say one last good bye to Grandma and Sophie. Nearing their destination Tinker was tiring, after all she never ran this far before. Being an indoor cat this was more exercise than she had ever done. She was panting and slowing in her pace and finally said, "Wait, I can't go on much more," Brutus was afraid they would be too late,

"Tink it's only a little ways further, jump on my back and hang onto my collar," Tinker slightly afraid because she had no claws, knew his intention and he was for sure big enough to ride. So as he lowered himself to the ground, Tinker jumped upon his back and fastened her jaw around his collar, digging her teeth into the fabric and using her front clawless toes to grip on tighter to the collar and her back toes in his deep fur to hang on. Brutus took careful yet swift steps to keep up the pace and Tinker held on for dear life. Her ears peeled back she was trying not to look yet a bolt of excitement was running through her. Just to think she was a passenger on what was claimed the biggest, meanest dog in the neighborhood, who was now one of her closest friends.

As they neared the Avink Funeral Home with swift intentions at hand, car accidents were barely avoided. Cars were halting at the sight of this group of four crossing busy streets and running along a highway on a side walk. They were a sight to be seen and an extraordinary one at that.

Jeremiah 31:13 Then young women will dance and be glad, young men and old as well. I will turn their mourning into gladness; I will give them comfort and joy instead of sorrow.

77

MISSION ACCOMPLISHED

Soon Dovie swooped down and they had arrived at the Avink Funeral Home. Everyone seemed to have arrived so they needed a plan to get inside. Tinker jumped off Brutus back and began meowing loud and strong, and then Brutus began barking as Kit chimed in. There was such a commotion, Dovie flew around to the window and looked in, she said, "Keep it up, and louder, I think they hear you!" Then a blonde haired woman, smartly dressed in a suit, came to the door and when she opened it, to her surprise there were three furry friends. As she peered over the top of her glasses, she did not believe her eyes. Before she could react, Brutus bolted in with Tinker and Kit right behind. The woman chased behind them not knowing what to do. They reached the door of the hall where the service was taking place and they slowly walked up the aisle. Brutus saw Ken on the end of the aisle and sat down next to him, Tinker and Kit sat in front of Brutus. Ken was so shocked and the woman in the suit was just raising her hands and shrugging her shoulders,

"How did you get here and where did Tinker and your buddy come from?" Ken whispered, Monica turned and with surprise and delight she stood up and picked up Tinker, stroking her fur,

"You're so special, how on earth did you get here?" There was a slight disruption for a minute or two until the new guests were distributed.

Tori went over to gather up and hold Tinker, Kayla took Kit upon her lap, Brutus sat next to Ken in the aisle while Blue was held by Steve, and Jlo was sitting on Joe's lap. The man speaking said, "This family sure includes their pets in all aspects of their lives and in death. Now everyone is here so let's return to our tribute to the lives of Ellie Marie Harper and Sophie Harper, her beloved little companion."

To say the least it was a sad funeral filled with wonderful hilarious stories of these two lives. Before closing the casket, the Avink's gave the family time to say their goodbyes. The entire family kissed them goodbye, Ken lowered Jlo to see them, she licked both Ellie and Sophie's face and did her best bark in salute, shaking she even said a prayer for help to not be afraid and be strong. Blue being held now by Kathy to have one last look into the casket, he pawed at Ellie and licked Sophie's nose, he said, "I'll miss you, Grandma and especially you runt cakes, I'll never forget you, not ever!" Tori picked up Tinker and held her over the casket to see Grandma and Sophie, Tinker was indeed pleased to be there. Gazing at Sophie, Tinker thought the little angel wings were fitting for her tiny little angelic friend whom she would miss terribly. Big cat tears were spilling from her eyes and dripping off her face, with her last energy she gave a howling meow. Kayla even held up Kit, as she looked on she said with confidence,

"Sof, I will protect your family to the best of my ability until I leave this earth, I give you my word!" And Brutus, well Brutus nearly tipped over the casket when he jumped up to put his paws on the side to see in. A few floral arrangements were lost but Ken and Monica stabilized it, and then Monica lifted Sophie's little body up so he could kiss her goodbye. With a big German shepherd dog lick and a choked back lump in his throat he said,

"I know you can hear me even better now that you're in heaven and Sophie or Rob, I can't wait to see you again someday,"

Lowering down from the side and trying to shake off the sadness, he just sauntered back a ways and sat staring in remembrance and honor of a loved human and a perfect tiny angel returning to heaven. This was Brutus first time he lost an angel friend that was returning to home.

Before walking out the entire family said their tearful goodbyes and caressed and kissed both Ellie's face and little Sophie. They joined together in a circle, holding hands and saying a prayer for strength to carry on in memory of their beloved mother and little Sof. Behind them the animals were in a circle paw to paw and with heads bowed, in flew Dovie and landed in the center of all of them. She actually flew in right before the lady funeral attendant closed the door as the threesome entered in, but hid in the back not to disrupt the service. As they bowed their heads, Dovie lead a prayer and gave them strength from above to help them continue on, cheer their owners up and encouraging them forward.

After the prayers everyone loaded up in the cars, there was no need for the animals to go on foot; they all jumped in with the family. All the pets were on their way home. Tinker pleaded to please get there fast, she was getting car sick. Brutus assured her they were close. Tinker even wanted to get out of the car and ride on his back the rest of the way. When they reached home, Brutus took Tinker from the car and carried her in on his back; she was still too woozy to walk from the ride. As the people were congregating at Monica's house the pets were all together reminiscing about Sophie and Grandma. Even though Brutus and Kit were angels and knew this was for the best they shared the same longing for their friends as the earthly pets did.

As the guests left that evening, all the pets took their place with a loved one. Jlo slept with Tori, Tinker with Kayla, Ken stayed with Monica so Brutus slept in her room on the floor, and they even let Kit stay tonight so she slept near Brutus on the rug.

As their prayers were answered in their sleep the Lord lifted their burden from their hearts and replaced their sadness with joyous memories. In the morning the family sat together during breakfast sharing their fondest memories, laughing and crying over the wonderful moments that Sophie brought Grandma. They all decided that Grandma's last years were truly blessed by her little side kick Sophie. They knew her little pup gave her so much joy and meaning to her days. They agreed and realized that most families don't have one tenth of the joy from grandparents that they had received from Ellie, that her love was truly special. They all agreed they were truly blessed by her presence in their lives, and she would not want them crying, but to carry on and be the happy family she created. This would be their task to rejoice in her and Sophie's life, they all hugged and kissed and were going to daily support each other in keeping their word and staying strong like Grandma would want.

Proverbs 31:31 Honor her for all that her hands have done, and let her works bring her praise at the city gate.

Proverbs 31:23 Her husband is respected at the city gate; where he takes his seat among the elders of the land.

78

I'M BACK WITH ELLIE

As I awoke the second time from my groggy state, it felt like I had slept for days. Thank goodness Hernandez was still by my side. "I was having quite a dream about my past," I said slightly shaking my head as to understand where I was. Suddenly I sprung to my feet in the realization that Ellie is here, here in Heaven. "Hernandez, I have to go, I have to get to her right now." As I stood up I felt a little woozy and dazed, Hernandez was saying,

"Slow down Rob, you have a little while longer and you will be ready," Ready? I thought I couldn't be more ready to meet Ellie. This was the first time I ever disobeyed my heavenly mentor,

"I really have to go now," I said as I bolted from the bedroom and ran towards where the new angels are processed, I was yelling, "Sorry Hernandez, Ellie is waiting to see me; she has to be wondering where I'm at," I was running as fast as I could and I finally could see her in the distance. She looked up and the first thing she said was,

"Oh my, what are you doing here you little thing?" Not thinking what I looked like, I ran harder and she was kneeling down to intercept me. As I looked down I saw my paws and could not understand why I was still Sophie. Nothing mattered now or could stop me; I had to be with her. Her eyes were big and shining; she was more beautiful than ever. I could see the luminous heavenly colors with gold radiating around her. As I grew near my heart was beating faster, my euphoria was raging inside me. I leapt to her and when I outstretched my paws, they became human arms and I reached under her arms to help lift her up to her feet and we stood together eye to eye. At that very moment she saw me as Rob and smiled the biggest smile in the world, "My love!" she sang, hugging me and laying her head upon my shoulder. My heart felt like it exploded! Then she held my face in her hands, "How in the world did this happen? Where is Sophie?" she asked,

"I will explain it all later," I told her. We hugged and kissed and held each other and could not stop looking at one another. I feel like I've waited an eternity for this. Now this is heaven and the reason for living a good life, to share with your loved ones forever. Instantly I conveyed my letter to her;

To the End of Time, I will Love You,

To my Beautiful Wife Ellie Marie Harper,

It has been decades since we have looked into each other's eyes.
I remember the very last touch and glance you gave me at the hospital.
Your love and concern has never been forgotten.

I have been with you in spirit every day since my passing and have watched over you daily with love and pride. You have been so strong with our family and children, I realize more every day why God allowed me to have you as my mate.

When we see each other again in heaven I can hardly wait to embrace you and hold you in my arms once more.

Ellie, I have been with you for the past years and even though you have not recognized me, I was with you as Sophie, your tiny side kick. I now have even greater appreciation for your enduring kindness, love and care you bless everyone with on a daily basis. Your ongoing generosity and love is so apparent, even for the pets like I was. God did not want you to be alone in your later years, and that's why he sent me to you as your little companion

Ellie, I am on my way to greet you and pass into Heaven with you, I will truly hold you forever and ever. I pray with all my Love and Strength, will our Lord and Heavenly Father be with you and I will soon be at your side,

Today I am with you whole as your husband; I will continue to honor and cherish you for the rest of our days. We will forever be united together in Heaven.

You are the love of my life and until the end of time; I will always love and adore you.

Forever your Loving Husband (and pet Sophie),
Robert George Harper

As we embraced, Ellie smiled and said, "Rob I've missed you so much but I will long for Sophie, she, you or her, was a big part of my day. You fulfilled my life the last few years and I was never lonely, thank you," I told her I used to be her guardian, that when I came as Sophie, I'm not sure who appointed me, but I was sure thankful to be with her on earth again.

We have now spent a few days together and did a lot of catching up. We reminisced both about our human years together, our children, grandchildren and our years together when I was Sophie. There were so much laughter and telling stories about these things to our loved ones here in heaven. This past time of sharing has made my mission complete. Ellie was asking about her mother Mable, she is an extremely important Executive Angel and could only greet Ellie momentarily when she arrived.

Soon, Hernandez came and told us we were going to be debriefed about the mission and earthly time I spent there. Ellie and I were ready and wanted to understand more. To our surprise Ellie's mother, Mable Rose, was our debriefing angel. Ellie ran and embraced her mother. Together their heavenly colors were spectacular and blindingly bright. Mable was always a saintly woman on earth and it was no surprise she was elevated to an Executive Angel in heaven. She is one of the angels in command who chooses the proper angels to go to earth for missions. We were so intrigued with her choices yet not surprised.

As we went to our debriefing appointment, we met in a kitchen type room, fitting since that was always Mable's favorite room in the house. We sat in the sparkling soft blue and silver chairs with Mable in the throne like gold and silver chair at the end of the table.

Ellie immediately noticed that her mother was wearing a shimmering gold apron, just like she did every day on earth. As she hugged her mother tightly and they shared mental exchanges she stepped back, "Mom, I wouldn't have imagined anything less, I knew you would hold an important position, definitely one that needed an apron," Mable smiled,

"I have a lot of angels and missions to keep track of, so this comes in handy," She then reached into a pocket and pulled out a gold tablet with a silver pen, as she talked she was noting the days in which the assigned angels were due to return to heaven and scratching off the finished details.

She informed us that no angels are misplaced on earth then began to explain her choices during Rob's mission. She said that Dovie, the assistant to the Angel of Death, was Ellie's oldest and only sister Irene, fitting since doves were her favorite bird. Ellie was so pleased to know her sister was watching over her on earth. By this choice, Mable wanted to ensure that Rob and Ellie came back together and she knew Irene would do this perfectly. She told us soon Irene's mission will end and there will be a reunion here in heaven when she returns, "She will remain until your oldest brother passes and then she will return with him," Mable said, this in itself made our hearts warm.

We learned Brutus was Ellie's cousin Sam, who was killed in the line of duty as a police officer and always wanted to serve his country, this mission was perfect and his protective nature would be useful to the tiny animals in Ellie's household. Ellie always had a special place in her heart for Sam. Kit was a family friend who used to be a neighbor down the street and is doing a duo purpose mission in that neighborhood and was an assistant to Darlene. Darlene, a superior human angel on earth and was a close friend of Mable's, she was always a dear friend of the families, Dorothy Flynn. Ellie adored all these people during her life and understood her mother's choices.

I asked her about Alfonso, the fuzzy dog at the mall, and low and behold it was "Huey," Gus's black lab. He and Gus became very active in the mission program to help the betterment of humans while on earth. *Well, I'll be*, I thought, "Oh, and the caterpillar?" I asked,

"That is another whole level of sub angels and a story for another day," Mable said. Wow, I thanked her again for appointing me to be with Ellie for her last years and knew that in any form no one could love her more. She knew that and nodded her head. I hugged her and she gave me that loving smile and pat like she always did as the wonderful mother in law she had always been to me.

1 Chronicles 16:34 Give thanks to the Lord, for he is good; his love endures forever.

79

THE SURPRISE

We laughed as we told her we would miss our Ellie-Sophie, relationship. But I told them, shaking my head that I won't miss the dress up days. Ellie smiled as we reminisced about the events that took place, we all were laughing, as I caressed Ellie's hand in mine. Mable told us she had one more surprise. As there was a knock on the door Mable greeted an angel with a bright white basket. Taking the basket from her she turned around, Ellie gasped as she squeezed my hand. I sat still in surprise as I looked at my hands to make sure I wasn't hallucinating. In the basket was Sophie, wagging her tail and staring at Ellie, she stood up in the basket as Mable handed the package to me. I took the basket and turned to Ellie, with open mouth and beaming eyes she scooped Sophie up slowly, examining her and smiling. Sophie's tail was wagging like mad. I reached over to pet her. It is amazing how animals' unconditional love continues forever, even into heaven.

Expressionless, Mable explained, "This tiny tot was going to only live a few days. She would have come to heaven without earthly experience, and since Monica was going to get another female Chihuahua, we knew she couldn't resist the littlest sickest pup. So I placed your spirit Rob, in her body to give you a way to Ellie, and you provided a life for this pup. I knew you could handle it, besides you must have told me a few times when I lived with you and Ellie on Robinson Street with Cindy and Tasha as your pets, that "if you couldn't be human you'd want to come back as a Harper pet." As she raised her eyebrows she looked at Rob, "Without a doubt, you of all people, needed to be with Ellie, let her love you and care for you like she has all your pets, and save this baby from an early death." Afterwards she smiled her big warm smile and enjoyed the sight she was beholding in front of her.

We listened intently sort of mesmerized by what we are holding in our hands. Smiling now I was holding what felt like me, rubbing my favorite spot under my belly, and I realized how small and frail Sophie was. Mable added, "Her memory is only of how much she loved Ellie, the family and the pets, her life in her mind was hers not yours, Rob she will have to get to know you, and I see that will be no problem," Ellie and I hugged with Sophie between us, she was licking our chins.

We sat back down and began talking about the family. Sophie snuggled right into Ellie's lap, she knew her place well and looking at her there I could almost feel her comfort. Then Mable showed us what was happening on earth with our loved ones. We saw that Ken had proposed to Monica so Brutus would be moving in to protect the family. Tori is excelling in soccer, and Kayla is in dance, they are both honor students in school. J.R. and Becky were expecting another baby which was going to be a girl and her name would be Cecilia Rose, and that would make their family complete. Courtney and Ron have been successful with their lives and now own a winery accompanied by several salons. Kathy and Steve are settled near J.R. and Becky in Texas to enjoy the grand babies and moving forward with their business and enjoying little Blue. Jlo runs around and tells her friends that her sister that died was an angel and that Sophie knew things that no other dog on earth knew. Tinker is best friends with Kit and is trying to convince her that they need to revenge the bad animal hating neighbor again. Oh, and Kit, she comes by every day and the family feeds her inside the house right along with the crew. We both knew what awesome pets we had and how fun it will be one day when we are all together in heaven.

Just seeing our whole family adjusting and doing well supporting each other is a blessing itself. After looking at all of them in thankfulness, and holding each other, with Sophie in her favorite spot on Ellie's left arm, Mable smiled, "So Ellie and Rob, each of you can now become the new guardians of someone on earth. Do you know who each of you will choose?" Ellie and Rob looked down upon their entire family and loved ones and looked into each other's eyes smiling,

"Yes, absolutely we do."

Ellie thanked her mom again and I gave her another hug and kiss for being so exuberantly thoughtful. We walked away hand in hand, calling to Sophie. She scampered along beside us. At that time we knew the three of us would be wonderful guardians in the future.

THE END

NIV, New International Version Bible Verses, Public Domain

Page	Verse	Page	Verse
2	Psalm 34:6	202	Zechariah 2:3
10	Proverbs 2:11	206	Luke 19:6
16	Psalm 49:18	210	Proverbs 24:27
20	Psalm 26:6	214	Psalm 33:11
24	3 John 1:14	220	Psalm 30:11, 30:12
28	Philemon 1:4	224	Ephesians 1:16
32	Ruth 3:12	228	Isaiah 46:8
36	Deuteronomy 15:16	232	Proverbs 27:10
42	Psalm 4:8	236	Proverbs 29:25
48	Job 19:13	240	Jeremiah 1:8
54	Genesis 27:23	246	Proverbs 3:24
60	Proverbs 6:30	250	Proverbs 2:2
64	Proverbs 15:30	254	2 Corinthians 2:4
68	Job 7:14	260	Proverbs 31:28
72	James 1:6	264	Proverbs 31:29
78	1 Chronicles 16:27	270	Ecclesiastes 3:12
84	Psalm 49:13	276	Proverbs 31:27
88	Job 12:7	280	Job 4:12
94	Romans 14:19	286	Job 36:29
100	Proverbs 5:21	292	Numbers 11:17
106	Jeremiah 10:19	298	I Kings 20:38
110	Luke 22:43	306	Ephesians 1:18
114	Philippians 4:13	312	Genesis 31:14
120	Job 21:6	316	Proverbs 17:6
126	Matthew 11:28	322	Romans 12:19
130	Proverbs 31:12	326	Psalm 98:4
134	Proverbs 22:6	330	Acts 5:20

"Oh! This is me after a tough day working on
the book. There are so many parts describing
my wonderful attributes, I just get exhausted.
I hope you read them all,
Thanks, Jlo"

Hello, This is Jlo and I wanted to share with you a little after book information. I knew that we were going to be famous stars so I have been trying to train Sophie and Blue to wear sunglasses so we are incognito for the paparazzi. These are our practice photos.

Oh, and this is our final post book photo. I just wanted you to know that we ALL are little angels, Blue, I, and Sophie. Get the picture? You have to admit I am the most beautiful, that's why I'm in the middle so my beauty can radiate . . . . JLO

For more information about this book, the Author and future books,

Please go to WWW.WRITEONTIME.ME

If you like this book please send a message!

God Bless all Readers of Heaven Sent, ☺ *Mischelle*

CPSIA information can be obtained at www.ICGtesting.com
Printed in the USA
BVOW070350140613

323269BV00002B/2/P

9 781481 714013